The author, Charmian Coates, who lives in Blackpool, was born in Ilford, Essex, in 1937.

Aged nine, she was taken to India and spent two-and-a half years there.

Charmian is married with four children, one sadly deceased, five grandchildren, and one great-grandchild. In 1972, she left Oxford to run, alongside her husband, Alan, a small private hotel in Blackpool.

This novel is inspired by a piece in a pre-war newspaper.

The author has had three previous novels published by Pegasus, 'Love Writes in Many Colours,' set in Oxford in the 1960s, and 'First Impressions', also set in Oxford in the 1950s. Also, 'The Virgin's Daughter', set in Tudor England.

By the same author

Love Writes In Many Colours
(Vanguard Press)
ISBN 978 1 84386 229 1

First Impressions
(Vanguard Press)
ISBN 978 1 84386 333 5

The Virgin's Daughter
(Vanguard Press)
ISBN 978 1 84386 354 0

THE VIEW FROM HER WINDOW

Charmian Coates

THE VIEW FROM HER WINDOW

Vanguard Press

VANGUARD PAPERBACK

© Copyright 2008
Charmian Coates

The right of Charmian Coates to be identified as author of
this work has been asserted by her in accordance with the
Copyright, Designs and Patents Act 1988.

A CIP catalogue record for this title is
available from the British Library.

ISBN 978 184386 449 3

*Vanguard Press is an imprint of
Pegasus Elliot MacKenzie Publishers Ltd.*

www.pegasuspublishers.com

First Published in 2008

**Vanguard Press
Sheraton House Castle Park
Cambridge England**

Printed & Bound in Great Britain

DEDICATION

Dedicated to the memory
of a good friend,
and talented artist, writer, and poet.

Patricia Butterworth
October 11th 1916 – 30th December 2007

Much missed!

ACKNOWLEDGEMENTS

With grateful thanks to Alan, my dear husband of almost
fifty-one years, for his love and understanding.
Also, thanks to my son Reg, daughter-in-law,
Caroline, and granddaughter, Sarah, for all their
care since Neil's death.

Also thanks to Jackie Buksh, Mary Cardwell, and
Elle Marie Hinchcliffe for their friendship.

And finally, I'd like to mention the
Lancashire Authors' Association,
Of which I've been a member
Since 1994.

CHAPTER ONE

"Laura! That child's crying again. You'd best give her a dose of Fennings Fever cure. Her row's making my head ache."

Laura groaned and dropped the wet baby vest and the wooden peg that she was just pegging it onto the line with, back into the bath at her feet. "Just coming!" She hurried indoors and unclipping Claire's safety-harness, picked the red-faced Claire out of her pram and cuddled her. The baby began to chuckle. Laura knew the reason she kept crying was because she was bored with being confined to her pram. But Claire let loose wouldn't suit Laura's mother-in-law. Noticing something beneath the pram, she bent and picked up the knitted doll she'd made and handed it back to Claire. "She seems all right, now, Mrs. Field. She'd just dropped Betty."

Doris Field's gnarled hands paused at their task of easing shirts and sheets through the rollers of the mangle, and her thin lips tightened. "If I say she should have Fennings, then she should have Fennings. If anyone should know babies, I should. I haven't had two of my own for nothing. I'll have you know I'm fifty-five and I knows everything."

And didn't Laura know it! Her mother-in-law with her bullet-brown eyes which only ever softened for her son, Sid or Claire, and straggly greying hair drawn tightly into a bun, looked every minute of her age. Knowing from experience that it did no good arguing with her, Laura found the medicine bottle and gave Claire a dose. "There you are, darling."

She put the baby back into her pram. Doris Field was always moaning about something. If it wasn't Claire who was making too much noise, it was that Laura hadn't swept in the corners when she'd cleaned the kitchen. Or else she'd not washed up properly; that there were still traces of food on the plates. All lies. If only Rod hadn't been killed in that fire like he had. She'd wished this a million times, but what was the good of wishing. What had happened had happened. Sometimes when she was particularly unhappy she would have little daydreams of Rod being still alive, and she and Claire happy with him in their own small home. Instead of here, in her parents-in-law's house, with its dark paint work and dreary atmosphere – the view from her window; flapping washing, a ramshackle shed where her father-in-law kept his barrow, a depressing small yard and a six-foot high wall. The only pleasant aspect of life in the terraced house near the railway station was the fruity smell from the burst plums in summer – though even this was spoilt by the fear she might be stung by the wasps.

Bert Field himself was okay, but he was henpecked. Why he didn't stick up for himself, tell his wife where to go when she laid down the law to him, Laura didn't know. Her father-in-law was twice his wife's size; the muscles on his arms alone stood out like duck-eggs from pushing his barrow. Bert, who always wore a cloth cap over the sparse grey hair that fringed his bald head and a disreputable jacket with leather patches at the elbows, made his living wheeling a barrow laden with fruit and vegetables that he hawked around the local houses and guest houses. To have someone stand up to her was perhaps what Laura's mother-in-law needed, but it was obvious that this person would never be Bert Field whose policy was to keep his mouth shut for a quiet life.

She heard in her head for the umpteenth time Doris Field's sharp voice, "You should be grateful to us, we took you in and we didn't have to, you know. Your widow's pension would have hardly kept you both, and you couldn't have worked with a baby to see to, you'd have had no choice but to let the child go."

Laura knew her mother-in-law was right, the ten shillings a week widow's pension would have gone nowhere, not if she'd had to pay rent for a room, but did the woman need to keep rubbing it in like she did?

Sidney put his head around the door.

What was he doing here? At this hour oughtn't he to be at work? Though she supposed with him being the manager at Woodhouses furniture shop, he could do as he pleased.

"Sid! I weren't expecting you, son," exclaimed his mother in a completely different tone to which she spoke to Laura. "Is there something wrong?"

"No. I just thought I'd tell you that Prue's in the Glenroyd. I took her in early this morning. Her mum's got our Tom and Bob."

"I thought the baby weren't due for a couple of weeks?"

"It weren't. It's darned inconvenient. January's our busiest time of year. We've got some knocked-down three-piece suites."

"Are those the ones that were seventeen guineas, son?"

"Aye. Nine pounds, five shillings now. Easy payments too, five shillings a month and no deposit. I'm expecting a rush."

Sid spoke as if five shillings a month were nothing. To Laura it was an impossible sum, and one she was certain she would never have to spare. She could just imagine her brother-in-law talking customers into spending money they'd not got. She'd no time for Slimy Sid in his check suits and dapper bowties. How different he was to Rod, his younger brother – the man she had loved and lost. Different not only in character. Dark-haired Rod with those clear-cut features and blue eyes. Sid, stocky with mousy hair and thin-lipped like his mother. Laura wondered if there was more than met the eye in the fact that Prue had gone into labour early. Prue had once told Laura that she was always 'late'. She recalled the bruise on Prue's face the last time Sid brought her to the house. Prue had made the excuse that her condition was making her accident prone; that she'd bumped into the door. But had she? Had it been Sid's fist she'd bumped into?

17

His mother wiped her hands in her apron and hurried over to the fire. "Still, you've time for a cuppa, son?" Without waiting for an answer, she lifted the kettle off the hob, and stirring the coals into life, placed it in the centre. She turned back to Laura. "For heaven's sakes, stop fiddling with that child. Make yourself useful. You can fetch me down a cup and saucer from the dresser for Sid for a start – one of the best ones, mind."

A skivvy wouldn't be treated any worse than she was. She tucked the sleepy Claire beneath her covers, before going over and unhooking a cup from her mother-in-law's treasured Wedgewood service. She placed the cup and saucer before her brother-in-law. "Ta, Laura." He smiled in his over-familiar manner, his hand slyly brushing hers.

She jerked away.

Her mother-in-law pretended not to notice. "And the milk jug and the sugar basin."

"I was just getting them."

"There's no need to answer back!"

Laura placed them on the table. "I wasn't."

Doris Field sniffed, and lifting the earthenware pot, poured. "There you are, son."

Sidney put down the cup for his mother to refill, wiping his whiskers with the back of his hand. "No one makes a cup of tea like you, Mum – or a meal."

His mother took the hint. "Why don't you come to us for your dinner tonight?"

He pretended reluctance. "I've got to go up the hospital to see Prue. Besides I don't want to make you extra work. I can do myself something when I get home. There's a heel of cheese in the larder. I can have some bread and cheese."

"Bread and cheese! That's not enough, not for a man, not after you've done a full day's work. I can keep something warm for you. Steak pie, mash and carrots do you, son?"

"If you're sure, Mum."

"Course I am."

"Lovely, I can't wait. I only wish Prue had a light touch with pastry like you, Mum."

Doris preened herself. "You've either got it, or you haven't. Look, son, if it's getting on when you get here, why don't you stay the night? That's if you don't mind sleeping on the sofa?" She looked meaningfully at Laura.

Laura flinched. She knew what her mother-in-law was implying. If they hadn't taken her and Claire in, they would have had a bedroom spare.

"A sofa doesn't bother me. And it would save me a long walk." His eyes lingered on Laura in a way she didn't care for.

She returned to pegging out Claire's washing; she couldn't bear to be in their company for another moment. Removing the pink matinee coat from the tin bath, her thoughts drifted back to happier times.

Laura had come to Blackpool from Chorley when her mother, suffering for many years from heart trouble, died. Her father had been killed in the trenches in the Great War before she was born, and she fancied a new start in the popular resort. She'd no relatives in Chorley, no one to stay for. In fact no relatives at all apart from a great aunt who lived in Manchester. Her mother's aunt, who had brought her mother up, hadn't approved of her niece's choice of husband, she considering Laura's mother to have married 'beneath her' because Laura's father had been brought up in a workhouse. Now the only contact was a card at Christmas.

Laura found lodgings and work as a cinema usherette at the Tivoli, Talbot Square. Showing some people to their seats, she accidentally shone her torch into the face of a young man. She apologised. But later, when she left work, he was waiting for her outside. This meeting was the start of things between her and Rod. They went for a cup of tea in a nearby cafe. He was a window cleaner.

Romance blossomed quicker than a snowdrop in spring. She hadn't cared too much for his mother when taken to meet his family, but brushed aside her misgivings, reasoning that it was her feelings for Rod which mattered, never expecting to have to live beneath the woman's roof.

Life seemed full of promise, when in August 1934, six months after their first meeting, they married at St Justin's Church. Laura in dress of Jubilee blue taffeta, a plaited head-dress over her fair hair and carrying sweet peas. Rod, beside her, in his best suit. Rod's mates from his snooker team at his local, forming a guard of honour, holding their snooker cues over the church door as the wedding party left for a slap-up reception at Stanley's Cafe. Even Doris Field, dressed in a feathered red hat and fox fur as she attempted to take charge, hadn't been able to spoil the magic for Laura.

A honeymoon at Southport followed, three wonderful, unforgettable days and nights in a small boarding house.

They returned to the rented rooms in North Shore that were to be their first home, and Laura swept and polished everything in sight. With satisfaction, she arranged the wedding presents they'd received, placing on the shelves of the dresser the twenty-six piece dinner service that the girls at the Tivoli had clubbed together for.

"That's enough. The place looks like a palace," Rod remarked, pulling her to him. "Let's try out the bed?"

She giggled. "It's still broad daylight. I'm a respectable married woman."

"So what? I like respectable married women – especially between the sheets."

"Sauce box!"

He pinched her bottom in reply.

"Well, at least let me put the polish and cloth away first."

Afterwards Rod went out and brought back fish and chips and they ate them off the new dinner service.

The following day would be etched in her memory forever. The painful events that happened later, that changed her life, making those moments with Rod especially poignant. It was his first day back at work. She got up early leaving her new husband still asleep to make sandwiches for his break. They were cheese and pickle, his favourite. Wrapping them carefully in greaseproof paper, she put them into his snap tin. Beneath the neat package, she placed a note, with a heart drawn on it and the words, *'I love you.'*

He kissed her before he left that morning. As it turned out, it was the last kiss he was ever to give her; his lips warm and tender, the kiss full of promise of future lovemaking, as he slipped his hand within the V neck of her nightgown and caressed a breast, teasing the nipple until it hardened.

She was planning in her head what she would make him for his meal when he finished his round as she heard Rod's footsteps go down the stairs, and the front door open and close. She would go to the market, and get a nice bit of neck of mutton; do a hot pot in the oven with baby carrots and potatoes.

No one had eaten the meal she'd prepared so carefully.

Laura saw again the headlines on the placards:

HERO SAVES CHILD FROM FIRE BUT DIES HIMSELF.
Tragedy of window-cleaner, Rod Field, who had just returned from his honeymoon. Sightseers stood with heads bowed and hats doffed as the twenty-five-year-olds body was removed. Many in tears.

She pegged the last garment securely and stepping back from the line, wiped her cheek, and picking up the bath and, with dragging steps, went back inside the house.

After the funeral, she returned to her job at the Tivoli; the sympathy of the other usherettes and having something to keep herself occupied, helping. The weeks passed in a blur; then she hadn't felt well. A touch of flu she imagined, until she realised with some surprise that she'd missed two periods. When she missed a third, she paid a visit to the doctor and learnt that she was pregnant. She'd fallen for a baby on honeymoon.

The next few months were a nightmare, especially when she'd no choice but to take up her mother-in-law's offer of a roof over her head. Living with her in-laws was worse than she could ever have anticipated. Doris Field constantly carped at her. Whatever she did, nothing was ever right. Even the little white booties and vests that she'd attempted to knit for the new arrival weren't knitted to the older woman's standards. Laura's unhappiness grew along with her thickening waistline.

Claire, though, when she was born at the Glenroyd, was wonderful. Laura fancied that the blue-eyed, six-pounds six-ounce baby had a look of Rod. How she wished Rod could have seen her, how proud he would have been to have such a beautiful daughter.

*   *   *

Laura was dreaming. In the dream she felt Rod's strong arms wrap themselves around her, pulling her close to his naked warm flesh. A hand slid downwards to her buttocks, pulling up her nightgown, kneading and caressing, the other moving round to her belly and into the small fair triangle between her thighs. She reached up to touch Rod's face: her fingers brushed a bristly moustache. Rod hadn't a moustache! She jerked awake as reality hit her. This was no dream! Someone was actually in bed with her, someone with a moustache. Sid!

Shocked, she wrenched herself free from him and shot from the bed and over to the light switch. With trembling fingers she flicked it on, and harsh light lit up the dishevelled bed, and her brother-in-law. "I might have known. How dare you!" Her voice dropped to a whisper. "Get out!" She grabbed up the rag rug by the bed and covered herself.

Sid leered. "Don't be daft, you know you want it! You must be starved for it. Don't deny yourself pleasure. I won't tell anyone, if you won't." He tapped his nose. "It'll be our little secret and I'll see you all right. I've always fancied you, you know. I don't know what you saw in our Rod, but whatever it was, he's dead and no good to no woman, and I'm very much alive, which you'd soon find out if you gave me half a chance. Now, come back to bed, let's enjoy ourselves. Don't worry about Prue, she's a cold fish. She doesn't like it anyway."

"Stop it! You sicken me."

"Oh, go on, there's no need to play hard to get."

"I'm not." Had she for one second been tempted to let Sid? She was a normal woman, and it had been ages. She shuddered. No! Definitely not with him. She felt like scrubbing her skin raw to rid herself of his touch. "Get out," she repeated, her voice rising. She eyed the cot in the corner of the room. "Before you wake up Claire – and not just her."

"And if I won't, you'll do what?" he jeered. "Tell my mother that I tried to force myself on you? Do you think she'd believe you? I'll just say that this was all your idea, that you invited me to your bed. Then, just as things were warming up, you suddenly got cold feet."

She gasped. "That's preposterous. She'd not believe such a wild story."

Sid smirked, stretching his arms above his head. "She'll believe anything I tell her, will my mum."

That was true. Sid could twist his mother around his little finger, Laura knew he could get her to believe that black was white.

"She certainly won't take your word over mine. You must know she never thought you good enough for our Rod; to see you in a bad light, to appear a husband-stealer, would just prove her right about you."

"I wouldn't! I'd never do such a thing to Prue. I don't even like you. The opposite, in fact. I feel sorry for Prue being married to someone so unfeeling and shallow."

His eyes narrowed. "You do, do you?"

"I certainly do. You'd not only cheat on her, but you beat her too, don't you? Admit it? All those bruises, I've never believed all those tales about her bumping into doors, I really don't know why she goes along with it. I wouldn't!"

"Well, what if I do give her the odd tap when she steps out of line?" retorted Sid. "She promised to obey me in church, didn't she? She's my property, I can do what I like with her. Anyway, it's her fault, she shouldn't annoy me so much. Now, come on, you're wasting time. Come back to bed. I promise you won't regret it if you do. I'm a good lover."

"I've already said *No!* For heaven's sake!"

"Suit yourself." Sid swung out of bed. "And don't think you can run to Dad to spill the beans about me. If you did, you'd be wasting your time." Suddenly he made a grab for her, and cornering her, flung the rug to one side, pushing her up against the wall, shoving his knee between her thighs. Laura struggled, reaching up in an attempt to scratch him, she opened her mouth to scream but nothing came out. Almost fainting, twisting her face away from his, she saw Claire yawn – was she about to wake? Sid slid his hands up her naked back. She felt his hardness pressing into her. Oh, God, no!

The door opened, framing Doris Field, her greying hair dangling in a wispy pigtail and wearing a misshapen knitted bed jacket over a vast white nightdress. Her brows drew together. "What on earth's going on here?"

Laura gasped. "It's not what you think. I didn't encourage him. I wouldn't!"

Sid soon recovered himself. "Course she did, Mum. She tempted me – been giving me the glad eye for weeks. And me a married man." He stretched out his hands. "I know I've been weak, but..."

His mother ignored him. Eyes narrowing, she grasped hold of Laura roughly. "Disgusting! This is a decent house, lady. I knew I'd regret taking you in and I was right. I'll not have such goings-on under my roof. You can get out – go and cool your hot blood on the streets." She pushed her towards the door.

"That's where she belongs. She's a tart," sneered Sid.

"I'm not!" I've not done anything." Laura tried to pull away but the older woman held her fast. Surely Doris Field didn't really mean to chuck her out, thought Laura in disbelief as despite her struggles she was frogmarched through the bedroom door, down the stairs and into the passage. "But, Claire!" She grabbed for a coat off the hook, but snatched empty air.

"I'll see to my granddaughter," said Doris grimly. Holding Laura securely with one hand, she pulled back the bolt on the front door with the other, opened it and thrust her outside.

The door slammed behind Laura – the bolt shooting into place. She stood shivering on the doorstep. It was raining and her nightdress became plastered to her legs. The blank windows and the sodden pavements seemed eerie in the pale light of the street lamp. At least there was no one about to see her humiliation, she thought. She began to cry – harsh sobs that racked her body. "Claire! Claire!"

She turned and rattled the door knocker, calling desperately through the letter box. "Oh, Mrs Field, please let me back in."

The house remained silent.

After what seemed like hours the bolt shot back and the door opened and Bert Field, wearing a coat over his nightshirt and with a concerned look on his face, draped a blanket over her shuddering shoulders. "Come in, lass, You're soaking. I'll get you a towel."

Thankfully, she followed him inside.

Laura hurried into the bedroom; a whimper came from the cot. She looked down at Claire, but she had put her thumb into her mouth and gone back to sleep.

Laura tidied up the bed and got back into it. She sat hunched with her fists pressed into her mouth, her knees up to her chin, her thoughts whirling through her head. Damn Sid, and damn his horrible mother – I'm going to get out of this place! Things had been bad enough before, but she couldn't go on living with her in-laws, not after this. But where could she go? If only her parents had still been alive. She'd no one to turn to. Who would take her in with a child in tow? She didn't think her great-aunt Hannah would welcome her and Claire if they turned up on her doorstep in Manchester.

Words of wisdom, half forgotten from childhood, flashed through her head. Hadn't Mum always said: *Put your problems in the hands of the Lord.* Should she? Maybe, just maybe, there was somebody listening? Laura had turned against God when Rod was killed – blaming God for allowing it to happen – thinking, that perhaps there wasn't even a God. She knew deep down that it was bitterness that had caused such thoughts. That was it, she decided, she must pray about this. She put her hands together and closed her eyes. 'Please, God, I know I've not been to church as much lately as I should have, but in the name of your son, the Lord Jesus Christ, please help me, tell me what to do?'

Suddenly in her mind's-eye, she saw Bert Field reading the Situations Vacant column of the *Evening Gazette*.

That was it! The paper. Why hadn't she thought before of trying to find a position where she could have Claire with her?

*   *   *

26

Both Sid and his mother acted as if the previous night's events hadn't happened when Laura came downstairs the following morning with Claire in her arms. With her mother-in-law hovering over Sid, refilling his cup even before he'd asked for more tea, he was coolly seated in his shirt sleeves at the breakfast table, tucking into bacon and eggs. As Laura placed Claire in her highchair, she noticed a trickle of egg yolk running down the sticking plaster on his chin and shuddered, then embarrassed at his close proximity, pretended there was something urgent she just had to do in the scullery. How relieved she was, when she returned to the kitchen to find him gone.

That day passed just like any other, filled with countless chores, though she did manage to slip away to take a walk along the promenade as she very often did, pushing Claire in her pram. As she left the house, she saw perched on a roof on the opposite side of the street, a flock of doves who, as if by some cue, suddenly took off and flew high into the sky to flutter in and out of an hourglass shape, before returning to the roof. At their soft cooing, as warm and deep as a chuckle, she felt her spirits lifting. She reached the prom. It had been raining earlier and there were pools of water about, but the sky was pale blue with banks of grey and white fluffy clouds, like ice floes on a waste of snow. She looked out over the sea wall and was dazzled by sunlight that lit a wide pathway of gold across the water. How mild it is for January, she thought, undoing the top button of her coat. A lone seagull flew overhead, and on a calm metal-grey sea, further out, were white patches of them swimming. In the distance stood the Tower, solitary and stately in its dull rust-coloured winter coat. Some way off to the left was Southport, to the right, Barrow; though the hump of its headland was not discernible. Despite it now being out of season, with many of the arcades shuttered, there were quite a few people about – who'd left not only pieces of bread for the birds – but also dog dirt – she had to manoeuvre hastily the pram wheels to avoid it. Shading her eyes, she looked out over the white-edged wavelets, seeing some way off a smudge of a steamer, with its smoke whiffling the sky. She wondered how long would it be before there would be something suitable in the *Gazette*? And if there was; on applying, would she get it? She was sure there was many other young women in her selfsame situation. What was so special about her that an employer would choose her from perhaps a dozen others?

She put Claire to bed, and at last had time to sit down and take up the newspaper. She studied again the advertisement she'd marked with a cross.

WANTED – Housekeeper – Central Drive.
To look after a middle-aged ex-Indian Army couple.
Widow with child acceptable. Live in. Terms negotiable.

This sounded just what she was looking for. As she wrote her application carefully in her best handwriting, she thought back to earlier that evening. Her father-in-law, with an understanding look in his eyes had patted her shoulder when she'd asked if she could borrow his *Gazette* when he'd finished with it. After his action of the previous night it was obvious he was sympathetic to her.

When she was satisfied with what she had written, she took the letter down to the post-box.

A couple of days passed.

Waiting for the arrival of the postman, she decided to change Claire's nappy. Anything to take her mind off staring at the clock on the mantle shelf, the hands of which seemed to take forever to get to eight am; his usual time. She was so on edge that when she heard the rattle of the letter box she almost pricked Claire with the pin. Putting the wriggling baby back into her pram, she dashed to the door. A brown envelope lay on the mat. She picked it up – her heart sank, it was addressed to her father-in-law. But the next day, when the box rattled and she put down Claire and rushed out, she saw a square white envelope. Could this be it at last? Could this be a letter for her, a reply to her application? With a shaking hand, Laura picked it up and turned it over. Across the envelope, in small neat handwriting was written her name *Mrs Laura Field*. The letter was hers! She tore open the envelope. Had they asked her to go for an interview?

> Secunderabad House,
> 11 Central Drive,
> Blackpool,
> 10th January 1937.

Dear Mrs Field,

Thank you for your letter. I think you might be just what my husband and myself are looking for. Do you think if I taught you how to do it, you'd be able to make us our favourite hot curries? While out in India, the brigadier and myself, became used to our native cook giving us curry at least once a week. If so, we'd like you to call to the above address with your child at three pm tomorrow.

> Yours sincerely,

Florence T Bradshaw.

*   *   *

Laura studied the contents of her wardrobe, she needed to make a good impression. At last pulling out a dress, she rejected the rest – they were only fit for the rag-and-bone man. If only she could afford to buy something new for the interview. She'd had this dress from before Claire's birth and although Rod had always said the colour blue suited her, matched her eyes, there was a darn where the moths had made a hole, and the seat of the skirt was baggy. Her summer coat would have to do – it was a bit thin for this time of year, but it was smarter than her everyday one – and also blue like her dress. Thank goodness she'd had her other pair of shoes mended recently, she wouldn't have wanted to appear down-at-heel. She removed a matching velour hat from the wardrobe shelf, pulling a face. She guessed she'd no other choice, her usual hat was so shapeless it looked as though the cat could have had her kittens in it – if only she could borrow a fetching hat like that worn by Joan Crawford in the film, *I Love My Life*. In such a hat, the job would most definitely be in the bag!

Laura stopped outside a detached house that was surrounded by a high laurel hedge. The wooden plaque attached to the gate post said, SECUNDERABAD HOUSE. She opened the well-oiled gate, and with cotton wool legs and a dry mouth, manoeuvred the pram through it and up a gravel path, bordered by rose bushes. With a shaking finger, she pressed the bell. A faint musical chime sounded from within.

The door opened on a woman in her fifties with faded blonde hair and a rather leathery skin. The effects of too much Indian sun, Laura supposed. She was smartly dressed in a silk floral afternoon tea gown and thin silver bangles slid up and down her arms. She smiled, looking closely at Laura. "You must be Mrs Field," she said, her accent cut-glass. "Do come in. I'm Florence Bradshaw."

Laura swallowed. "How do you do, Mrs Bradshaw." She gingerly pushed the pram into the hall, careful not to scrape the shining cream paintwork of the skirting board, and praying that the wheels had not picked up any muck to soil the red carpet.

Mrs Bradshaw tickled Claire beneath her chin. "Aren't you a little poppit."

Claire chuckled, reaching out to the friendly stranger, hoping to be picked up, and chattering in baby talk.

Mrs Bradshaw turned to Laura with a sigh, saying, "You're very lucky, my dear. You've got what I always wanted – a dear little girl, but sadly the brigadier and myself weren't blessed. Still, I've got my two corgis, Toby and Bobby. They sleep at night at the foot of my bed."

The idea shot into Laura's head that the Bradshaws might expect her to see to them as part of her duties.

Mrs Bradshaw must have read her thoughts. "I always see to my 'babies' myself. I was just about to give them their weekly bath." A yapping came from the rear of the house. "Coming darlings, Mummy's coming," she called out.

Laura regarded the delicate fabric of the elegant dress that Mrs Bradshaw was wearing and hoped, that at least, she would cover it with a rubber-backed apron.

"My husband will interview you. You can leave your pram in the hall."

"Thank you." Laura glanced critically at her reflection in the full-length mirror as she lifted Claire out of the pram. She frowned. The hat, despite sponging, brushing, and new braid trimming, still looked shabby.

"This way," said Mrs Bradshaw, opening a door.

Clutching Claire's hand, Laura entered. A man with a cloud of smoke around his head, and in a bottle-green velvet-collared smoking jacket rose from an armchair. He was tall and spare, and by his bearing, obviously a military man. He'd iron-grey hair and a waxed moustache, and if anything his skin was even more leathery than his wife's. He removed a fat cigar. "I'm Brigadier Bradshaw." He briskly shook Laura's hand and asked her to sit down. With Claire perched on her lap, she did so.

He shivered. "Excuse me, this English weather," he said, going over and poking vigorously at the already blazing fire.

Laura took in the room. The first thing that struck her was its Eastern appearance. The floor-length windows drapes were of pale green silk-edged with gold brocade; there were brass vases on the sill, and several elaborately carved wooden occasional tables. On one was a sandalwood cigarette box. In the centre of the mantelpiece was an elephant with ivory tusks. Alongside it was a framed photograph which showed a troop of mounted white-clad topeed soldiers. She guessed the officer leading them was the brigadier.

He settled himself back in his chair. "That's better."

"I'll go and see to Toby and Bobby," said Mrs Bradshaw. The door closed behind her.

The brigadier proceeded to interview Laura, but his manner had changed. To her disbelief, she realised his hot eyes were on her knees, where Claire had ruched up her skirt. Wet-lipped he was regarding her in a way that could only mean one thing. Hastily she pulled at her skirt to cover them. She brushed aside her misgivings. He was old enough to be her father. Besides he was a gentleman, gentlemen were above that sort of behaviour, weren't they? Not only that, he was offering her seven shillings a week, all found. He didn't seem to be bothered about interviewing anyone else. He was saying the job was hers if she wanted it. On top of her widow's pension, seven shillings was a fortune, and not to be sneezed at. She'd be able to put by quite a bit on that. Mrs Bradshaw seemed a kind lady who'd be a pleasure to work for. And not everyone would accept a child. Besides she just had to get away from Doris Field. She'd work for Frankenstein himself, to get away from her!

The room which would be hers and Claire's was on the floor above where the brigadier and Mrs Bradshaw slept. It contained a double bed, oak wardrobe and dressing table, and next to it, was a lavatory-cum-bathroom for the housekeeper's use. Compared to what she was used to, it would be like living in a palace. The view, too, was attractive, with lawn, flower beds and at the bottom of the garden, a greenhouse. She could just see herself on fine days taking a chair outside to pod peas or top-and-tail gooseberries.

She was just congratulating herself that she'd fallen on her feet when the brigadier, fingering the ends of his waxed moustache, moved closer, and to Laura's horror, ran his finger tips lightly over her arm, saying in a peculiar voice, "My wife takes sleeping pills for her nerves. You'll not mind, will you, if I come and tap on your door if I need anything?"

His meaning was all too clear.

Mrs Bradshaw appeared. Oblivious of the atmosphere, she asked if everything was fixed up for Laura to start. How Laura managed to get away, what excuse she gave for suddenly changing her mind about the position, she couldn't remember afterwards.

Feeling sick, she returned to her in-laws'. After such a disappointment, her mother-in-law's acid tongue seemed worse than ever. And it was at least a week before she could get up the courage to take another look at the Situations Vacant column.

*   *   *

Laura was about to be interviewed for the third time in so many weeks. Her second interview, she was certain had come to nothing because of the sort of people her prospective employers were.

The front door had been opened by a stiff-faced, dark-clad man. "It's the back door for domestics," he summed up.

Startled, she recalled Mrs Moggs, her neighbour in Chorley, who as a young woman had been in service, telling her how things had once been. She'd thought times had changed. Obviously they'd not changed enough.

33

The mistress of the house appeared to be from the same mould as her manservant. When Laura rang up later, she'd not been surprised to be told she wasn't suitable.

This latest was for a housekeeper to look after a business man, his invalid wife and small daughter. There was a nurse in attendance. She thought of the letter in her handbag written in a strong purposeful handwriting – she knew its contents by heart:

> The Cedars,
> 23 Westcliffe Drive,
> Blackpool,
> 4th February 1937.

Dear Mrs Field,

Thank you for your letter. If you're a good plain cook, then you could be what I'm looking for. I would like you to call for an interview with your little daughter tomorrow afternoon at two pm.

Yours sincerely,
Geoffrey Roberts.
P.S. If this isn't convenient, please contact me.

She halted outside a detached house with neatly kept flower beds and a huge cedar tree in which was an old bird's nest not yet blown down by the wind. "This must be it, Claire – look, there on that white-painted board – The Cedars." Claire chuckled. Laura opened the gate, and manoeuvred the pram through it and up the gravel path, which was bordered with laurel. Having learnt her lesson, this time she went around to the back. She tapped on the door. Please God, she thought, let this be third time lucky!

It opened on a smiling young woman. Over a green linen dress, she wore a white starched apron, and pinned to her glossy brown curls, a nurses' cap. "You must be Mrs Field," she said. "Do come in. I'm Rosemary Wilde, Mrs Roberts's nurse."

"How do you do," replied Laura nervously.

"Why have you come to the back door?"

She explained.

"The Roberts aren't like that. They treat their staff as equals."

Laura relaxed, and pushed the pram over the doorway and into the house.

Rosemary reached out and tickled Claire under the chin, who lifting up her arms, began talking in baby talk. "And this must be Claire? Isn't she a sweet little thing? You can leave the pram in the hall," she added.

"Thank you."

Rosemary held open a door. "Go right in."

Clutching Claire's hand, Laura entered a well-furnished, high-ceilinged room with tall windows curtained in red velvet. From behind a large desk, a man rose. He had brown hair, pleasant features and was in his middle thirties. Smiling, he put out a hand. "Mrs Field?"

"Yes."

His handshake was firm. "I'm Geoffrey Roberts." He pointed to a chair. "Do sit down."

"Thank you, Mr Roberts." She made herself comfortable, seating Claire upon her lap. She, suddenly shy, solemnly placed her finger into her mouth and refused to be drawn when the 'frightening stranger' spoke to her. Until, from a desk drawer, he produced a rag picture book.

With a whoop of delight, she took the book from him, and seated on the floor at her mother's feet was soon engrossed in looking at it.

"Now, where were we?" smiled Geoffrey Roberts.

"You were telling me that your wife would normally do the interviewing."

"That's right, but unfortunately, it's one of Mrs Roberts's bad days. She's got multiple sclerosis."

"Sorry, sir, but could you tell me what that is?"

"Simply, it's a disease of the central nervous system."

"Curable, sir?"

"Unfortunately, no." He dropped silent a moment, before continuing, "Mrs Roberts has been like this since the birth of our daughter Mollie."

Laura told him about herself. He explained the duties she would be expected to carry out if she got the post. She found herself warming to him.

"The wages will be five shillings a week, all found," he said, "would that be satisfactory?"

More than satisfactory, she thought, answering in the affirmative. Five wasn't as good as seven, but it was still a decent amount.

"Perhaps you would you like to see the housekeeper's room, Mrs Field?"

"I certainly should, Mr Roberts."

He led the way up a wide staircase carpeted in red-and-black patterned Axminster, and secured by shiny brass rods, to a pleasant room on the second floor. Next to this was a bathroom containing a bath, lavatory and wash basin for the housekeeper's use. No more lugging a tin bath into the scullery from the shed if she got this job, Laura told herself; considering it the height of luxury to have a special room for bathing. No more going out back and having to sit there with the wind whistling around her feet in winter either.

Though she had to admit that her 'in-laws lav' compared favourably to the one she and Mum had once shared with three other families. In memory a sickening stench of ammonia filled her nostrils. Mum had been the only one to clean it. Daily pouring Jeyes Fluid into the bowl and brushing it around with the lavatory brush. She had mopped the piddled floor with carbolic. Within hours it had stunk as bad as ever. Laura shrugged, thankful that the past was in the past.

The room itself had a single bed which was covered by a pink cretonne bedspread, and matched the curtains at the window. There was a mahogany wardrobe and dressing table. And, if Mr Roberts did take her on, another bed would fit in easily for Claire. But it was the excellent view of the rear garden that looked out onto trees, shrubs and a trim lawn that most impressed her.

"I've got a few more applicants to interview," said Geoffrey Roberts, seeing her to the door. "Here's my card with my phone number." He put out his hand. "If you could give me a ring tomorrow, I should have made my decision by then."

*   *   *

Pushing Claire, Laura made her way to the phone box. She parked the pram outside, securing the brake. Inside, with a trembling hand she picked up the phone, put in a coin and dialled. Mr Roberts had seemed favourably impressed when he'd interviewed her the previous day, but mightn't he have seen someone else since he'd liked better? It would be just her luck if he had. She didn't think she could bear the disappointment if she didn't get this position.

She registered the phone ringing at his end, then his voice said, "Roberts speaking."

Perspiring, she pressed button A. "This is Laura Field," she said shakily. "You asked me to ring you about the job of housekeeper."

Holding her breath, she waited. What if he said he was taking on someone else? She'd be stuck at her mother-in-law's

37

forever – a nightmare fate. She willed him to give her the answer she wanted.

A skeletal finger of a tree branch moved in the fresh breeze and tapped against the glass of the phone box.

"Oh, yes," came back his voice. "Well, I've got good news for you, Mrs Field. I've decided to take you on. Can you start as soon as possible? Your little girl will be company for mine."

CHAPTER TWO

The door creaked open.

"What do you think you're doing, my girl?"

Her chest tightened and her hands stilled on the garment she was folding. She knew that behind her, in the open doorway, with arms akimbo, was her mother-in-law, who would never think that she needed to knock on any door before entering in her own house.

"I'm waiting. Come on, I've not got all day."

Laura swallowed. She knew she would have to tell her in-laws' sometime that she was going. To just leave a note on the chest-of-drawers, was the coward's way out. Well, she was a coward. Far stronger people than her she was certain would be cowed at being on the receiving end of Doris Field's tongue and she knew that what she was about to do, wouldn't please the woman one little bit. "I'm... I'm packing."

"Packing! What on earth for?"

She took a deep breath and turned. "I'm... I'm very grateful for all you and Mr Field have done for me and Claire, but, well, I feel it's time that I stood on my own two feet, so Claire and I are leaving here." Trying to control her shaking hand, Laura carefully placed the neatly-folded garment into her suitcase. She felt sick, she'd never been much good at confrontation.

"Leaving! Leaving this house? Going where? Who on earth would take you in?" The thin lips clamped together like a steel trap.

Laura reached for another garment and began to smooth and fold it. "I've got a position as a live-in cook-housekeeper at the Cedars in Westcliffe Drive. I saw it in the *Gazette*. I start immediately." She placed the blouse into the case.

"Cook-housekeeper, indeed! I've never heard such nonsense. You've got no experience. You must have spun them a cock-and-bull story to get the position."

"I didn't!"

"No?" Her mother-in-law clicked her teeth. "What about references? Surely they asked to see them? They usually do."

"No." Was it odd that Mr Roberts hadn't asked her about references? If he had, she supposed she could have got the manager of the Tivoli to write her a character reference. But would that have helped? She had never been in Service; as far as domestic experience went, she was grassy-green.

Doris Field sniffed. "That sounds fishy to me for a start. Are you sure these people are respectable? That they haven't got some ulterior motive in taking you on?"

The brigadier definitely had, she thought. "Of course they're respectable. What ulterior motive could they have? Besides Mr Roberts is a partner at Osborne and Parkinson, stockbrokers in Queen Street. He's ever so nice."

"They say Doctor Crippen was a nice man too. Well, all I can say is I hope the Roberts' like their meals burnt or underdone."

Trust her mother-in-law to exaggerate. Dr Crippen, indeed! This insult was the last straw. The sooner she was away from here the better! If it wasn't for her child, she'd prefer to sleep under the pier than spend another second beneath her in-laws' roof.

Doris Field's manner suddenly changed. "Look, don't go rushing into anything," she said slyly, eyeing Claire, who was banging the bars of her cot with a spoon. "You don't really know these people in Westcliffe Drive. They could work you like a packhorse. I've heard some tales, I can tell you. I've been thinking of buying a wireless. I saw a five valve all-electric one in the window of the Radio Shop in Cedar Square. Paying cash down, I should be able to knock a bit off the price – get myself a bargain. You'd be very welcome to listen with us of an evening. Mrs Fisher next door has a wireless; she says there are some very good programmes broadcast."

"That won't tempt me to stay on here."

"No? Well, I think you're being very silly. You've got a comfortable room." She looked around. "You've even got a fireplace in here."

Laura eyed the small black grate. *Which, even in the coldest weather you've never allowed us to have a fire in.* It wasn't for lack of money either – it was meanness – she knew for a fact that each week several pounds from the greengrocery business went into her mother-in-law's post office book. And as for the room, not only was it poky, and the deal furniture scratched, but the green bug-splodged wallpaper, looked more like grey, it was so dingy. And though she'd tried, she'd never been able to open the window. In summer, she and Claire were stifled. "I'm leaving," Laura replied firmly, "and so is Claire."

Thick black eyebrows drew together. "Well, you can go where you like, lady, but you're not taking our Rod's child with you." She moved towards the cot. "You don't want to leave 'ums your old grandma, do you?" she said, putting on a sickly-sweet voice. "No, of course, you don't, Mummy's just being selfish, and not thinking of you at all." She turned back to Laura. "Claire's our grandchild, and her place is here with us, in this house."

"You can't stop me taking her! And her place is with me. I'm her mother."

"Well, of all the ungrateful," exploded the older woman, "and after all we've done for you. If I'd have known what I know now, that you'd take all we've got left of our Rod off without so much as a by-your-leave, I'd not have taken you in when you'd nowhere to go. It's shocking, that's what it is." Her eyes gleamed. "Anyway, how do you imagine you are going to get all your things to Westcliffe Drive? You needn't think our

41

Sid'll put himself out for you; shift everything in his van – not after the way you plan on treating us, your poor dead husband's long-suffering parents."

God forbid! She'd not risk herself in any vehicle with Sid. "We're being fetched. Sid's not the only one with his own transport, Mr Roberts, my future employer should be here soon." As Laura spoke there was a sharp rat-a-tat at the front door. "That's probably him."

From the street came the sound of a hooting car horn and shrill childish voices, followed by a man's, proving her right.

Her mother-in-law snorted. "You'd best go and see then, I'm certainly not going to answer the door like a maidservant. And, another thing, you'll have to hump your stuff downstairs on your own, that man's not to step over my threshold to help you either. This is my house, and I says who comes into it, and he's not. And don't think you can take the cot with you."

Laura eyed the cot. It was rickety and dented with the baby teeth marks of generations of Fields. They were welcome to it!

Turning on her heel, Doris Field stumped from the room. She turned. "Or come back here when things don't work out. Just wait till Mr Field learns about your 'goings-on', he'll have something to say."

That'd be a first! Laura threw the last few garments into the case, and plonking down onto the lid, attempted to close it.

*   *   *

It was Mr Roberts at the door. Laura explained the situation, and he waited outside while she carried down, first the wide-eyed Claire, and then two heavy shopping bags filled with toys and other necessary items. Finally she dragged down the bulging suitcase. After stowing everything, they drove off with the pram secured to the roof of his Austin. As the car moved smoothly along Lytham Road, Laura felt almost breathless with

42

relief at having at last actually escaped from Doris Field. Claire bounced up and down beside her upon the back seat. She looked around with interest. This was only the second time she had ever been in an automobile, the first time was on the most wonderful day of her life, her wedding day.

*   *   *

The kitchen of the Cedars was unbelievable compared to her mother-in-law's. For a start it was light and airy, with white-painted cupboards. The porcelain sink with its twin draining boards, had two taps; one of them actually being for hot water. This was provided by a solid-fuel boiler which stayed alight all the time, although it needed to be made up and the ashes emptied, night and morning. Easier work than what she was used to. It was the Economy Gas cooker itself that impressed Laura the most. She had seen an identical cooker in the window of Walmsley Brothers in Birley Street when shopping in town, but had then never expected to ever cook on one.

She ran her hands down the blue cotton overall which was her uniform as cook-housekeeper, its colour complementing her hair that she had fashioned into a chignon. Hearing laughter, she glanced through the kitchen window. Two small girls, both fair-haired and muffled up against the chill, were busily engaged in feeding their dollies with the raw carrots she had given them to eat. Claire and her employer's daughter, Mollie, were getting on even better than she could have hoped for.

It was three days since Laura and Claire's arrival at the Cedars, and after settling in, Laura had been taken by the nurse, Rosemary, into her mistress's room to learn her duties.

"Mrs Field?"

"Yes." Laura moved towards the bed, trying to ignore the fusty smell of the invalid, seeing a pale drawn woman with sparse fair hair in an elegant lemon satin nightdress and matching angora bed jacket, and beside her, on a bedside table, was a stack of well-thumbed paperbacks. Nearby was another table with medicine and cordial bottles, pill boxes, spoons and tumblers.

Her employer nodded towards a chair. "Do sit down."

Laura did so. Was this woman really only in her middle thirties? She looked far older. The trembling hands were almost as white as the lace-edged bed sheet and disfigured with knotted veins. How awful that someone so young should be so afflicted. To be bedridden was bad enough, but for Mrs Roberts to be unable to do anything for her own child was even worse. She would have hated it if she couldn't have cared for Claire and had needed to rely on someone else to do the mothering for her.

"As my husband has no doubt already told you," said Mrs Roberts, "you will be required to provide three meals a day, as well as look after Mollie. Mr Roberts will not usually require a midday meal. The tradesmen all deliver. You can ring them from the phone in the hall to place your orders. The laundry service calls once a week for the heavy washing. Rosemary will fill you in on anything else."

Her duties didn't sound too heavy – lighter in fact, than those she was expected to do at her mother-in-law's. She thought of the recipes she'd found in the kitchen drawer, left, she imagined by their previous cook. They would be a big help in planning her menus. And at least she didn't think she'd be expected to cook up any outlandish curries. She suspected that poor Mrs Roberts's appetite wouldn't run to things like that. But what, if what she cooked, didn't come up to scratch? Of course it would, thoughts like this were defeatist; she just couldn't fail.

"All the accounts are to be given to Mr Roberts for him to settle at the end of each week," continued Mrs Roberts. "You will eat in the kitchen, with the children and Rosemary, after you have served Mr Roberts in the dining room. I, of course, will take mine in here." She sank back onto her pillows.

Saddened, Laura returned to the kitchen. How unfair life was for some people. She'd really needed to concentrate to hear her mistress's low voice, as if even talking was a great effort. The only lively thing about Mrs Roberts were her brown eyes.

As the weeks passed she became used to her new life and surroundings. Her mother-in-law had soon turned up, insisting that she see Claire. Doris Field was her old overbearing self, but despite this Laura decided to allow her to take Claire to her house one afternoon a week – after all, the woman was Rod's mother, and Laura didn't want to deprive Claire of a relationship with her grandparents. Winter turned to spring. Laura's worries about her culinary skills proved groundless; her roasts, hot pots and suet roly-polys were more than acceptable, as were her spotted dicks, apple pies, crumbles and milk puddings. Claire grew and flourished on her mother's cooking and so did Mollie. Though it must be said that Mrs Roberts's appetite was no bigger than a bird's.

Laura saw quite a lot of both her employers. At breakfast time she served Mr Roberts with his bacon and eggs and pot of tea. At around ten-thirty, after a pleasant evening spent with Rosemary in the small sitting room allowed for their personal use, with herself knitting a cardigan for Claire and Rosemary knitting one for Mollie, while listening to the wireless, or laughing and chattering, Laura would make herself and Rosemary, a milky bedtime drink. At the same time she would take her employer a cup to the drawing room, where, relaxing from the pressures of his day, he listened to classical records. He always tried to engage her in conversation. Was he just being pleasant? Or was it something more than this? After all, Mrs Roberts was too sick to be much of a companion to him and he was probably lonely? A little voice said, she'd not be able to be a proper wife either as regards the intimate side of marriage, and Mr Roberts (who slept in a separate bedroom to his wife) was still quite a young man. No, she mustn't think such thoughts. An unaccountable warm feeling stirred within her breast, as she visualised him; a lock of brown hair falling over his brow, as he rose, smiling, from behind his desk to greet her that first afternoon. She shook herself, what was all this about? Apart from any disloyalty to the memory of Rod, Mr Roberts was not only middle-class, but a married man and off limits to her. So what? retorted the voice, he was also extremely attractive.

She had always fought shy of married men in the past, not that she'd ever been that tempted by any of them – the ones eyeing her up were mostly twice her age, paunchy, and with pink scalps showing through carefully arranged hair. She knew, though that several of her colleagues at the Tivoli had had affairs with married men. And look how those affairs had ended up. Either the girls were left with a broken heart when the man got cold feet and dumped her, or worse still, they ended up with a baby, which having no choice, being unable to afford to keep it, they had to give up for adoption.

Months passed. There was the abdication and the Coronation of King George VI, and his Queen, Elizabeth. The streets of Blackpool were decked with red, white and blue bunting and Claire was fetched by Doris Field to attend a party in her street. She'd wanted to keep Claire for the night, but Laura had put her foot down, it didn't hurt for her mother-in-law to be reminded whose child Claire actually was.

When Rosemary had her half-day off, Laura would sometimes wheel Mrs Roberts in her bath chair, when she was well enough, around Stanley Park, Claire and Mollie running on ahead of them, giggling, as they played tag on the grass or picked the daisies. On these trips, Gloria Roberts, her spindly legs covered by a crochet blanket would come alive as she reminisced about her girlhood in the South of England and the dances in country houses where she'd been belle of the ball. As time passed, Laura began to feel a rapport was developing between herself and the sick woman. Especially when she started reading aloud to Mrs Roberts, her condition having worsened so much that she was now unable to hold a book herself. She was always so grateful; praising her, saying that she'd an excellent reading voice. They were halfway through the recently published best seller from America, *Gone with the Wind*, and both of them on tenterhooks to learn more of Scarlett O'Hara's adventures.

Laura also helped Rosemary to set up a waterbed to prevent bedsores, when Mrs Roberts suffered one of her turns. To do this they had to lift her off her bed on her mattress, so for a while she lay on the floor on the mattress while they heaved the waterbed into place. They'd spent some time filling it with water from the bathroom tap. It was an unwieldy object; it leapt about convulsively as the water swelled up into its various compartments. They then lifted her up, Laura at her head, supporting the frail shoulders, and Rosemary at her feet, and laid her on the strange new balloon of a mattress. Mrs Roberts was exhausted by the process, but smiled at them and insisted she was more comfortable.

As the friendship between Rosemary and Laura grew, they disclosed to each other the details of their past lives. Rosemary had been born and bred in Essex, where her parents and elder married sister still lived. She, like Laura had loved, but unlike Laura, been jilted. After this, deciding to train as a nurse, she'd qualified in London. Later, an advertisement for a live in nurse in the *Times* brought her to Blackpool. "So you see, it was all for the best in the long run," she concluded brightly.

"Still, it must have been awful to be jilted," said Laura.

"I was very upset at the time, I must admit. But compared to you losing your Rod like you did; well, it puts it into perspective."

"It was like being in the middle of a nightmare at first," said Laura, her voice thickening, "Pete, the young lad Rod had taken on, filled me in on what actually happened. They were

47

wheeling Rod's bike with his ladders tied to it, past this house in Bloomfield Road, when they saw it was on fire, and that a child was at the upstairs window. Rod never hesitated. He had a ladder up in a flash and smashing the glass, climbed in and got the kiddy, handing her down to Pete. But before Rod could climb down himself, he was overcome by smoke. By this time the fire brigade had been called. They found him on the bedroom floor. He was taken to hospital. Everything was done that could be done, but he was already dead."

Rosemary put an arm around Laura's shoulders. "What a tragedy, you poor thing."

"Rod's funeral service was at the same church as our marriage, only ten days before." Her wedding day had been glorious with sunshine, whereas the sky was overcast on the darkest day of her life, mirroring her feelings. It seemed impossible that one moment she could be deliriously happy, and the next, plunged to such despair. At Layton cemetery, with the vicar leading, friends and family, two by two, followed behind Rod's deal coffin, shouldered by his snooker-playing mates towards the waiting grave, with herself in borrowed black, supported by the arm of her father-in-law.

"I don't know how you managed to come through it all," said Rosemary.

"I had no choice, had I?" She'd thrown a handful of dirt that rattled onto the coffin lid, the harsh sobs of her mother-in-law beside her somehow intrusive, as were all the well-meaning words of condolence from so many solemn-faced strangers at the funeral meal at the Fields. What a relief it had been to be able at last to escape to grieve on her own.

"Still, at least you've got Claire. She must be a big comfort to you."

"She's my reason for carrying on."

Laura discovered where Rosemary went on her half-days off. Rosemary's humming as she straightened the seams of her silk stockings before leaving the house, had got Laura wondering. Maybe Rosemary was meeting a man? She wasn't. She was meeting a girl like herself, who nursed an elderly gentleman in St Annes. Ethel would meet Rosemary in Blackpool town centre and they would usually go to see a film.

They were relaxing in their sitting room, the days chores over. "Look, Rosemary... LMS cheap Sunday excursions to Rhyl, Colwyn Bay, and Llandudno."

Rosemary took the paper and read, "Why do you want to go on a trip?"

"It'd be a change, for me and for Claire. I haven't had a holiday since my honeymoon in Southport."

Rosemary's brow creased. "Your Claire wouldn't want to go unless Mollie went too, now, would she? They're as thick as thieves, those two, but even if Mr and Mrs Roberts agreed, would you want to handle both children on your own? They're a handful at the best of times, especially when they're together."

"Couldn't you come too? You're due some time off, aren't you?"

"Yes, but..."

"But, what? I'd enjoy the trip twice as much if you came too, Rosemary. It'll make all the difference to have someone to share the experience with. I know I'd have the children, but its hardly the same as an adult, is it?"

"No, I suppose not. I'd like to come with you. Mrs Roberts hasn't been so poorly of late, and on a Sunday Mr Roberts would be at home and he could give her her medicine."

"Yes, of course he could. And I could leave them a ham salad and trifle for their lunch, and perhaps some sandwiches and cake for later. I'm sure it would all work out," said Laura.

"We'll ask them, see what they say. I won't go if they don't think they can manage."

"Of course you wouldn't, but I can't see that they would object. Claire and Mollie would be keen, I'm sure."

"Keen's an understatement!" Both laughed.

"What about food for us? Those two can eat a horse and then some – I really don't know where they put it all. We could have a meal in a cafe but that would make things far more expensive. And where do you want to go? Llandudno, Colwyn Bay, or Rhyl? I can't say I've any real preference, one way or the other."

Laura folded up the newspaper. "I can do a picnic to take with us. And as for our destination, I'm in the same mind as you."

Mr and Mrs Roberts agreed to their suggestion, not only for them to go on the trip, but for Mollie to accompany Claire, and a coin decided their destination – Llandudno.

Tickets were bought, all arrangements made, and the days were counted off eagerly. But on the morning of the trip, just as Laura was helping the excited Claire to get dressed, Rosemary tapped on their door and said she was sorry, but Mrs Roberts had had one of her bad turns in the night; she had, in fact, just called the doctor, so she didn't feel she ought to go on the excursion.

What should she do? thought Laura. Should she go on her own with Claire and Mollie? She didn't fancy coping with them alone. Or should she give the trip a miss altogether? It seemed a shame to have to disappoint the girls, though, both of them had been so looking forward to it; besides there was the tickets. There was no way she could get the cost of them back, she'd just have to lose the money, and she didn't really like to waste money. Even though she was better off than she'd ever been, the old habit of watching the pennies was ingrained in her.

Laura had almost made up her mind to tell the children that the trip was off, when to her astonishment, Mr Roberts said that he and Mrs Roberts had been discussing the situation, and between them, they'd decided that rather than disappoint both Claire and Mollie, he would use Rosemary's ticket, which he would pay Rosemary for, and accompany the children and Laura to Llandudno instead.

It was all hustle after that, Laura had no time to consider the way her pulse raced at the thought of spending a whole day, with only two small girls as chaperones, in her employer's company. Or to wonder if the latest hairstyle that was all the rave, the Eugene, with its waves which swept off the forehead, became her. Or for that matter, the pink-and-white floral dress she'd bought especially for the trip. The food she'd prepared, sandwiches, pork pie, cake and iced biscuits, as well as a large flask of tea were placed in a wicker hamper and Mr Roberts carried it out to his Austin, which he would park at the station for when they returned. After the *goodbyes,* they left, with Mr Roberts at the wheel, Claire and Mollie, giggling excitedly, bouncing about on the back seat, Laura vainly trying to restrain them.

The platform was crowded with home-going holidaymakers, their youngsters' buckets filled with small crabs and seashells. With the hamper and folded pushchair beside them, Claire held Laura's hand, and Mollie her father's. Spotting a chocolate machine, the children tugged their parents over to it. Smiling, Mr Roberts pressed two pennies into each girl's hand. Carefully, Mollie, and then Claire, inserted their coins into the slot, squealing with delight, as with a whirr, a second Fry's chocolate sandwich appeared.

Hardly had they torn off the wrappings, than the train steamed into the station; it jolted to a halt, brakes squealing. Everyone surged towards it. Mr Roberts opened the door of an empty compartment and helped Laura and the children up into it, placing the hamper and pushchair on the overhead rack. Beneath was a sepia print of Morecambe pier.

Both Claire and Mollie headed for seats nearest the windows, and scrambling onto them, knelt with faces pressed to the glass. A whistle blew. The train shuddered. Then with a

51

clatter, the wheels began turning. Gazing out of the window, they watched the terraced houses and small backyards with criss-crossed washing lines rapidly change to fields, bushes, and trees, with brown and white cows and woolly sheep nibbling grass. They licked their lips and fingers of the last of the chocolate. Laura, with a clicking of her tongue, cleaned their smeared faces with a spit-dampened hanky, they wriggling, turning back to the window. Eventually, tiring, and rocked by the regular motion of the train, they slumped against the adults and fell asleep.

Mr Roberts put aside his newspaper. "They look like angels," he remarked with a smile.

"I have to admit it's a treat to have them quiet." Her employer looked so different today. He wore a green-and-brown herringbone tweed sports jacket and brown trousers, and his emerald-coloured tie was fastened by a silver pin. His usual dark business suits and striped shirts, though smart, made him look older than he actually was.

"Would you mind if I smoked?" he asked.

"Why should I mind? I like to see a man smoking." Most men smoked and like the majority of women she thought it added to their attractiveness.

"That's all right, then." He held towards her his open cigarette case. "Do you? They're Du Maurier."

She shook her head.

He lit up and taking a satisfying pull of the cigarette, exhaled.

She breathed in its aroma with pleasure. Was he about to engage her in conversation? What on earth could someone like herself, who had left school at fourteen, find to say to an educated man like he was? She knew nothing about stocks and shares or classical music for that matter, though she had enjoyed the Viennese waltzes by Strauss.

"So do you like being at the Cedars?" he asked.

She took a deep breath. "I certainly do." For the first time in years she felt content, happy even. She had never expected to again, not after losing Rod, and being obliged to live with her in-laws. Now, she not only had understanding employers' and a comfortable home for herself and Claire, but best of all she had made a good friend in Rosemary.

"I'm glad. Both Mrs Roberts and myself hope that you and Claire will stay on with us on a permanent basis. I suppose life wasn't easy for you after your husband died?" he added sympathetically, as if reading her thoughts. "Your mother-in-law, well..."

Mr Roberts had been at home once when Doris Field had called to see Claire. No doubt he'd summed up her character correctly. "No, far from easy." She found herself confiding her life story, starting with her childhood: how she'd won a scholarship to Chorley Grammar School, but that her mother couldn't afford to let her go – her first job in a wool shop; her coming to Blackpool and her meeting Rod – ending with her unhappiness at the Fields'.

The train was slowing, with a jerk, and a squealing of brakes, it halted at a station. She realised that she'd been talking about herself for ages. How could she have gone on like she had? Was he bored? He didn't look it. She thought of what she hadn't told him; the poverty she and Mum had lived in with her father not returning from the war? Her mother had taken in washing. It was her job after school to deliver it in the big ramshackle pram. Though perhaps they'd not been as poor as some in their neighbourhood whose fathers had returned, or hadn't gone. In some households there was a new baby every year. Many in her class had gone to school with their backsides hanging out of their trousers, or in a cast-off too-large dress. She'd seen them run after mill workers when they came off shift, begging for leftover bread from their lunches. She had felt slightly superior, until her mother was ill in bed and not able to earn anything. Then she'd been so hungry, she'd joined them!

There was a commotion on the platform; the compartment door was wrenched open. A family party, mum, dad, grandma and several boys of assorted ages, wearing short trousers and with scabby knees and socks that concertinaed down legs prepared to enter. Laura groaned inwardly, knowing that with others present, any further conversation between her and Mr Roberts would be out of the question. Hardly had she thought this, than the door was slammed-to.

The train moved off. They began to talk again – this time Mr Roberts told her about himself – that he was born and bred in Birmingham, and had come to Blackpool some years earlier for his wife's health – the sea air.

Claire and Mollie were stirring, and close-packed blackened trees and undergrowth were flashing past the compartment window. Were they in North Wales already? Were they approaching their destination?

It was bedlam. He pulled down the hamper and pushchair from the rack. She helped the girls to their feet. Getting off, with the two youngsters jiggling about, Laura was struck not only by the fact that it was a lovely sunny day with white clouds in a blue sky, but by the singsong accent of a vendor as Mr Roberts bought a map of Llandudno from a platform kiosk. Shoulder to shoulder, they studied it together, looking for places of interest. She breathed in the pleasant smell of her employer's shaving soap. Accidentally, their cheeks brushed. Laura jerked back – feeling a strange sensation in her chest. "How about the 'White Rabbit' memorial to Lewis Carroll?" she said faintly.

He touched the side of his face. "A good idea, haven't you just begun reading *Alice In Wonderland* to Claire and Mollie?"

Claire pulled at Laura's skirt. "We're hungry, Mummy, we're both hungry."

"Hungy, Hungy," chanted Mollie, dancing around them.

Mr Roberts pointed to the map. This time Laura kept her distance. "Well, let's go and find this Haulfre Public Gardens and have our picnic. There are swings and roundabouts there too. We can see the 'White Rabbit' later."

"Hurrah!" cheered the girls.

Despite the gardens being no distance, first Mollie and then Claire, wanted to go in the pushchair. Laura was glad she'd brought one.

Both children livened up when they got to the play area and they had to try everything in sight.

After pushing the squealing youngsters on the swings, both Laura and Mr Roberts sank down thankfully onto the grass. Later, Laura, opening the hamper, spread a tablecloth, laying it neatly with crockery and cutlery.

Mollie and Claire came running over.

"They should have a good appetite after all their exertions. I only hope I've packed enough food?"

"Looks like there's enough to feed an army."

Laura smiled. She turned to the girls. "Now, sit down properly, you can't have anything to eat unless you do."

They both pulled a face, but seated themselves cross-legged and Laura tied napkins around their necks, before handing each of them a plate of food.

As she passed Mr Roberts a piled plate, their hands touched. Something, almost like a charge of electricity seemed to run up her arm. By the gleam in his eyes, this had affected him too. Or was she imagining it? Surely she was imagining it? If not, what did it all mean? She brushed aside the notion that she might be falling for him. And worse still, that he might be falling for her. This just couldn't happen. It would spoil everything. She was happy where she was, she didn't want to have to leave, to need to find another position, that's if she could find one? For in such circumstances, she would have to leave the Cedars.

Her mother had sent her to Sunday School as a child. She knew right from wrong. There was no way she could have some cheap affair with her employer – commit adultery – while under the same roof as his wife, whom she not only respected, but was becoming fond of.

Not a crumb was left from their tea, and as she tidied everything away in the hamper, she pushed the problem to the back of her mind. She just wouldn't think about it and then it would go away. There was no overwhelming attraction between her and her employer – it was all in her imagination.

The 'White Rabbit' memorial was followed by a trip to the beach, making sandcastles, and paddling in the shallows. As they watched the happy, excited girls, Mr Roberts suddenly said, "When I was their age, I wouldn't have been allowed to paddle or play with sand, my nanny was a real gorgon. I was never allowed to get dirty."

"That's a shame." Hearing this, she was glad her childhood hadn't been a middle class one.

Before returning to the station, they went around the small gift shops on the promenade to buy keepsakes. Laura helped Mollie choose a green leaf enamel brooch for her mother. They bought sticks of pink peppermint rock with Llandudno stamped through the centre. Suddenly Mr Roberts disappeared into a shop and came out a minute later with a shell necklace that Laura had admired. "This is for you, Laura."

"Oh, no, I can't accept a present."

"It's just for giving us such a wonderful day. And Mrs Roberts suggested that I buy you a 'thank you'."

For a moment, his words blunted her overwhelming feelings of happiness, until she saw the way he was looking at her – which said clearly that this was 'his' gift, and not his wife's.

The children danced around and Claire said, "Wear it now, Mummy, wear it now."

"Here," he said, "let me fasten it for you."

She blushed, but agreed. His fingers lingering on the back of her neck caused delicious shivers. As the compartment swayed rhythmically on their homeward journey; the girls slumped asleep against them, she looked up to find that Mr Roberts's hazel eyes were fixed on her in a most personal manner.

Brushing the shells at her throat with a finger, she couldn't help but feel pleased.

CHAPTER THREE

Laura tried to avoid him as much as she could. This wasn't easy. Her sleep, too, was disturbed; she kept dreaming about Geoffrey, as she called him to herself. They would be making love. She would jerk awake, pleasure turning to pain, feeling despicable and in a cold sweat, with the bedclothes tangled around her. She shouldn't be having such dreams, it just wasn't right. Geoffrey could never be hers! He belonged to a sick woman. A woman who had always treated her with kindness and consideration, and whom she'd never want to hurt.

Then she made the mistake of telling Mrs Roberts that her twenty-third birthday was coming up. Laura had been reading to her.

The brown eyes glistened. "You should have seen me when I was twenty-three," said Mrs Roberts softly. "It's all of twelve years ago, 1925 in fact, but it feels like yesterday. My parents gave a party for me in the grounds of our house. They hired a marquee as there were so many guests invited. I had a wonderful dress from Worth, white taffeta, with tiny pink rosebuds on the shoulders. It was at that party that I first met Mr Roberts. He was brought by my cousin, Jack; he and Jack were both studying at St John's College, Cambridge. Mr Roberts and I danced every dance – I tore up my dance-card so that every dance could be his. We were married before the year was out. There's a photograph…" She sank back weakly onto her pillows.

"Shall I continue?" asked Laura.

"No, not yet. I want you to see the photo – the one of me wearing that dress. They said I was beautiful then, you know. The album's in there, in the top one." She indicated a chest of drawers.

Laura put a marker between the pages of the book. She wasn't certain she wanted to see any photographs – perhaps one of them together, young and very much love. She could hardly refuse though. She'd no right to feel jealousy at the idea of him being in love with someone else. It was awful to be jealous of a woman so ill, anyway, but despite the physical side between Geoffrey and his wife of necessity being very much in the past, mightn't she feel jealousy with the evidence before her? Opening the drawer, she found a red leather-covered album. "Is this it?"

"Yes, bring it over to the bed."

She placed the album in front of Mrs Roberts; she had to open it for her and slowly turn the pages which were covered in semi-transparent paper.

"There's one of Pater."

Laura looked closer at the photograph, registering a jovial-looking portly man of about sixty in dark dress clothes. With a glass in his hand, he was toasting the camera.

"And there's Mater. She's stood next to her elder sister, my Aunt Jane; that's the taller one on the right," explained Mrs Roberts, moist-eyed.

Two smartly-dressed, almost identical white-haired women in slightly old-fashioned clothing, smiled out from the snapshot in question.

"Aunt Jane lost her young man in the Boer War and so never married. They're all gone now. My dear parents in a car crash eight years ago, and Aunt Jane of cancer, three years after that." She sighed.

Laura was studying the photograph of a young couple. Seated on a chaise longue in some sort of floral arbour, Geoffrey, some pounds lighter than he was now, had an arm around the shoulders of a very pretty girl in a white dress. From what she'd been told of the dress, she realised that the girl, whose eyes shone with joy, had to be Mrs Roberts, dressed up in all her finery for her birthday party. The tender look on Geoffrey's face as he bent towards her was unmistakable.

"Yes, that's me," confirmed Mrs Roberts.

"You were lovely!"

"To look at me now you wouldn't think it the same person, would you?"

Laura denied this, although she thought it herself.

Mrs Roberts patted Laura's hand. "Now, your birthday. Next week, you said?"

"Next Saturday, the 19th of September."

"Hmm. I think your birthday should be a day to remember, as mine was. You're only twenty-three once. What would you say to having a meal out to celebrate – I was thinking, afternoon tea at Lewis's? My treat."

She'd seen Lewis's advertising in the *Gazette*. For such a posh place, their teas at 1/6d a head, were excellent value. "That's very kind of you, but, well, I shouldn't want to go on my own, and anyway if I went, who would mind Claire and Mollie? I couldn't be missing all afternoon."

"Why not? I'm sure Rosemary would look after the children," said Mrs Roberts. "You certainly don't need to worry about them. And as for you having to go there on your own, you don't need to."

"I don't, but who…?"

"I'm sure Mr Roberts would be only too pleased to accompany you."

Mr Roberts! Laura panicked. She had to get out of this, she just couldn't spend any more time alone with Geoffrey. Why was Mrs Roberts pushing them together like she was? "I've nothing suitable to wear to somewhere like Lewis's."

Mrs Roberts laughed. "An excuse like that won't wash with me." She nodded towards the massive oak wardrobe. "That's filled with clothes that I'll never wear again. You are about the size I used to be. Help yourself!"

Laura had no choice but to give in gracefully.

The day of her twenty-third birthday dawned. She was woken by Rosemary with a cup of tea, and a parcel wrapped in red tissue paper that contained a pair of black suede gloves. Claire and Mollie, too, had presents for her and home-made cards that they'd drawn with coloured crayons. Claire's present to her mummy was a handkerchief with a rather crooked *Laura* embroidered in pink silk in one corner, and Mollie's, a tiny bottle of *Evening in Paris*, which Laura suspected had been obtained for Mollie by her father. She'd also given her a card, a large, lace-edged one on which was written in masterful handwriting, Best wishes from Geoffrey and Gloria Roberts.

Laura took as long as she could to clear up after lunch, but in the end she had no option but to get ready for the outing to Lewis's and the afternoon tea with another woman's husband. The borrowed dress, coat and hat lay on her bed. Obviously haute couture, they were of a quality she'd never expected to wear herself. She had with difficulty picked them from all the other expensive outfits in Mrs Roberts's wardrobe. The full-skirted dress with the sweetheart neckline and narrow sleeves was of pale green wool. The coat, with a half-belt at the back was three-quarters in length and cream-coloured. The matching velour hat had a perky green feather.

She put on the dress and ran her hands down herself, feeling with pleasure the softness of the wool. Taking the imitation pearl necklace, Rod's wedding gift, and thinking tenderly of him, she fastened it around her neck, before putting on the coat and hat. She studied herself in the mirror – a stranger, a rather stylish stranger, looked back at her.

Gloria Roberts was so enthusiastic when she saw her. "I knew that coat and dress would really suit you. I shall want to know exactly what happens at Lewis's – what you have to eat, and what music the band plays. I do hope you have a good time."

"I do too," said Rosemary. "And don't worry about the children, I'll take them for a walk, it's a nice afternoon."

Laura, embarrassed at the warm appraisal of Geoffrey Roberts's eyes, said she wouldn't worry – she knew Rosemary was more than capable. Clutching her handbag to her, as if it were a shield to protect her from the turmoil churning through her, Laura followed him out to his car.

Surrounded by tall ferns in Chinese-looking vases and mirrored-walls that reflected and enhanced; the atmosphere of the restaurant heavy with perfume and cigarette smoke, she faced Geoffrey across a white-clothed table for two, upon which cutlery glinted – too apprehensive to enjoy the medley of popular tunes that were being played by *Johnny Rose and his band*.

Laura had to make an effort to take in the scene, the other tables and their occupants, many of them stylishly-dressed women of all ages, who chattered as noisily as parrots in a parrot-house. Mrs Roberts would want a full description of everything and everyone.

A waiter handed them thick cream-coloured menus. Geoffrey's eyes ran down the list of high-teas on offer. He turned to Laura. "What would you like?" he asked.

She looked:

> Fried fillet of plaice and chips,
> or salmon mayonnaise. Or choice
> of ham, tongue, beef or lamb, with salad,
> brown or white bread and butter.
> Pot of tea and fancy cakes.

She laid the menu aside. "It all sounds absolutely delicious, but I'm not sure I'm very hungry, Mr Roberts."

"Geoffrey. You can't keep calling me Mr Roberts." He smiled at her encouragingly.

What would he think if he knew that she always thought of him as Geoffrey? "I suppose not, er… Geoffrey."

"Good! This is your treat, Laura. You've got to eat something. Mrs Roberts would be very disappointed if she thought you hadn't enjoyed yourself. Look, why don't I order us both plaice and chips?"

"If you like."

"Brown bread or white?"

"Brown, please."

"For me, too." He turned to the waiter. "Two plaice and chips, brown bread and butter, a pot of tea and a selection of fancy cakes."

"Certainly, sir." The waiter scribbled onto his pad.

The food, and the rest of the order set before them, she poured the tea and passed Geoffrey his cup. She took a slice of brown bread from the lower willow-patterned plate of the cake stand and nervously picked up her fish knife and fork. How was she going to manage to get through all this? Her stomach was full of butterflies. Geoffrey was tucking in with gusto. Their tête-à-tête meal was obviously not affecting him as it did her.

He put down his knife. "Now, come on, I can't eat if you don't." He picked up her fork, and putting a little bit of her fish onto the prong, he offered it to her. She had no option but to take it from him.

He smiled. "That was tasty, wasn't it?"

She couldn't reply. He laughed, and somehow, as she finished her high-tea with a chocolate éclair oozing with cream – the magic of his company, coupled with the strains of *These Foolish Things* had such an effect on her, that she found that not only was she enjoying herself, but she was wishing that the afternoon would never end.

Gloria Roberts couldn't get enough of Laura's account of all she had seen and heard at Lewis's; wanting to know every little detail, especially those of the latest ladies' fashions. By the time, she retired for the night, her throat was quite dry, despite having emptied a pot of tea and drunk a cup of Ovaltine.

She tossed fretfully, her sleep disturbed by a shameful dream of Geoffrey and herself. She jerked awake. Claire was calling! She bent over her bed. "What is it, darling?"

"Thirsty, Mummy."

"I'll get you a drink of water." Perhaps Claire was coming down with a cold? Mollie had just had one.

"No, Mummy, not water, can I have a drink of milk?"

"Milk! It'll mean Mummy going down to the kitchen to get it. Can't you make do with water?"

"Please, Mummy."

Laura yawned. She'd better do what Claire asked, it would be quicker in the long run, and then they could both get back to sleep. "All right, love. I'll not be long."

Slipping on her dressing gown, she went downstairs. There was a crack of light showing from beneath the drawing room door. Geoffrey! It could only be him burning the midnight oil, no doubt attempting to catch up with work he should have done earlier at his office instead of entertaining her. She hugged herself at the notion of the two of them being the only ones awake in the house. What would she do if he should suddenly come out of the drawing room? What she was wearing was hardly indecent, but all the same the rayon material did rather cling to her figure – making her feel uneasy. She went into the kitchen, and opening the door of the walk-in pantry, reached the milk jug down from the marble shelf. She was just leaving the kitchen, with a tumbler of milk in her hand, when she almost collided with Geoffrey.

"Good Grief!" he exclaimed, moving aside. "I thought we'd got a burglar."

She laughed nervously, clutching the neck of her dressing gown together. "Claire's restless," she explained. "I was just getting her a drink of milk."

"That's fine. I was just going to make myself a cup of coffee. I've still got a stack of paperwork to get through, and well, the figures were dancing before my eyes. I thought my brain might work better."

"Good idea." He was stood too close, his breath, warm on her cheek. "Let me make it for you?" she said faintly, placing the tumbler on the table and half-turning towards the pantry.

His hand whitened on the back of a chair. "Thank you," he said, "but, no, you'd best get back to Claire, I can manage."

"If you're sure?"

"I am."

She picked up the milk.

"You did enjoy yourself this afternoon?" he suddenly asked, his voice strangely hoarse.

She turned back to him. A muscle was working in his throat, and there was a faint beading of sweat on his brow. "Yes, it was wonderful." Their eyes met, his hot with something dark and unfathomable. Hardly realising what she was doing, she put down the tumbler and moved closer. Their lips met in a long sweet kiss and his arms came around, clasping her tightly, pressing her breasts into the roughness of his tweed jacket. "Oh, Laura!"

Appalled, they both drew back. "I'm sorry," he said shakily. "I shouldn't have done that."

How on earth would she be able to face Mrs Roberts after this? Mrs Roberts had been so kind to her; what a way to repay her kindness. "No, no, it wasn't your fault," she mumbled stiffly, "it was just as much mine."

"I must take the blame. A man should be responsible for his actions. I've got a wife that I care about, I've got no right to kiss anyone else." He turned away.

"I shall have to leave here."

He turned back. "No, you mustn't do that," he said urgently.

65

"But after this, I shall have to."

"I don't want you to go. Neither would Gloria; why she considers you part of the family. Look, Laura, it was only one kiss. It doesn't have to lead to anything. Besides, if you gave in your notice, how would you explain why you wanted to leave? She thinks you're happy here."

"It wouldn't be easy."

"Then why do it? Surely we can try and forget what has just happened? We must make sure it goes no further."

"Can we do that?"

"We've got to."

Was it possible for herself and Geoffrey to live under the same roof, feeling as they obviously did for each other, and deny themselves? She wasn't at all certain. A cry came from upstairs. "Mummy! Mummy!"

"There's Claire, I must go" – picking up the tumbler, and hurrying from the room.

She pushed open the bedroom door. "Here you are, darling," she said, in what she hoped was a natural manner.

The next morning when she placed Geoffrey's breakfast in front of him she tried to pretend that those moments in the kitchen had never happened. This wasn't easy, just being in the same room as he was made her go hot all over. It was obvious too, by the way his hand shook on his teacup that he was also finding the situation difficult. He certainly didn't hang about over his breakfast. But for Laura the worst moment came when she entered Mrs Roberts's room to receive her orders for the day. Although, as Geoffrey insisted, nothing had actually occurred between them, guilt-pangs made her stomach churn so much that she needed to visit the lavatory.

In the afternoon, her chores finished for a few hours, she read from *Gone with the Wind* to Mrs Roberts. By the time everything was cleared up from the evening meal, and she was enjoying a programme on the wireless with Rosemary, she began to feel that perhaps this *forgetting* what had happened, might work after all. She was so happy at the Cedars, she didn't want to have to leave. There was Claire to consider too. If they left here, Claire would also have to leave Mollie. And why should the children lose out? At ten, Laura laid down her knitting, and went to make the bedtime drinks. As was usual, she took Geoffrey in his Ovaltine.

She entered the drawing room. He was turning back from putting on a record. "Thank you," he said, averting his head.

With a shaking hand and flushed face, she put the cup down on the table by his chair. "Is there anything else you need?" she asked, not looking at him.

He hesitated. "No. Well, not at present." He picked up his Du Maurier cigarette from the ashtray and taking a pull on it, exhaled.

Despite the tension she was feeling, she breathed in its aroma with pleasure.

The record on the turnstile began to play. To her astonishment it was Bing Crosby singing her favourite song. Geoffrey must have remembered her saying that she liked it. He'd said he'd not got it.

> "A cigarette that bears a lipstick traces
> An airline ticket to romantic places,
> And still my heart has wings,
> These foolish things remind me of you."

She went to pass him, but he wouldn't let her.

"I must go."

"Laura!"

She looked up at him. Then she was in his arms, his lips pressed hers, their kisses, tinged with desperation; so sweet, so tender… Her senses swam – she felt as light as the down of a dandelion drifting over the silky sand dunes. Did he feel the same? If the pressure of his fingertips caressing her back was anything to go by, he did!

"You came," sung Bing,
"You conquered me!
"When you did that to me,
"I knew somehow this had to be… had to be… had to be…"

Footsteps broke through her consciousness. Rosemary! Geoffrey had heard her too, and they sprang guiltily apart.

Rosemary carried on straight past the open doorway; they catching a glimpse of her green overall in the long mirror. It was only then that they realised that the gramophone needle was stuck.

Geoffrey stopped the record. "I don't think she saw us."

"Are you sure?"

"Pretty certain," he said shakily.

"I don't know where I'd have put myself if she'd walked straight in on us," said Laura.

"Well, she didn't. I don't think we've anything to worry about."

"How can you say that? If she'd seen us kissing, she'd probably think she ought to tell Mrs Roberts what she'd seen."

"I don't think so, Gloria's a very sick woman, she wouldn't want to cause her such stress. I'm sure she'd think that least said, soonest mended."

"Oh, would she now. That would be very convenient for you, wouldn't it?"

"Don't! It's not like that at all. All this is as hard for me as it is for you. I don't make a habit of it, you know."

"How do I know?" Her mouth trembled. "Mrs Roberts would be so upset if she knew what was going on right under her nose. Now, wouldn't she? I think, taking everything into consideration, I should look for another position immediately."

"No, no, Laura. You mustn't!"

"You know I've got to. I've no choice."

"I know it's not going to be easy, you staying on here after this, but, well, I don't think I can do without you."

Could this be true? He was an educated man. What had they really in common? "But what about your wife," she stammered, "don't you love her anymore?"

He looked confused. "Yes, of course I do; but, well, it's different, different to what I feel for you. What has happened won't happen again. I won't let it. From now on, I'll be strong, I'll keep things platonic. You'll see."

"Do you think that's possible?" she asked, weakening.

He nodded. "The most important thing is that you remain here, in this house. We've got to be able to at least see each other; you want to keep on seeing me, don't you?"

She had to admit she did; that she would be devastated at the alternative. In the end, she came round to his way of thinking, relieved in truth to have had her mind changed by him.

Laura returned to Rosemary with their milky drinks, considering her demeanour slyly as she placed the tray in front of her, and was satisfied that Rosemary was no wiser by the way she blithely tucked into Laura's home-made ginger biscuits.

But in reality, she was still worried. Several nights running footsteps woke her. As Rosemary slept in the next room to her patient on the ground floor, they could only belong to Geoffrey. After a few moments, she heard him descend the stairs, then a door close. Following this, she longed for him so much, for the feel of his arms around her and his lips on hers, that couldn't get off to sleep again, and each morning as she fried eggs and buttered toast, she kept on yawning.

Rosemary, taking the breakfast tray for Mrs Roberts from Laura, looked at her knowingly. "Not sleeping very well, are you?"

"It's Claire, she keeps waking up and then she wakes me."

Rosemary put down the tray again. "Don't give me that. It's because you've got something on your mind."

Laura reddened. "I don't know what you mean?" She busied herself with scrubbing out a scrambled egg saucepan.

"Oh, no? I saw you and Mr Roberts, you know. The other evening in the drawing room."

"I was just taking him in his Ovaltine."

"And that wasn't all you were doing. I saw your reflections in the mirror, you were both wrapped around each other."

Laura's hand stilled on the saucepan.

"You thought I'd not seen you?"

"I'd hoped you hadn't. Why didn't you say something before?"

"I was waiting for you to tell me." Rosemary regarded Laura intently. "Look, something like this happened to me once."

"Did it?"

"Yes, it was after Peter, my fiancé jilted me. I was on the rebound. I fell hook, line and sinker for a married man. He was my boss at the office where I was a typist."

"So what did you do?"

"I had to be strong. It hurt like hell, but ending it was the only way. I knew in my heart of hearts there was no chance of it ever going anywhere. He had kids, you see. So I left and went to train for a nurse. Look, won't you confide in me? I had thought we were friends."

"We are."

"Then why haven't you confided in me? Before things got so far as they obviously have."

"It's happened so quickly."

"That's what they all say! Apart from anything else, I really would have thought you'd have more sense in the first place."

"I'm in love."

"Love! Infatuation more like!"

"It's not! How dare you. Allow me to know my own feelings."

"I shouldn't have said that. You're not offended, are you? I wouldn't want to do that. I don't want to damage our friendship, and you've had such a sad life, I suppose I can understand how you might be susceptible."

"Don't patronise me!"

"I'm sorry, Laura. I'm just making things worse. Please forgive me."

Her hand tightened on the handle of the saucepan. She smiled briefly. "Of course; no doubt I'd have said the same to you."

"That's all right then. He's told you how he feels?"

"Not exactly." Did Geoffrey really feel as strongly for her as she did for him?

"Anyone who gets mixed up with a married man is a fool. I've seen it time and again and it always ends badly."

"Do you think I don't know that, Rosemary? Nothing's really happened between us. Not what you think, anyway."

"Maybe, not yet!"

"Neither of us want it to. It seems wrong."

"It is!"

"Mr Roberts is an honourable man."

"Oh, Laura. Don't be so naive. No one's that honourable. If he had been, he wouldn't have made a pass at you in the first place. And of course something will happen. It's only a matter of time. I know he's very attractive. I could have fallen for him myself, given half a chance. I'm not his type. His type, I reckon is more like you. Someone similar to what Mrs Roberts must once have been like."

Did she resemble her? She'd never considered this before. She recalled the photo of the young girl in the white dress; yes, perhaps there was some resemblance. Still, she refused to believe that all this had come about because he was

71

subconsciously looking for a younger and physically fit substitute.

"I don't know how you can do this to Mrs Roberts? He's hers, not yours. He belongs to a sick woman. A woman who's never done you any harm, the opposite in fact."

"Don't you think I know that, Rosemary? I feel awful, but what can I do?"

"You know that without me telling you. You've got to leave here; find another position. I don't want you to, I would really miss our cosy evenings together, but it's the only way, you know that, don't you? You must never ever see him again."

Never see Geoffrey again! That was easy for her to say, it wasn't her that was going to have to bear the pain. That's if she could bear it! Oh why did things have to be so difficult? Why should she have to lose out on love yet again? "But I don't want to leave. I feel settled here, or at least, I did. And what if I can't find something else? I've got Claire to think of. It's not as if it's just me. "

"It shouldn't be that difficult for you to find a post. You've got experience now. No doubt, Mr Roberts will write you a good reference. It's the least he can do."

"But, Rosemary, what excuse can I give to Mrs Roberts for wanting to leave? She thinks I'm happy here. I can't tell her the truth, can I? I just don't know how I'm going to face her."

"You'll think of something." Rosemary picked up the tray. She turned at the door. "Why not tell her that you need to move further away from your mother-in-law. Tell Mrs Roberts that the woman is interfering too much in Claire's life."

As Laura finished washing the saucepan, tears mixed with the sudsy water in the sink.

*   *   *

She entered the sick room, her chest palpitating, the palms of her hands sweating.

"What is it?" asked Mrs Roberts. "You don't look too well. You're not coming down with the flu?"

"I'm okay; it's just, well, I… I need to give in my notice."

"Notice! Why? I thought you were settled here. I don't know what Mr Roberts will say about this? Both of us have been really pleased with your work. What on earth has brought this on?"

Laura shot a look at Mrs Roberts. Did she really not know? Had she no suspicions? "I was settled – I've been very happy working here. I'd rather not leave. But, well, it's my mother-in-law; living at the Cedars, I'm too close to her. She keeps coming round, and telling me how to bring up Claire," she finished in a rush. She felt sick. She didn't like lying, but what else could she do?

Mrs Roberts had taken it better than Laura could have hoped for, saying she would miss her and that she couldn't expect that the new cook-housekeeper would be as good a reader as Laura had proved to be – even if the woman should be willing to read to her. Also that she would have a little something for Laura before she went.

A money gift? Was this what Mrs Roberts meant? How very kind she was! It would certainly come in handy, even if undeserved. She definitely couldn't suspect anything. She wouldn't be sympathetic if she did – no wife would. Relieved, Laura left the room with a lighter step.

Apart from seeing her present position advertised, she found nothing suitable when scouring the *Situations Vacant* column in the *Gazette*. She knew Rosemary was right, she needed to make a clean break from Geoffrey and leave his employ, but all the same, she couldn't very well go until she found somewhere to go to.

She was becoming desperate, when, one evening, Rosemary returned from her half-day off with news of a position, having been told of it over the teacups by Ethel, her friend who nursed in St Annes. Next door to her, the cook-housekeeper to a lady in her seventies, was leaving to get married.

This was too good a chance to miss. Rosemary confided Laura's problem to Ethel. A broad-minded young woman, she sympathetically promised to put in a good word for Laura with the *bride-to-be* who was looking out for a reliable replacement to take over from herself.

With mixed feelings, Laura looked through her window at the shrubs and well-rollered lawn, the scene which was now so familiar and she was going to miss.

CHAPTER FOUR

There was a sharp rapping on the back door.

Laura answered it. Her heart sank, on the step was Doris Field, the expression on her face as black as the hat she wore crammed over her forehead. "So, this is where you're hiding. You've given me a right wild-goose-chase!"

It was three weeks since Laura and Claire's arrival at Freemantle House. Laura had come for her interview which had gone better than she ever could have expected – especially once she'd shown Mrs Mullet the glowing references from Geoffrey. On the day she had taken up her new position, she and Claire, with their belongings, were driven over to the inner promenade area of St Annes by Mrs Mullet's chauffeur, bald-headed Mr Bicker. Geoffrey had wanted to take them himself, but Rosemary, when Laura told her of the offer, said it was best that he didn't know where she was going to, as then he wouldn't be tempted to seek her out. Laura knew Rosemary was right. With Mr Bicker waiting in the car, she and Geoffrey said their painful goodbyes, he with a tight face, she tearfully.

"Mrs Field," faltered Laura.

"Yes, your mother-in-law. Don't suppose you expected to see me. Aren't you going to ask me in?"

She hadn't really given Rod's mother much thought. All she had been bothered with was getting out of temptation's way. "Of course." She showed her into the kitchen.

"No consideration," grumbled Doris Field, seating herself ramrod-stiff on a straight-backed chair. "Moving all the way over here; costing me a fortune in bus fares. I'm not made of money you know."

"You've come on the bus?"

"No, I've flown over on the back of a gull!"

On the back of a broomstick, more like!

"Despite it being far from convenient for him, this time Sidney's brought me over in his van; he's parked by the front gate. Soon as I told him I had to come all the way over here to see our Claire, he offered to bring me." The brown-bullet eyes softened. "He's such a good son is my Sid – always considering his poor old mother."

A rotten husband, though! She wondered if Prue had any fresh bruises. "How's Prue?" she said.

"Pregnant again! She's another one with no consideration, as if my Sid hasn't got enough mouths to feed already."

Trust her mother-in-law to blame Prue. Did she never think that this pregnancy might be the fault of her precious Sid? More than likely in fact!

"And why St Annes? – as if I didn't know."

Laura poured boiling water into the teapot. "What do you mean?"

"Coming all over here. You thought to make it awkward for me to see Claire."

She slammed down the kettle. "I wouldn't do that! It's not that at all."

"No? What was it then? Why did you change positions? Was you found with your hand where it shouldn't be?"

Fingers whitened around the handle of the pot. *The cheek of the woman!* "Of course not! I'll have you know I'm no thief. I'd rather do like it says in the Bible, 'If your hand offends you, cut it off, than take something that wasn't mine." If she'd not left her previous place when she had, she could have done just that. Her conscience told her that she would have been just as much a thief to take another woman's man, as to take her money. "Why I left the Cedars is my business. Claire's outside playing in the garden, I'll get her."

"About time too!" Doris Field pulled out the long pin securing her hat to her grey bun, and taking it off, placed it beside her cup and saucer. "She'll be that pleased to see her old grandma will my little love." She opened her shopping bag and took out a paper cone of sweets.

*   *   *

Mr Bicker changed gears. "You've settled in well," he remarked, eyeing Laura in the mirror.

"How could I not, when I've got such a considerate employer?" A rapport had soon grown between Laura and Mrs Mullet. She didn't have to read to her as she had to Mrs Roberts, but Mrs Mullet was keen on jigsaws, and Laura would help her with them, finding the right place where a difficult piece of puzzle should go. If it hadn't been for the constant dull ache in her chest as if a stone was lodged in her heart, she could have been content.

"Oh, aye," said Mr Bicker, "she's considerate to everyone."

Laura nodded. "Life's far easier than where I was before; not only is Freemantle House smaller, but there's other help." Although built at the end of the previous century, Freemantle House was modernised, the kitchen well equipped. The view from her bedroom window was as attractive as the Cedars, with flower beds, shrubs, a trim lawn and even a stone sundial, on which birds perched.

Mr Bicker frowned into the mirror. "Poor Mrs Hughes, it's a darned shame. She has to provide for an invalid husband, you know."

"Has she?"

"Oh, aye. Fred Hughes was gassed in the Great War. Can't work at all. He spends his time stamp collecting, listening to the wireless and pottering round the house."

"Not much of a life for him, then."

"You've said it." They were on their way back from Blackpool, Mr Bicker having driven her in so she could get some new underwear from Hills for Mrs Mullet.

"I can't understand why she needs to send you such a distance for her shopping, what's Hills got that the shops in St Annes haven't? – that's what I'd like to know," he said.

"It's because Hills is where Mrs Mullet got her trousseau as a new bride before going to India," explained Laura.

He hooted his horn. "There's a road hog if ever I saw one! I didn't know her in those days," he continued. "She were widowed when I first saw her. Came here in the 20s to live with Mr Cecil, her bachelor brother, when her husband, a colonel, was killed on the North West Frontier. Mr Cecil had private means. Loved literature he did – kept a room just for his books."

Laura had seen the room – there were books from floor to ceiling. She'd tried reading one called *Crime and Punishment*, and written by an author with an unpronounceable foreign name, Dostoevsky, or something. It was really too highbrow for her taste, but somehow she persevered, hoping to get something out of it, thinking that perhaps the reading of such a book might fit her for Geoffrey. How stupid could she get? As if such a thing could ever matter. Geoffrey and whatever they'd once felt for each other was most definitely a thing of the past.

Mr Bicker turned into the drive. "Mr Cecil died from a stroke, ten years back, leaving Freemantle House to Mrs Mullet. A fact that pleases young Nigel I reckon."

"Nigel, who's Nigel?"

He turned off the ignition, and getting out of the car, came round to open the door for Laura. "He's Mrs Mullet's nephew. She's childless, so naturally Nigel, who's a bit of a charmer, at least as far as the ladies are concerned, keeps in with her."

"Surely not?"

He tapped the side of his nose. "Perhaps I'm speaking out of turn? But, all I can say is I wonder just how often he would visit her if she'd nothing to leave?"

*   *   *

"My nephew Nigel is coming to stay next week for a few days. Will you get the blue room ready for him?"

"Of course, Mrs Mullet." Laura took the tray of tea things from the table which fitted over the knees of the sweet-faced, grey-haired woman who was resting with her feet up on a stool. She carried it back to the kitchen. She had heard so much of this Nigel and wondered what he would really be like? Mrs Hughes, the charwoman, when she and Laura were out of earshot of Mrs Mullet, would raise her eyebrows.

Since saying goodbye to Geoffrey, Laura had heard nothing of him or his wife. She'd received some letters from Rosemary, and even met her twice in Blackpool town centre for a cup of tea – but when Laura asked her about the Roberts, she just replied, "Fine, fine"; immediately changing the subject. Consequently, they had rather drifted apart. Laura was sad about this and though sometimes she went next door for a chat of an evening with Ethel, it wasn't the same.

Claire was now at the nearby nursery school, which not only meant that she couldn't be taken off so often by Doris Field, much to Laura's relief – the less she saw of her mother-in-law the better she liked it, but also that Claire made some new little friends. She'd really missed Mollie, and for a long time kept asking when they would be going to see her? Laura had found it hard to keep making excuses as to why they couldn't. Now, every day, Claire, in her miniature siren suit with a zip up the front and blue knitted pixie bonnet, edged with white angora wool, chattering about her classmates, came home with pictures she had crayoned, proudly presenting them to her mother. These were then fixed to the dressing-table mirror.

Laura made up the bed in the spare room with clean sheets and blankets, cutting a few pink and white carnations from the garden and placing them with a bit of green fern in a little vase on the windowsill.

Nigel arrived. The only son of Mrs Mullet's younger sister who lived in Oxford, he worked as an assistant manager at the Morris car factory, and tall, dark and more than presentable, was in his late twenties. He put down his suitcase and smiled at Laura confidently. "Well, and who might you be?"

Taking him in to Mrs Mullet, she explained.

"You're certainly an improvement on auntie's last housekeeper." She flushed at the warm regard in his eyes.

Mrs Mullet, to Laura's surprise immediately began encouraging a friendship between her nephew and her housekeeper, suggesting that she go with him one evening to the cinema, and that she would get Mrs Hughes to come in to listen out for Claire. Laura hadn't liked to refuse Mrs Mullet. Then too, she usually enjoyed going to see a film, and Nigel seemed pleasant enough. Besides, she wasn't so old, that she couldn't feel rather smug at being seen on the arm of such a good-looking man. The matter was clinched when Mrs Hughes said that the extra money Mrs Mullet had promised her would come in useful.

Nigel commandeered his aunt's car and chauffeur, and he and Laura went to see the *Ghost Goes West* with Robert Donat.

"Aren't they a scream?" she laughed, turning to Nigel.

He laughed too, and offered her again the box of chocolates. "Here, try that one – its toffee-and-cream."

She nibbled it with enjoyment – she was glad she'd come – how foolish to be so reluctant – until under the cover of darkness, he tried to slip an arm around her. She wriggled away. Most girls would find him attractive, but when she glanced at his profile, she kept seeing Geoffrey; kept wishing it was Geoffrey beside her, instead of Nigel. She knew it was daft to still be dwelling on what could never be, but she just couldn't help it.

Nigel didn't seem at all put out by her reluctance; no doubt he regarded her as a challenge. When Mr Bicker pulled up at Freemantle House, Nigel drew her to him. Anticipating his action, she swiftly moved her head and his lips just brushed her cheek.

This didn't deter him. Over the next few days he kept appearing in the kitchen, pleading to be allowed to clean out mixing bowls, just as if he was still a small boy, even asking if he could have a piece of pie straight from the oven? On one occasion, ignoring her advice, he burnt his mouth. Any ploy it seemed to get to know her better.

To a certain extent, it worked. She was lonely, and he had a wealth of amusing stories. By the time his stay came to an end, Laura was certain how he felt about her, although she hadn't encouraged him and couldn't return his regard.

*   *   *

He returned a few weeks later, Mrs Mullet didn't seem surprised that Nigel should visit again so soon. Outings followed. They went to see *Only Angels Have Wings* starring Rita Hayworth.

At the box office, as Nigel paid for their tickets, something fell from his wallet. She picked it up – it was a snapshot of a smiling, but rather flashy looking young woman. She turned it over. On the back was written, 'With love from Rita'.

What a coincidence, this girl had the same name as the star they were about to see. Laura handed the photo back to him. "A girl friend?" she asked.

"Not now," he mumbled, avoiding her eyes.

81

Idly she wondered at his manner, then as they followed the usherette's flickering torch into the darkened auditorium, promptly forgot it.

* * *

In early September there was an Indian Summer. There were also chilling headlines on placards, *Germany invades Poland*. Workmen were painting white lines down the road and around tree trunks. When she asked, one of them told her that these lines were in preparation for the blackout.

That Sunday Laura had planned to take Claire to Sunday School while she went to the church service, but opted to sit instead with bated breath around the wireless set with Mrs Mullet and Mrs Hughes as the sombre tones of the Prime Minister crackled around the room. "…and that consequently, this country is at war with Germany."

Mrs Hughes twisted her hands in her lap. "I'd hoped it wouldn't come to this. More young fellows sent off to the trenches to be gassed and have their lives ruined."

Mrs Mullet nodded. "Their womenfolk's lives ruined too. I only hope Nigel will have enough sense not to volunteer. It would be just like him to go before he needs to."

"Perhaps this time, they'll be calling up the girls as well. I'm thankful now I never had a family. All that work and expense to bring them up, and then have them taken off to be slaughtered." Mrs Hughes loved children, and never missed a chance to make a fuss of Claire, confiding to Laura the reason for her having no babies of her own was because of needing to be the breadwinner.

They listened in silence to the rest of Neville Chamberlain's message. Laura turned off the wireless. They sat stunned, each with their own thoughts. What would happen now? Would Hitler's bombs fall soon? Would Germany invade

England? What would happen to her and Claire if they were overrun with Nazis?

Mrs Mullet's words as regards Nigel were prophetic, as some weeks later, just as the finishing touches were being put to the air-raid shelter in the back garden, she got a letter from him from Aldershot telling her that he was in the Oxford and Bucks Light Infantry, he having signed up the day after war was declared. On finishing his basic training, he was to join a special unit – eventually to be posted abroad.

It was the following August before Mrs Mullet got a letter from Nigel saying that he was soon to leave England for an unknown destination, but would visit his favourite auntie to say goodbye before setting sail.

It was a Saturday some weeks later when he arrived, looking even more handsome than ever in his officer's uniform. That afternoon, as his aunt was taking her usual nap, he asked Laura to go with him to the park for a bit of fresh air. She didn't like to refuse, not with him going away, and possibly going into danger. And what reason did she really have? He was good company.

Red and gold leaves fluttered from the trees and crunched underfoot as he and Laura strolled along, with Claire running just ahead. There were a few other couples nearby, some of them with children in prams and pushchairs, or trailing them by the hand. It was that warm that the women wore summer dresses, while many of the men, like Nigel, were also in uniform. Suddenly he drew her to him. "You must know how I feel about you?"

Laura pulled away, too embarrassed to speak. She only wished she could say she felt the same. She liked him well enough, but liking wasn't love. There were no fireworks as far as she was concerned, not as there'd been with Rod and Geoffrey. If only one could fall in love to order. Why was it that love very often struck where and when it shouldn't?

"Couldn't you try to love me, just a little?" he pleaded.

"I'm fond of you, but…"

"I'm probably going into danger. I've got to face it, I may not come back."

"Don't say that!"

"It's got to be said, Laura. War is war. Before I leave England I'd like to see you and Claire all right."

"How can you do that?"

"If we were married you'd be entitled to an army allowance. It would make life a lot easier for you."

"Married! – you want to marry me?"

"Yes."

Marriage was a serious step and one many men were wary of taking, unless they thought they'd not get what they wanted any other way. Was this taking care of her and Claire so much guff? Wasn't it more likely he was hoping to get his pleasures while he could? Perhaps she was being unfair and he was genuine? "But I'm only working class. You're middle class."

"What's that got to do with anything?"

"I would be out of place as regards your family."

"It's me you would be marrying, not them. I wouldn't let 'class' make a difference. If you were my wife they'd have to accept you as you are."

"A cook-housekeeper!"

"Yes."

"I don't love you."

"You said you were fond of me," said Nigel.

"Yes, I am, but that's not enough."

"I'll take what I can get."

"You think that now, but later you'd regret it."

"If there is a *later*."

Laura flinched at his words. What with all the bombing at Manchester, Liverpool and Preston docks, it was beginning to look as if there wouldn't be any future. One had even fallen as close as Seed Street in Blackpool – killing some locals. How long did any of them have? Wouldn't it be wiser to grab at life while she could?

"Anyway," he added, "love can grow you know."

They left it at that and returned to Freemantle House. Using the recipe that she'd got from 'The Kitchen Front', Laura diced potatoes, carrots, cauliflower, onions and swedes for a Woolton pie. Nigel's words ran through her head. Was what he'd suggested possible? If she should agree to marry him, mightn't she grow to love him in time? That's if there was any time? Besides how did she know whether the *fireworks* with Rod and Geoffrey would have stayed at the same intensity? Things might have died down to mere fondness after a while. That's if she was lucky, there was no guarantee of *fondness* even. Into her head flashed a picture of mother-in-law, Doris Field. Had she once felt fireworks for her husband? Had he felt them for her? It was very hard to imagine either way. It was equally hard to imagine Doris Field as young and in love. Of course she could have married for other reasons than love? Laura supposed some did. She also supposed that many of those marriages worked out successfully. As she was at present, she had no security. If something should happen to Mrs Mullet, where did that leave her? Facing another upheaval. She bit her lip; she didn't think she could take a further change of employment. But did she need to? If she were to marry Nigel, all that would be over. She would be his wife, and as he said, the recipient of his army allowance which had to be more than the widow's pension which she'd lose. Also, said a little voice, as Mrs Mullet's favourite nephew's wife, no doubt Mrs Mullet would see her provided for in the event of her death. Could she marry for such a reason? What other option had she now? No, she argued with herself, if she married again, she wanted it to be for more than just convenience.

She reached down a frying pan, tipped in the prepared vegetables to which she'd added oatmeal, stirred in gravy browning and cooked the mixture on top of the stove. She sniffed – it smelt all right – she'd strangle that Lord Woolton if it didn't taste good too – rationing made the life of a cook-housekeeper a nightmare. She put the lot into a pie dish, covered it with pastry, and popped it into the oven. As she straightened up, a picture of Geoffrey, his brown hair falling across his brow flashed before her eyes, making her recall the passion of his kiss and the way it had made her feel. She couldn't afford such a luxury she told herself sternly. Besides it wasn't as if she were on her own, she had to consider Claire.

To Laura's relief, the Woolton pie came in for compliments from both Mrs Mullet and Nigel. After everything was cleared away, he and Laura went on the bus to Blackpool to see the 'Show of 1940' at the Opera House.

Still laughing, some hours later, they entered a nearby pub. The lounge bar was packed; buzzing like a beehive from scores of conversations and thick with cigarette smoke. Airforce blue dominated the room. The population of Blackpool had trebled due to the coming of the RAF. The private hotels in South Shore near to her in-laws, were now heaving with Brylcreem Boys. There were extra women too, workers at the aircraft factory and civil servants from the ministries in London. Nigel struggled up to the bar, while she admired the low-beamed ceilings; the brass warming pans, rosy with electric light; the fishing nets which draped the walls. He came back carrying her port-and-lemon in one hand and his pint in the other and placed them on the round table in front of them. She sipped at her drink. Removing two cigarettes from a silver case, he offered her one which she refused. He replaced it, slotting the other into his mouth and lighting up. He drew on it deeply; exhaling, a spiral of smoke swirled upwards and around his head.

"Well, then, Laura, did you enjoy the show?"

"I should say so; it was excellent. The Mad Hatters band were hilarious." She began to hum one of their numbers under her breath. "I'd almost forgotten the war, you know, until I kicked my gas-mask case." She eyed it ruefully.

"And Arthur Askey?"

"He was funny, wasn't he?"

"He's only short, but he's not short on jokes. Richard Murdoch's the perfect foil, don't you think?"

The door opened, and a stockily-built, well-dressed man with a bushy moustache entered. He pushed his way up to the bar and ordered a whisky-and-soda. It was the familiarity of his strident voice that alerted her. It couldn't be, could it? She took a quick look at the man. Her stomach lurched. It was her brother-in-law, Sid! Was this his local? If not, what bad luck that he should be here at the same time as they were. She shrank back into her seat, hoping against hope that he wouldn't see her. She certainly didn't want to speak to him. She'd prefer never to see him ever again.

But his bold eyes came to rest on her. "If it isn't our Laura!"

Our Laura, indeed! She noted that Sid was still in civvies – trust him to wriggle out of joining up – she only hoped someone would give him a *white feather* like in the Great War. Still, knowing her brother-in-law, he'd no doubt be too thick-skinned for such an insult to have any effect. She'd no choice but to acknowledge him, after all, he was Rod's brother and Claire's uncle. Hopefully he would go off after exchanging a few words. She swallowed. "Hello, Sid." She turned to Nigel. "This is my brother-in-law," she said. "My late husband's elder brother."

Nigel rose and put out a hand. "Pleased to meet you."

Sid made no effort to shake it. "More than our Laura appears to be, I reckon."

"What else do you expect?" she muttered.

"A few more manners."

"I did acknowledge you."

His bullet-brown eyes darkened. "Only just. And I know why. You're scared I'll let on about you."

"I don't know what you mean?"

"I reckon you do. You've always acted like such a goody-goody, such a little innocent, but we know better, don't we, Laura."

"What?" Why was Sid speaking like this? The answer hit her straight-on. He must be still smarting from having been thwarted in his evil designs on her that time.

"No? You're certainly not above picking up soldiers," he sneered.

"Picking up soldiers!" This was worse than she could have imagined. He must really mean to get his own back on her. "What rubbish! I've not picked anyone up. I wouldn't. I don't care for your insinuations – this is the nephew of... I've known him...I don't have to explain myself to you, Sidney Field."

Sid turned to Nigel. "If I were you, mate, I'd drop this one like a hot cake. She might give the impression that she's a respectable widow. But you can't rely on impressions. She *had* to marry my brother, you know. Why, she even made a pass at me, a married man – and under my parents' roof, too – I refused of course."

"What! It was you, you who tried to force yourself on me!"

"You would say that, wouldn't you?"

"I'm not a liar," said Laura stiffly. "And I never had to get married neither."

"No?"

Her face flamed and anger bubbled up within her "Well, really!" She threw the remains of her port-and-lemon into Sid's leering face.

Voices stilled around them. She felt the heat from avid eyes.

Spluttering, he pulled out his handkerchief and wiping his cheek, grated, "Temper! Temper!"

Eyes hardening, Nigel purposely stubbed out his cigarette in the ashtray. His fists tightened at his side, and he said in a low voice. "You swine! How dare you insult Laura like this?"

"All true, mate," snarled Sid smugly. "My wife was only in hospital having our third when this one came on strong. Laura's no better than a tart."

Tart! She choked. Surely Nigel wouldn't believe him? She shot a questioning look at Nigel. If he did, well, that would be the end of it. At this thought she felt almost put-out.

"I've heard enough. I'll give you, true, mate." Nigel's fist exploded. It connected with Sid's nose. "Now, clear off!"

Sid yelled. Blood spurted onto the spotted bow-tie and white shirt front. Wobbling like a drunk, desperately trying to staunch the flow, his face creased with pain and astonishment. He spat out a tooth. It pinged as it hit Nigel's beer glass – it was a molar. "I'll bloody well get you for this, mate," Sid snarled. He shot out a fist, following it up with another. The first glanced past Nigel's ear, but the second sunk into his midriff. Nigel doubled over, but shot up as Sid closed on him. They grappled. Laura, meanwhile was hitting Sid with her handbag, and making herself felt too. All three went lurching against the customers at the other tables, they snatching up their drinks out of harm's way. The landlord pulled the battling threesome apart. "This is a respectable pub, if you want to fight, go outside!" He turned to Nigel. "You should be fighting Jerry, not your own countrymen." He jerked a thumb at Sid. "And as for you, scarper, quick, before I call the police."

"I'm going." Sid glared at Laura and Nigel. "I'll get even with the both of you," he snarled.

"On your way," put in the landlord.

The door slammed behind Sid.

As the hum of conversation started up again, he passed the window, looking very disgruntled, and holding to his nose the red and sodden handkerchief. Seeing them, he shook his fist.

Laura turned. "Oh, thank you," she said.

"What for?"

"For not believing his lies."

"You've no need to thank me for that. Anyway, thank you too."

"What for?"

"For swinging your handbag, of course."

She laughed. "Are you all right?"

"I'll live. Now, shall I get you another port-and-lemon?"

"Yes, please. I need something to calm me down – that's if the landlord will serve us?"

They returned to Freemantle House, and Nigel again asked her to marry him. Grateful of his support, and feeling somewhat light-headed from several port-and-lemons, she found herself weakening. On the way back from the bus stop she had let him kiss her and she'd found it quite enjoyable.

"Auntie would be so pleased if we had good news for her in the morning," he said.

"You really think Mrs Mullet would be pleased?"

"Auntie Maude is very fond of you. It would mean a lot to her for you to become one of the family."

"Would it really?" She was fond of Mrs Mullet too. She had never known either of her grandmothers, but if she'd had a grandmother, she would have liked her to be exactly like her. Yes, it would be very pleasant indeed to make her employer happy. Of course her mother-in-law wouldn't be pleased. Doris Field would be far from keen on the idea of Laura marrying again, probably thought she should be a nun for the rest of her life. Still, it was too bad what Doris Field thought. Her mother-in-law had no right to tell her how to live her life. Her private life was her private life. And Nigel seemed to get on well with

Claire, he had even told her a bedtime story when Laura tucked her up for the night. Yes, it would be good for her daughter to have a father. She'd missed out herself on a father; in fact she had always felt somewhat cheated at not having one, and she didn't want Claire to miss out too. "All right, then."

"You agree?

"I said *Yes*, didn't I?"

"Yippee! Laura! Oh, darling." He swung her around the kitchen and planted a smouldering kiss on her cheek. "I'll arrange a special licence first thing tomorrow. We'll be married as soon as possible."

She shook her head in an attempt to clear it. Married! She really shouldn't have drunk so much. What had she said?

Putting her back down, Nigel pulled out his wallet and removed a large white fiver. "Take this, darling and buy yourself a stunning outfit for the wedding."

She goggled at the bank note in her hand. She had never seen such a sum of money close to before. Why, it was a couple of weeks wages for most men. There was easily enough here to buy Claire a special dress as well as something for herself. She could just see her little darling with flowers in her hair, wearing a blue taffeta dress with a frilled skirt and puffed sleeves and looking like a princess. "But, Nigel, I can't take this. It wouldn't be right."

He laughed and pulling her close, his lips found hers. "Why not? You're going to be my wife. I can't tell you how proud and happy you've just made me."

But Laura felt uneasy. She'd given her word that she would marry Nigel, but oughtn't she to have slept on it?

CHAPTER FIVE

In the bathroom, Laura undressed and put on her new blue rayon nightdress. She pulled a face at her reflection in the mirror; her eyes resembled two holes burnt in a blanket – she looked as if she were about to go to her execution instead of spending a night in a high-class hotel with her new bridegroom. She pinched her cheeks to give them some colour. Was that better? It would have to be. In the bedroom, Nigel was seated on the bed. "Your turn," she said lightly. She didn't want to hurt his feelings, to let him see how reluctant she was. Now all the excitement of the actual wedding was over she felt rather flat, knowing, all of a sudden that she should have listened to Mrs Hughes and not let herself be rushed into marriage. How well did she really know Nigel? And why should Mrs Hughes have such strong misgivings about him? There was no reason that she could see. Mrs Hughes could give no satisfactory explanation. Mr Bicker felt the same way; hadn't he said as much to her before she'd even met Nigel?

At the sound of running water from the bathroom, she relaxed sufficiently to look around the stylish room. The honeymoon she'd shared with Rod returned; the happiest few days in her entire life. Their Southport boarding house had been basic compared to this. In their room there'd been a white china chamber-pot beneath the bed. She'd been too embarrassed to use it with Rod present, and putting her coat on over her nightdress, would go downstairs and out-back to the lavatory. There'd also been a wash-hand-stand with a marble top and a flowery jug and basin. The landlady would tap on their door and take the jug down to the kitchen to fill it with hot water so Laura could wash and Rod shave. On their wedding night, as she and Rod shyly turned their backs on each other to get undressed, she'd been bubbling up with excitement, and feeling exactly the opposite to how she felt now.

Moving slowly, Mr Hughes, with the bride on his arm, entered the Registry Office, his chest wheezing like a concertina, to where a beaming Nigel, in his dress-uniform, waited. She knew she looked good in her wedding outfit, a grey-and-white dress and swagger coat from Gladys Whittaker in Queen Street, Blackpool. She wore with her coat and dress, a veiled white-hat, gloves and a fox-fur stole with lovely golden eyes; the latter, a wedding gift from her new aunt, Mrs Mullet. Determined to ignore the faint feeling of disquiet which was rapidly growing, she concentrated on the excited Claire who was following on behind them with her posy of sweet peas. She could have passed for Shirley Temple in her frilly bridesmaid's dress and with her hair done up in matching blue ribbons. Claire was to spend the night at the Hughes' home.

At the wedding breakfast, they cut the cake and read the telegrams. Mrs Mullet, who'd indeed been pleased at their news, had brought in caterers to provide the buffet. From somewhere (black market, perhaps), dried fruit had been obtained to make a modest cake, which beneath a fancy white cardboard and silver-foil cover was as good as the pre-war wedding cakes. Slivers of cake were passed around and everyone toasted them in champagne. The Brigadier General whom Ethel nursed, produced a Box Brownie camera, and took snapshots, guffawing, 'that the happy couple' could put them in their family album to show their grandchildren. Laura relaxed, but waving from the taxicab as they left for their honeymoon hotel, she couldn't help wondering at the look of relief on Mrs Mullet's face.

The toilet was flushing. She turned down the bedclothes and climbing in, pulled them up to her chin. She felt goose-pimply all over, although the room was warm enough. The moment of truth was fast approaching. With the feelings she still had for Geoffrey, what if she couldn't respond to Nigel? He might be angry? She couldn't really blame him, a man had a right to expect that his bride would want him. Perhaps if she squeezed her eyes shut and pretended it was Geoffrey making love to her, all would be well? Would that work? Nigel climbed in beside her. He fingered her nightdress. "How about taking that off?"

She winced. "Must I? I'm freezing."

He laughed. "Not for long, I'll soon warm you up, darling."

She wiped away the tears that were seeping from the corner of her eyes as she stared through the darkness of the bedroom at the shadowy humps of furniture. In the distance, she heard a church clock strike three times.

Nigel was not Geoffrey, no good pretending that he was. She'd not become aroused. He had hurt her, leaving her sore. In desperation, she'd even prayed for the wail of the air-raid siren, for them to have to get up and put on their gas-masks and leave the bedroom for the safety of the hotel's basement. Even if the siren had sounded it would have solved nothing. She knew the failure of their wedding night was her fault, but she couldn't help it. Did he realise? She hoped not. She'd done him a great disservice. She owed it to him to try and make it up to him, even if she found the doing of it distasteful. But how could she? There was no time left.

Later that morning, at the railway station, amidst the crowds of other servicemen and their wives and girlfriends, they said their goodbyes. She turned her head away at the last moment and Nigel, bending over the compartment door to kiss her, found her cheek instead of her lips. "I'll write as often as I can, darling," he promised. "And, don't worry, things will turn out right between us."

Nearby a soldier and his girl embraced passionately. Laura concentrated on the dusty train, its windows criss-crossed with strips of brown paper. What had she done? She knew now for certain that this marriage was a mistake. "I'll… I'll look forward to them. I'll reply by return of post." Nigel had used French Letters, she'd been a bit embarrassed when he'd produced the packet. Still, without them, she might very well now be pregnant. She certainly didn't want another baby, especially not in such uncertain times – and certainly not with Nigel.

The whistle blew.

Awkwardly, she added. "Just you look after yourself, Nigel."

* * *

Autumn turned to winter. Laura's daily round went on the same as always. If it hadn't been for the snapshot of herself and Nigel she would have begun to feel that she had imagined that marriage ceremony. Certainly she'd received no letters from him. But that, she knew, didn't mean anything in wartime.

* * *

The day started like any other – the hours filled with getting Claire ready for school, and seeing to her usual chores.

Just after she had taken in Mrs Mullet's elevenses, the front door bell buzzed. Laura put down the potato that she was peeling, wiped her hands on the dishcloth and patted her hair. Mrs Mullet didn't get that many visitors, especially before midday. The tradesmen delivered to the back door – so who could it be?

Laura gasped. "Geoffrey!!"

"Laura."

She supported herself on the doorjamb. "What are you doing here? How did you find me? I'd thought as far as you and I were concerned, that was that!" His officer's uniform added to his attractiveness. He removed his peaked hat, and a lock of hair

95

fell over his brow, but now there was the odd grey one mixed with the brown. Her attention was drawn to his wiry wrist which was covered by a golden down. Was it like that all the way up his arm? Was his body the same? She felt hot all over at her thoughts. She wriggled uncomfortably – her cami-knickers were sticking to her. "Did Rose…? I guess she must have."

He cut in. "Yes. Rosemary told me where you were."

"But she said she wouldn't, that it would be best." She couldn't let all that start up again – especially now – as well as Mrs Roberts there was Nigel to consider.

He cut in. "That was then. Look, Laura, can I come in? We can't talk on the doorstep, and I've such a lot to tell you."

"I can't see what good it would do… oh, all right then. But only for a moment or two – I'm very busy." With a trembling hand, she held the door open for him, and turning on her heel, led the way to the kitchen.

"Is that someone for me, dear?" called out Mrs Mullet from the drawing room.

"No, Mrs Mullet." Laura tried to keep her voice steady. "It's for me – a friend," she added.

He laid his hat, gloves and stick on the scrubbed table. "You're looking well," he said.

"So why are you here?" she asked breathlessly. "It's been so long, I never expected…"

He eyed her keenly. "To see me again? I had to come. I would have come before, but Rosemary only gave me your address a few days ago – I bumped into her in town – she wouldn't give me your address at the funeral – said it was too soon. She was right. I had to grieve."

"Funeral!"

"Yes." A muscle moved in his throat. "Nine months ago. Gloria's condition rapidly worsened after you left, there was nothing anyone could do. She got weaker and weaker. She died at home in my arms."

"I'm so sorry, Geoffrey." Laura reached out and took one of his hands in hers and patted it briefly. "Mrs Roberts was lovely. I was very fond of her."

"She was very fond of you. She told me more than once." He put his hand over hers.

The shock was electric – she withdrew her hand quickly. "You talked about me?"

"We did…" Nervously he touched his inside pocket. "I really do need a cigarette. Do you mind if I smoke?"

"No, of course not."

He offered her a cigarette, she nodded her agreement, he took one himself; then with trembling fingers, lit the cigarettes, passing one to her. They both drew deeply and exhaled, the smoke intermingling over their heads.

"I see you still smoke the same brand. I always liked the smell of Du Maurier cigarettes," she said faintly.

"Gloria missed you when you left – especially your reading to her. She knew, you know."

"About us?"

"Yes."

"How awful. Was she very upset? I would have been, if it had been my husband. Devastated, I think."

"I think she'd gone beyond that," he said quietly. "Or, if not, she managed to hide it successfully. She was a wonderful woman, so caring – caring only about Mollie and myself, and how her death was going to affect us. I'm sure I never deserved such devotion. She told me I was not to pine. I was to come and find you. She said she was certain that you would make me happy."

Laura wiped her damp cheek. "She said that?"

"She did. She said you'd make a good mother for Mollie. That your Claire and our Mollie would enjoy being sisters."

"Sisters!"

"She said that."

"Where… where is Mollie?"

"In Cleethorpes. Stopping with my cousin. Hermione's got two small daughters."

"I'm glad she's okay. And I'm sure she and my Claire would have liked being sisters, but…"

"But, what?"

She bit her lip. "It… it's too late."

His brow creased. "Too late? Why? I don't understand."

"If only you had come a few weeks earlier."

"Earlier – why? Would that have made any difference?"

"All the difference in the world!" Her voice went off-key. "I'm married. I've married again."

He jerked to his feet, his chair tipping backwards. "Married! No! You're not, are you?" he added tightly.

"I'm afraid I am."

"When… when was this?"

Laura swallowed. "A month ago. I married my employer's nephew – Nigel was on embarkation leave."

Geoffrey righted his chair and seated himself stiffly. "Like me. I see. You love him, this Nigel?"

"I don't know. He's been very kind to me and Claire. I like him, maybe I'm even fond of him, but…"

"Then, why?"

"He begged and pleaded with me. He seemed so keen. I never expected to see you ever again. Maybe I was flattered that he should want me so much. Perhaps I was lonely. I know I've got Claire, but I need more than just a child in my life, and he offered me security. He said that if I was his wife, he'd look after me and Claire. I had to think of Claire. You do understand?"

He stubbed out his cigarette and rose to his feet. "So that's it, then," he said dully, picking up his belongings.

She rose too. "I'm afraid so."

"I'm off tomorrow."

"So soon?"

"Yes. I had hoped…" His voice trailed away.

"What?"

"That you and I – well, I thought that with there no longer being any barrier between us; at least, I thought then, there wasn't, and with the very real chance I may not return."

"That's what Nigel said."

"Well, he's right in both our cases."

"Please, don't! I can't bear to think of you not coming back."

"Sorry."

"Never mind about that." She stretched out a hand. "Go on."

He shook his head. "I can't! It's hopeless, Laura. You're a decent woman. I can't ask, can't expect something like this of you. Especially now."

She could read in his eyes what he was hesitant to say. He wanted her to sleep with him. He'd hoped to take with him the memory of a few hours of bliss. She wanted what he wanted. Wanted the fulfilment she would get from him with an intensity that couldn't be denied. How had he managed without sex for so long? Her own hand beneath the bedclothes wasn't satisfactory. Or had he managed? Mightn't he have gone to a brothel from time to time? – she guessed there were such places in Blackpool. She didn't want to think about him and those sort of women, or in fact, any other woman. "Because I've a husband?"

"Yes, of course. I'm no wife stealer. I've got a few principles."

"But… what if I say it's what I want."

His jaw dropped. "What! You want me to…? But, I mean… Are you sure?

Was she sure? She felt her heart throb. Of course she was! "Yes. I'm definitely sure."

"You're certain about taking such a step?"

"I am. Now, come on. Say it, please!"

A muscle moved in his throat. "Well, I had hoped when I came here that you would agree to me booking a room for us in a hotel. That we could have one night of love together before I went."

Laura's pulse raced. She knew that a night with Geoffrey would be so different to the one spent with Nigel. She wanted more than anything to say, *Yes*. Dare she? Would it be really that wrong, when she loved Geoffrey so very much? It didn't seem wrong. Sunday School and the Ten Commandments flashed through her mind. The lovemaking that she longed for was still Adultery – only the opposite way round to what it had been before – this time it was her who was married to someone else. She wondered if it were the Devil who was tempting her? Urging her to sin? Oh, blow the Devil!

He shook his head. "No, Laura, forget it. I've no right to say such things to you."

She eyed his clean-cut features, her eyes lingering on his firm mouth. "You have every right. I love you. And you love me. You do, don't you?"

"More than I can say!"

Suddenly she thought of her mother, she swallowed. What would mum think of her, what she was about to do. She knew it was a shocking thing she was agreeing to. She couldn't help it though.

"Then that's all that matters." Whether it was a sin or not a sin didn't seem important. Neither did her mother's disapproval. All she wanted was to lie in his arms – enjoy his kisses, feel his hands on her body – this might be her last chance – their very last chance to be together. And neither man might return. Even if they did, would she be alive? Would any of them still be alive? This dreadful war was hotting up. All the major cities were being devastated by bombs. Who could say whether St Annes mightn't suddenly be flattened and she be killed? What harm would a few hours with the man she adored do in the scheme of things?

"What about Nigel?"

She flushed, shame sweeping over her. How could she consider doing something like this? She forced down her guilt. She just had to – or explode! "I'm sorry about him. I know that he doesn't deserve to be treated so shabbily. I know I owe him loyalty, but what I feel for you is stronger. It's too strong to be denied."

"Are you sure? I keep saying that. I'm sorry."

"I'm more than sure!"

His hat, gloves and stick, slipped from his hands; she found herself folded into his warm embrace, their lips meeting in a long sweet kiss – in which the reality of the kitchen faded... They came up for air. "I'll need to find someone to mind Claire," she murmured, suddenly ecstatic.

"Do you think you can?"

"I hope so. I'm pretty certain I know who'll do it."

His face brightened. "You do. That's wonderful. I'll make the arrangements then, shall I? Tomorrow night? Would that be enough time for you to make yours?"

"I think so." How wicked she was planning a night of passion. She should be strong and tell him to go. Tell him firmly that she never wanted to see him ever again. What would Rosemary say if she knew that Laura was intending to cheat on her new husband? When she was hesitating about leaving the Cedars, Rosemary had remarked, 'No backbone!' Well, blow Rosemary! All that mattered was Geoffrey and their love – and its consummation.

*　　*　　*

Laura tossed and turned, and got up before her alarm rang. Would everything go according to plan? She would ask Mrs

Hughes when she arrived if she'd have Claire for the night – praying it wouldn't be too short a notice. She had come up with an idea, one which she hoped Mrs Hughes would swallow. Though the older woman had tried to talk her out of marrying Nigel, Laura was certain that she wouldn't approve of her cheating on him.

Her excuse for a night away from Freemantle House was the engagement of one of the girls from the Tivoli, her story being that the party was unlikely to end before midnight. She didn't like to spin a yarn, but what else could she do? She had to have this time with Geoffrey or regret it forever. And it was wartime.

Mrs Hughes had been more than keen to have Claire, as was Mrs Mullet, for her to have some fun. "You're only young once. You go off and enjoy yourself with your friends; don't worry about me, I'll be all right."

The day's chores seemed endless, but by late afternoon, she was becoming increasingly nervous. Surely she should have heard by now that everything was set – he'd promised to phone. Claire's things were packed. And her own. What if he had changed his mind? What if he couldn't find a room? What if he should now think her *fast*; had in fact decided he wanted nothing more to do with her?

She worried for nothing. At twenty to five, Geoffrey rang to say he would meet her at six pm inside the Sandbach Cafe. Laura had passed the beribboned lace-curtained windows of this cafe in St Annes Square, but never been in.

Having seen Claire go off happily with Mrs Hughes, she walked there, with her gas-mask slung across her shoulder and carrying an overnight bag. Would he think she looked okay? Her blue dress and three-quarter-length matching woollen jacket were almost new, and she was wearing her hair loose, having washed it the previous night in rainwater, using an Amami sachet she'd been saving for a special occasion. She didn't normally use much make-up, just a pale pink lipstick and a light dusting of face powder, but to help her confidence, she'd smeared a trace of blue eye-shadow onto her eyelids.

Two Land Army girls, with muscular legs, cycled past, followed by a convoy of army lorries. On the opposite side of the road, elderly couples, hand-in-hand, strolled by in the early evening sunshine. She almost envied them. They seemed content. She began worrying again. What if the hotel he'd booked for them was the same one she'd stayed in with Nigel? She would be so embarrassed if the receptionist, recognising her with a different man, should think her a *tart*. Of course it wouldn't be the same hotel, there must be hundreds in St Annes.

She halted at the gold-lettered, SANDBACH CAFE. This was it; was Geoffrey already inside? In the discreetly-lit interior, a hum of conversation and clattering cups met her. A lady was scraping a violin, and hovering between the stylishly-dressed men and women were waitresses in lace-edged white caps and aprons over black satin dresses. Attached to their waistbands by cords, hung small notepads and pencils. The atmosphere of the cafe brought to mind her twenty-third birthday, unbelievably, all of four years ago, and the meal with Geoffrey at Lewis's.

Laura saw him waving.

Shoving her belongings beneath the table, she forced a smile, feeling her cheeks become heated at the sharp looks she was getting from a middle-aged couple. Did they find it odd that she and Geoffrey should both have an overnight bag with them? Could that prune-faced woman in fussy twin-set and pearls, and her pinstriped companion have put two and two together and guessed they were up to no good? Too bad! It didn't matter what they thought, they were nothing to her. She concentrated on Geoffrey. He looked as relieved to see her as she was to see him. Had he half-expected her not to turn up? He reached out and took her hands. "It's lovely to see you. I thought perhaps you mightn't come in the end."

103

"I had to!" She poured the tea, but her hand shook – some slopped into the saucer.

"Go on, take a cake," he urged.

Sipping her tea, she shook her head, she was far too tense to eat...

He held out his arm; nervously, she took it. They crossed the road and turned up a side street. Wobbling on her three inch high heels, she wished she'd not tried to be fashionable, hoping they'd not got far to walk. "What's the hotel called?"

"Ashby Lodge. Why?"

She breathed out. "No reason." The one she'd stay at with Nigel had been The Melbourne.

He halted. "I think that's it."

A rather lopsided sign on a white gate said Ashby Lodge.

"Good Heavens. It's no more than a glorified boarding house," he said. "You don't mind, do you? I just got the phone number from the *Gazette*, I'd no idea of the actual place."

"To tell the truth, I'm relieved." Ashby Lodge was two terraced houses joined together, and modest when compared to The Melbourne. Still, as far as she was concerned the less people to stare at them, staff or guests, the better. He unclipped the gate for them to enter a front garden with vivid golden and white chrysanths beds. They ascended the three steps to the entrance. Taking up much of the foyer was a shiny-leaved aspidistra in a brass pot. The walls were panelled in dark wood, and on one hung an ornately-framed picture of Highland cattle. There was a squat black telephone on the reception desk – it burst into life, startling them. Almost immediately, a door opened and a plump woman appeared. They waited while she answered it. She wore a floral wrap-around overall, too much lipstick, and her peroxide-blonde hair was arranged in bangs. Tut-tutting, she put down the phone and turned to them, smiling. "Can I help you?"

104

"Mr and Mrs Brown from Southport," said Geoffrey, "I phoned to book a double room for tonight."

She eyed them knowingly. "Of course, Mr Brown. Did you and Mrs Brown have a good journey?"

Laura mumbled a *yes*, averting her face. Mr and Mrs Brown, indeed! He may as well have said Smith. She was certain the woman could tell they weren't married. With his intelligence, she'd have thought he could have done better than that. Still, maybe it just showed he wasn't used to this sort of thing.

The receptionist handed them a key. "Room Five, straight up the stairs to the first floor, turn left, then along the corridor; it's the fourth door on your right. Breakfast is between eight and nine. Would you like early morning tea, sir?"

"Yes, tea would be very acceptable."

"At what time, sir?"

"At eight am, I should think." He turned to Laura. "That won't be too early for you, will it, darling?"

"N… no…"

"Eight it is, sir. Could you both sign the register, please?" The woman pushed an open book towards them.

With a flourish, he wrote GEOFFREY BROWN. She noticed with some surprise as she signed herself, LAURA BROWN, that there seemed to be quite a few Mr and Mrs Browns already on the page.

Their free hands drifted together as they climbed the steep staircase, up the centre of which ran a strip of frayed carpeting, to the first floor. At the touch of his fingers threading through hers, Laura became woozy with emotion, mixed with excitement. Trembling, she almost lost her balance. He threw down the bags and grabbed hold of her. "Careful! – hold onto the banister." He dropped a kiss on her forehead.

"I am holding it!"

"Good!" They continued on up the stairs, turning left at the top. He paused outside a door. "Five. This must be it, darling."

Laura swallowed. "Yes."

He turned the key – the door swung open, the room was almost completely filled by a double bed and wardrobe. In the corner was a washbasin. He pushed the door to with his heel; with great relief, they dumped their bags and gas masks. He turned to her, and folded her into his embrace. "At last!"

Their lips met in a lingering kiss. Again emotion swept through Laura. All that mattered was the moment – these few precious moments that might be all they would ever have. They sank to the bed.

She heard a tapping. "There's someone at the door."

Helping her off with her dress, he groaned. "Ignore it!"

The tapping became more insistent. "You'll have to answer it, Geoffrey."

A voice called. "Mr Brown! Mr Brown, telephone!" Footsteps receded.

"I'll have to go," he said, buttoning up his shirt.

"Be quick, then. I want you!"

"I want you, too, darling. I can't tell you how much. I'll be no longer than I can help, you can be certain of that." He hurried out. She heard his footsteps descending the stairs.

She lay there in her petticoat, gazing at the ceiling – listening – something was swinging on a thread. Oh, no, a bad omen, a death watch! She moved her head restlessly – willing it away. How daft; it's only a spider.

She heard heavy footsteps and Geoffrey came slowly back into the room. "Sod it! I'm sorry, love, but I've got to go. I've been recalled."

"Recalled! Oh, no!" She pulled herself upright on her pillows.

"'Fraid so. They didn't say why, it's an emergency of some kind. There's a train at ten from St Annes Station." He checked his watch. "It's almost that!"

"How did they know where you were?"

"I had to leave a phone number where I could be contacted."

Laura got off the bed. "I'll come with you."

"No, no. Best not. It's better you don't. It's best we say our goodbyes here."

"Yes. You're right." With a sinking heart and trembling fingers she re-fastened his shirt and corrected his tie.

He looked around the room sadly – gave her a final kiss. She clung to him in desperation. He unloosed her arms. "There'll be other times, darling. I'll write. Phone, if I can."

Then he was gone.

Laura lay on the bed, too upset to even cry. She felt cheated. Why did this awful war have to spoil everything? If only this summons had come an hour later! In the distance she heard a whistle. Was it his train? She got out of bed and looked out of the window, but all was pitch-black. Her toe stubbed against something. His swagger stick, he'd forgotten it! She picked it up and getting back into the bed, tears streaming down her face, nursed the stick for comfort. Eventually, she fell into a fitful sleep.

She turned over, and awoke. A sliver of light pierced the curtains where they didn't quite meet.

"Geoffrey," she murmured. Then the awful truth hit her. He was gone!

CHAPTER SIX

Laura blew her nose, and wiping her eyes, tucked her handkerchief back up her sleeve. She looked around the room; the same one in which her wedding to Nigel had been celebrated six months earlier. How she was going to miss Mrs Mullet, or Aunty Maude as she'd insisted on being called. It couldn't be possible, she couldn't be gone.

It was Mrs Mullet's funeral meal. The scene at the graveside, the floral tributes, banked earth and gaping hole; all combining to return her to those dark days when she'd lost Rod – and to asking those unanswerable questions about whether or not, there was actually an 'afterlife'. Mrs Mullet believed there was and never once missed the Sunday morning service at St Annes Church, despite needing a stick to get there. Was she now in Paradise and reunited with her beloved husband? Laura hoped so. She also hoped that one day, at some distant date, she would again meet Rod and her parents.

Unlike Rod at his funeral, Mrs Mullet didn't have many mourners; most of her friends and family were already dead. Apart from Mr Clegg, the solicitor; Nigel's mother, Leonora Norris; Mrs Hughes and Mr Bicker, and herself, there was only the Brigadier General and some ancient neighbours.

She put the fish-paste sandwich back onto the plate. She just wasn't hungry. The other mourners, didn't seem to have her problem, as they were wolfing down the sandwiches which she and Mrs Hughes had made straight after breakfast, first removing the crusts and cutting them into triangles, before covering them with damp tea towels.

Five evenings ago, Mrs Mullet seemed fine – no different than usual. In fact, earlier in the day, quite lively, flirting with the Brigadier General when he called. That evening, after helping her with her latest jigsaw, Laura made them both a milky drink. Afterwards, she helped her up to her room. "Thank you, and sleep well," Mrs Mullet patted Laura's shoulder. On a sudden impulse, she kissed the thin papery cheek.

At eight, when she took Mrs Mullet in a cup of tea, no movement came from the bed – despite her cheery, "Wakey, wakey, it's a beautiful morning." After drawing the curtains, she turned towards it. She knew immediately something was wrong, and when she touched Mrs Mullet, she found her cold.

Flying downstairs, her chest tight as if bound by a steel band, she phoned the doctor. Maybe Mrs Mullet wasn't really dead? After all, Laura was no nurse, what did she know? Maybe he could give her an injection, or something to bring her round. Please God, let him be able to give her something!

Her hopes were dashed. After a routine examination, the doctor informed her that Mrs Mullet had suffered a fatal heart attack in the early hours of the morning.

Laura glanced across to where Mr Clegg, the solicitor, who half-choked by his high-wing-collar, was deep in conversation with the fur-clad and classy, Leonora Norris. She was over fifty, but trimmed-out to look younger. With bleached hair, too much make-up and long painted fingernails, she was gushing in manner. Laura wasn't certain whether she liked her or not? She seemed false somehow. Despite her over friendliness, and saying Laura was the daughter-in-law she'd hoped for – that she was pleased that the rumour she'd heard of Nigel marrying some gold digger had proved to be false, she'd not invited Laura to visit her in Oxford. No doubt she didn't think Laura good enough to mix with. Was Mr Clegg telling Nigel's mother that she, Laura was to be present at the reading of the will? She felt guilty at anticipating a legacy. Whoever came in for Freemantle House would no doubt sell it. She'd have to get out. She was trying not to think what she could do next, or where she and

Claire could go? It might all depend on the amount she was left in the will.

They were seated in the drawing room. Her throat felt tight, and the palms of her hands were moist. Surreptitiously she wiped them down her skirt. She'd never felt so nervous in all her life. Not even the first time that Rod had taken her to meet her prospective in-laws. *Or the second!* The solicitor cleared his throat and began:

"This is the last will and testament of Maude Mullet
of Freemantle House, St Annes on Sea," he read.

The smaller legacies came first. "To Lilian Hughes, who has proved to be honest and trustworthy while working diligently for me for the last fifteen years, I leave the sum of £200."

Mrs Hughes's face lit up. Seated on the edge of her chair, she got to her feet. "I never expected to get that much! How very very good of Mrs Mullet!"

"Quite!" said Mr Clegg severely, continuing. "To William Bicker, who has driven me safely to wherever I wanted to go for the last twenty years and more, I leave the sum of £200."

Mr Bicker, rubbing his palms over his knees, looked equally pleased.

Laura smiled. She was glad that Mrs Hughes and Mr Bicker had been left a reasonable amount. If anyone deserved to gain from such a sad event, they did. Mrs Hughes might be able to retire now. She was over sixty and it was high time she could put her feet up. Mr Bicker wasn't getting any younger either. He'd once told Laura that he had fought in the Boer War.

Mr Clegg was mentioning her name. "To Laura Norris, my dear nephew Nigel's wife, who with her culinary skills should go far, I leave the sum of £100 and my gold locket."

Laura couldn't believe it! How generous! The gold locket Mrs Mullet had always worn. And money too! She felt like dancing and singing. With the £20 she'd saved from Nigel's army allowance, such a reasonable sum might open up a whole new world. If she could borrow a bit more from the bank, she might be able to buy herself and Claire a house of their own. Or better still, something that could provide not only accommodation but also a living. An idea shot into her head. A boarding house! What better business for her to run with her catering experience? She wondered how much money one would need to get one? A leasehold place in Blackpool wouldn't cost so much. But could she do it? The cooking and cleaning was one thing, but what about the business side of things? Of course she could, she told herself firmly. First thing tomorrow, she'd make an appointment with the manager of the bank in St Annes Square – get things rolling.

Suddenly she felt guilty. If Mrs Mullet had known what she'd almost got up to with another man, she certainly wouldn't have left her anything in her will. Well, Mrs Mullet hadn't known, she told herself firmly, and her only regret was that Geoffrey had been called away before they could actually do it. Besides, guilt or no guilt, she couldn't hand the money, or the locket back, could she? No, of course, she couldn't! Though, if she and Geoffrey had made love, how on earth would she have gone on if there'd been any repercussions? – she was certain that loving him so much the sex would have been wonderful. She'd heard that enjoyment could make a difference to whether one conceived or not. French letters weren't always reliable. If she had found herself pregnant, she'd have had no choice but to blame her condition onto Nigel.

Nigel's mother seemed pleased with herself. Had Mr Clegg just said that she'd come in for Freemantle House and the bulk of Mrs Mullet's money? Laura hadn't actually heard him, being too full of her own thoughts. He was looking up from packing papers away in his briefcase, to shake the beaming woman's hand. But Nigel's name wasn't mentioned in the will. That's odd. He was Mrs Mullet's favourite nephew. Why hasn't something been left to him? This was something she would often mull over in the wee small hours, but not come up with an answer.

*   *   *

Two days later, dressed in her best, but with her insides feeling like an unset jelly, Laura stepped into Mr Potter's office – a room dominated by filing cabinets and a heavy oak desk on which was a squat black telephone, a metal inkwell, and a square pad of white blotting paper.

She glanced apprehensively at the middle-aged man who rose from behind the desk as she entered. Thickset and balding, he wore a navy pinstriped three-piece suit and across his chest was a gold watch chain. The ruddy face above the high white collar was full of self-importance.

"Do sit down, Mrs Norris," he said briefly. His handshake was like a limp lettuce leaf. "What can I do for you?"

She took a deep breath, and perched on the edge of the seat. Everything depended on how this interview went. She just had to convince him of her ability. "I'd like to borrow some money to buy a business," she said in a rush – "I know I've not got a bank account with you."

He frowned. "A business!"

"Yes."

"What sort of business?"

"A boarding house," stammered Laura.

"I see." He steepled his hands together. "And what sort of experience have you had in running such a business?"

"Well, none, but I am a cook-housekeeper. I've got quite a bit of catering experience."

"For how many people?"

"Well, recently, to only three. Though in my last place I cooked for six."

"Six! Wouldn't the number be several times that in a guest house?"

"Yes." She clutched to her tightly the handbag balanced on her lap. "B... but I'm sure I could do it. I'm very adaptable."

"Hmm. And what about your husband? Has he finances? Have you got his permission to approach the bank?"

"My husband's abroad, with the army – he's a lieutenant."

"An officer! I see. What sort of money are we talking about?"

"£200?"

"£200! You want to borrow £200. That's an awful lot of money. Have you thought of what sort of interest you'd be paying back to the bank on an amount like that?"

"I hadn't really."

He raised his eyebrows. "And what collateral have you got?"

"Collateral?"

"Have you any money, property, anything of value – the bank can't lend out money willy-nilly."

"I've got £120 – and a gold locket." Unbuttoning her coat, she slipped her hand inside and fingered it. "But I'll never sell it – it's got sentimental value."

"The problem, Mrs Norris, is that you need your husband's permission to get a loan, and at least one guarantor. And we would need to see a detailed plan of how you would run the business. Have you got a boarding house in mind, or plans?"

Laura's face fell. It was all far more complicated than she'd expected. "Well, not as yet, Mr Potter."

He tut-tutted, again steepling his hands and looking blankly at her. "I'm sorry, Mrs Norris, but at this moment I'm afraid the bank would not authorise me to help you." He rose. "If you could come back at some future date with something more concrete, we'd be pleased to consider you. Good morning."

Choking on her disappointment, she rose too. What on earth could she do now? She didn't fancy living once more under Doris Field's domination. That's if the Fields would take her in now she had remarried? Nowadays there was even less love lost between herself and her former mother-in-law. When Laura finally got up enough courage to tell her that she was going to marry again, the woman accused her of forgetting Rod. She'd replied that she'd not forgotten him, that she'd never forget him; in fact, she would always love him, but that life had to go on. Her answer wasn't well received by that *battle-axe*. Bullet-brown eyes narrowing, she said snappily, "If it weren't for our Claire, I'd not even cross the street for a faithless hussy like you." She'd lost her temper, too, retorting, "And if it weren't for our Claire, I wouldn't cross the street for you!" Doris Field, turning on her heel, stumped off.

*   *   *

Laura walked back to Freemantle House with dragging steps. Was there really no one else she could borrow money from? Of course there was Mr Bicker and Mrs Hughes – but she wouldn't ask them, they needed what they had for themselves. Suddenly it came to her. Her mother's aunt, Hannah Entwistle, in Manchester. Mum used to say that Aunt Hannah was well-lined – not that any of it had ever come their way. She'd only remembered ever seeing this aunt once, and that was when she was seven. Why Aunt Hannah had turned up when she did, Laura didn't know. All she could remember was a large woman in a black hat, with a strident voice, and with a purple stain covering one side of her face. This disfigurement had quite frightened Laura at the time. Would she help her? There probably wasn't much chance, but, all the same, it was worth a try. Laura made up her mind. She would go to Manchester and throw herself on Aunt Hannah's mercy.

*   *   *

Laura alighted at Victoria Station and glanced around in confusion. The noise was deafening. Everywhere she looked she saw the blue and khaki of servicemen and women, as in full voice they humped their kit bags on and off trains, or drank cups of tea provided by the WVS free canteen. Having no idea where the street her great-aunt lived in was, she bought a map of Manchester from the station kiosk. With her index finger she pinpointed what she was looking for. According to the map, Daphne Street seemed to be within walking distance, and was one of the side streets that led off Bellington Avenue at the far end of Market Street. Leaving the station, she headed in what she hoped was the right direction. As she turned into Market Street she realised it was almost dusk. The train had been delayed by more than an hour; consequently she was later arriving than she'd planned. She only hoped she could find her way in a strange place in the blackout. She wished now she'd come straight after taking Claire to school, but there'd been chores to do. Next thing it was dinner time. With relief she saw a sign saying, Bellington Avenue. Not long, now, she thought, turning into it.

As she passed houses and shops, studying each street sign as she came to it, she averted her eyes from the ominous gaps filled with rubble, wrinkling her nose at a stench which smelt she thought, like a combination of gas and drains and thanked God that she lived in Blackpool and not Manchester. Suddenly she heard the unearthly wailing of a siren. Oh, no! – that's all she needed, to be caught in an air raid. She began to shake and struggle with her gas mask case. This would be the first time she'd actually worn it. Hearing a droning overhead, she looked

115

up fearfully, seeing through the perspex window the shapes of planes – her imagination providing the swastikas. Something was falling with a whine – bombs? She looked around in terror and confusion. Where was the nearest shelter? People were shouting and running past her – mothers desperately wheeling prams at breakneck speed, or half-dragging sobbing children. A young lad with a tousled head and concertina socks appeared with a yelping mongrel on the end of a piece of string. A bus ground to a halt, and all the passengers piled off, and like the others, ran past her. An old man, hobbling on a walking stick, turned back, cap awry, his head wagging in his gas mask, as he yelled at her, "Come on, lass. Get under cover!" He shook his fist at the sky. "Bloody Huns! Trying to catch us on the hop like this. Usually the bastards don't put in an appearance 'till it's completely dark. They'll be coming in daylight next."

Laura needed no second invitation and followed him. At the end of the street was a purpose-built concrete shelter – its flat roof packed with sand bags. Everyone crowded into it, and only just in time as somewhere, from quite close by, came several deafening explosions.

They were squashed together on the hard narrow benches, the women trying to comfort the frightened children, everyone sweating in their gas masks, as they listened with bated breath to the sinister throbbing overhead, the crump of bombs, the ack-ack guns' reply, hoping and praying that none of the bombs would have their number on. After a particularly loud explosion, which sounded like hundreds of tea trays clattering downstairs, or cart loads of coal being tipped into cellars, the shelter shuddered and moved on its foundations, and clouds of dust and masonry showered down on them. She felt sick, what would happen to her Claire if the shelter should get a direct hit? Laura supposed if she was killed Doris Field would give Claire a home. Whatever her faults, she didn't think the woman would turn away her own flesh and blood. This was little comfort. She closed her eyes and prayed as hard as she could.

At last the All Clear sounded. Stiffly, she got to her feet, dusting herself down. The street outside was a shambles. Everywhere she looked she could see fires raging, hell couldn't be any worse, she thought. Beneath her feet was a sea of shattered glass and rubble. As well as smoke, there was a strong smell of gas in the air from the fractured pipes. Disorientated, she'd really no idea where she was going, or if it was possible now to find Daphne Street. She wandered around, skirting rubble, which, an hour or so before had been houses and shops. She passed a house where only one wall remained, like a stark sentinel. A curtain flapped from the dead eye of a frameless window. A chimney breast papered in childish motifs revealed that this had been the nursery. As did the child's cot hanging at a crazy angle over an abyss. To the furious clanging of ambulances and fire engine bells, she threaded her way through miles of telephone wire which lay on the ground looking like the entrails ripped out of pianos. Men were digging frantically with whatever they could use trying to save people buried under the rubble of their homes and businesses. Bodies, in some cases, parts of bodies of people, lay strewn around, cats and dogs – even horses who would no longer pull milk, bread and coal carts. The sight of so much gore turned her stomach, and she brought up her last meal.

It was just by luck that she recognised the street sign half buried in a pile of debris. But where there had once been a row of houses there was nothing but rubble. A couple of men, wearing tin helmets, and with blackened faces and hands were leaning wearily on their shovels. "Were there any survivors?" she asked one of them hesitatingly.

He lifted his helmet and wiped his brow with his sleeve. "All dead, apart from old Miss Entwistle. She was in a bad way when we dug her out, though. They've taken her to Salford Royal."

How Laura got to the hospital, she never knew. The Casualty Department was frantic. There were stretchers end-to-end along the corridor. Traumatised patients, groaning and writhing, their skin blistered and with huge raw welts – the colour of fire were waiting to be seen by the nurses and doctors who scurried hither and thither. It seemed like hours before she could find out what had happened to her great-aunt. Was she dead?

In the end they came to tell her that the woman she'd been asking about had died on the way to the hospital, and would she like to identify her? At first Laura didn't think that she could, after all it had been years since she'd actually set eyes on Aunt Hannah. Then she remembered the wine-stain on her cheek.

In the morgue, they pulled away the soiled sheet covering the body. Laura held her breath. Perhaps this wasn't her great-aunt? There must have been more than one elderly woman living in Aunt Hannah's street. Perhaps the man was wrong? It was unlikely, but she might have gone out for the evening, or away for a few days? She knew it was mercenary to hope that this wasn't her great-aunt, but she couldn't help it. For if this was Aunt Hannah, all her hopes and plans for the future would be dashed. There was no way she could ask a dead woman for a loan.

Somehow, she hardly knew how, she eventually got back to St Annes. With a sinking heart, she picked up the half-asleep Claire from Mrs Hughes. There was no doubt; the birth mark covering the right cheek had proved it. What on earth was she going to do now?

*   *   *

The following morning, while Claire was at school, she went over on the bus to see Doris Field. She didn't want to go 'cap-in-hand' to the woman, but she didn't see what else she could do.

As she passed a newsagents she saw a placard saying, DEVASTATION IN MANCHESTER.

She went in and bought an *Express*. The news item leapt out at her from the front page. In last night's raid the docks as well as the town centre had been badly damaged. It was believed that the latter was due to the Luftwaffe targeting the mills, many of which had been turned into armament factories. But what made her shiver was that an air raid shelter had taken a direct hit – and everyone inside, killed. Still feeling unsteady, she reached her destination.

Doris opened the door to her knock. "Well, this is a turn up for the book, you coming to see me!"

Laura shuffled her feet and struggled to find the right words. "As you know, my employer, Mrs Mullet has died and I'm no longer needed. Claire and I can't stay where we are. We've been given a month to find alternative accommodation."

"So?"

"I wondered if you could do me a favour?"

"Me do you a favour?" she snorted "Why should I want to do that?"

"Please, Mrs Field, can we come back here for a while? Just until I can find another place where I can have Claire – I've looked and looked in the paper but there's nothing. I'm desperate!" She'd thought of finding a house to rent, but houses to let were rare. The few that were, were too pricey. She didn't want to make inroads on her nest egg. As for a room in someone else's house, she could have got one for herself, but once she had mentioned having a child, no one wanted to know.

Arms-akimbo, Doris Field eyed Laura grimly. "You've got a cheek, lady, coming to me for help after the way you went off

119

that time without a by-your-leave. I really don't see why me and Mr Field should take you in again – especially now – can't some of your 'new' husband's in-laws give you house room?"

Laura shook her head.

"I see. So now you think you can come crawling back here! Getting a job with the toffs, indeed! Thought you were going to be better than us, did you? Well, pride goes before a fall. Your posh place didn't last long. He soon realised you were no better than a floosie."

"He didn't! I'm not!"

"Oh, no? Leading my Sid on like you did. And him a decent God-fearing man."

The devil's disciple, more like! "I didn't! It wasn't like that."

"I don't know why my Rod chose to marry you when he could have had a Blackpool girl. I've never believed that story about you having no parents – no father, more like. I reckon you were a by-blow – illegitimate!"

Illegitimate! That's a lie! This was worse than she expected. She had no choice though, but to take the insult. It was a terrible thing to be illegitimate. Society shunned you for the whole of your life. You were an outcast. Oh, please, must we talk on the step?" She saw a curtain twitch. "Your neighbours…"

"Hmm." The older woman looked at Laura hard, then turned on her heel. "You'd best come in – and mind you wipe your feet!"

Laura followed her into the back kitchen.

They faced each other across the scrubbed table.

"So you expect me to let you move in here again?"

"For Claire's sake, if not mine. You surely don't want Claire without a roof over her head?" Laura felt tears welling up and struggled to control them.

"If I agreed, and I'm not saying that I will, it definitely wouldn't be for your sake, lady. As far as I'm concerned, you could sleep on the street!" The bullet-brown eyes softened. "But our Claire's a different kettle-of-fish. I'll not have her suffering. All right, then, I agree, for Claire's sake. But if you're coming back here I'll insist on having new ground rules. This time, I'll expect you to really pull your weight, and do exactly as I think fit concerning 'my' granddaughter. Do you agree?"

Laura nodded. What other choice did she have?

"So when do you want to come?"

She didn't want to come at all! "In ten days time," she faltered. She might as well get it over with. "Mr Bicker, Mrs Mullet's former chauffeur will bring us over."

*   *   *

As the time drew closer, Laura's spirits dropped; she felt unhappier and unhappier. How was she going to bear being ordered about from dawn to dusk? If it hadn't been for Claire she would have willingly put her head into the gas oven.

The dreaded day arrived. The birds were singing when she emptied the ashes from the fire. She didn't feel like singing. Didn't feel she'd want to ever again. If only her parents were still alive. If only she had someone else to turn to, a sister, or even another aunt. But what was the good of wishing. There was no one.

Laura answered the door bell. She opened the registered letter that the postman had just handed over and gasped:

Dear Mrs Norris,

I have pleasure in informing you that as the only living relative
of the late Miss Hannah Entwistle, you are sole beneficiary to
her estate. Enclosed is a cheque for £150.

Yours faithfully,
George Fanshawe Gubbing. (Jnr)

With tears in her eyes, Laura fingered the cheque in
disbelief, her hands were so shaky that she dropped it. It
fluttered towards the open fire. Her heart missed a beat as she
snatched the cheque up out of harms way and soundly kissed it,
£150 – it was a fortune! Turning to Claire who was eating her
corn flakes, she hugged her. With this unexpected legacy added
to her savings and the £100 from Mrs Mullet, she didn't think
she'd need to go to the Fields. She might, she just might have
enough to get a leasehold boarding house? It looked like
someone up there was on her side, after all.

*   *   *

In the *Evening Gazette*, several guest houses were
advertised which might be suitable. Mr Clegg and the estate
agent between them would see to the financial side for her, but
she still needed someone to talk things over with, and to go with
her to look at them. A man would be best. Business people
always took more notice of a man. But who? There wasn't really

122

anyone. As she puzzled this over, a picture of her former father-in-law, Bert Field, in his old cap, flashed before her. She remembered how he had patted her shoulder that time in his house. She'd felt then he was sympathetic towards her. But would he help her now? Only if his wife didn't find out! But why should she? She certainly wouldn't tell her. The less that woman knew of her business the better. Doris Field had been very put out when she knew that Laura, and more importantly, Claire, no longer planned to move back to her house.

Still, maybe she would be seeing Bert before long? Sometimes, when Claire visited her grandparents in Blackpool, he came, instead of his wife. Claire was due to go for the day to them this Saturday. She crossed her fingers, with a bit of luck, it would be him who came to pick her up.

*   *   *

When she asked Bert Field to help her find a suitable boarding house, he immediately agreed. They mulled over the Property page in the *Gazette* together, picking out several *possibles*, advertised by Bing, Estate Agents. He then took Claire over on the bus to Blackpool and her grandmother, first arranging to meet Laura that afternoon outside the agent's office in Central Drive, adding with a grin, that he would tell his wife he was visiting his wholesaler.

Mr Bing accompanied Laura and Bert to view a boarding house in Trafalgar Terrace, near to South Shore Station. They had already seen two others nearby. Both of them, built during Victoria's reign, and into which you walked straight off the street, had very poky rooms, and no bathroom. There was also no back yard for Claire to play in, or for Laura to hang out her washing.

She stood with Bert on the opposite pavement and studied the two-storey terraced house. It looked solid enough, and in front of it there was a pocket-sized garden with a low wall and a wooden gate. Weeds ran riot in the garden, but she could soon change that, she'd plant some flowering lobelia, they were a real touch of colour; and maybe begonias. Early May was just the right time to put in bedding plants.

"Not bad, not bad at all, Laura," summed up Bert.

"My opinion, exactly."

"Solid Accrington brick. Window frames seem okay. A touch a paint perhaps. Of course it needs pointing in places, but that's not urgent." He eyed the house next door. "Not like there. It's a wonder the bricks don't fall out." He laughed.

Laura laughed too.

"We'd want what needs doing reflected in the selling price. But let's look inside first," said Bert.

She crossed back over. Mr Bing consulted his clipboard. "This one's a bargain, Mrs Norris. Not only is it Freehold, which means not having to pay an annual ground rent, but it's larger than the others that you've already seen. It has ten letting bedrooms, two of which are family rooms, a bathroom – a separate inside lavatory – plus one out-back, and a good-sized yard. Mrs Dixon, the landlady, died some time ago of a brain tumour. Quite unexpected it was. A tragedy for Mr Dixon. Mrs Dixon was only fifty."

"How sad."

"Yes, I agree, but maybe lucky for you. Mr Dixon can't cope with the RAF lads billeted with him – he's had to pay the woman next door to send in meals for him to heat up for them – consequently for a quick sale, he's willing to let the place go for a song."

"How much is a song?" asked Bert.

Mr Bing stroked his chin. "If Mrs Norris were to offer two hundred pounds cash for the place, which would naturally include all fixtures and fittings, plus stock, well I reckon, she'd get her hand bit off."

Excitement raced through Laura. Two hundred! At a pinch she could just manage that. They went inside and met Mr Dixon. Surely he had to be older than his late wife? He looked sixty if a day with his sunken eyes and sallow cheeks, though, she supposed, grief could have aged him. The guests being out, he showed them round the whole house. The rooms were all of a reasonable size. The beds too were good. She lifted the counterpanes to take a look. A back boiler behind the fireplace in the owner's private room provided hot water. There was an immersion heater for when the fire wasn't lit. All the same, she did wonder if there would be sufficient hot water for so many airmen to have their weekly bath, until she learnt that they bathed at the Lido Baths. The lounge where the Brylcreem boys ate their meals, played cards, or read, or wrote letters, contained two long dining tables laid up ready for the evening meal. Several armchairs, ancient though comfy-looking, a long settee covered with a black-and-yellow woven throw over, and also an old upright piano, around which, Mr Dixon said, the lads would gather of an evening for singsongs. He opened the scullery door into a yard, too small to need gardening, but big enough for a clothes line, and also for a swing for Claire. Facing Laura was a six-foot wall with no footholds – so there was no need to worry about her *little minx* clambering over onto the railway line.

Back inside, she eyed the scullery. The cooker was electric. She'd only ever cooked on gas, but she was sure she'd soon get used to it. She opened the oven door, and flinched. Well, elbow grease and hot water and soda would soon see off the accumulated grease. Beneath the window was a yellow-stone sink with a double draining board. The furniture, a large scrubbed kitchen table and four dining-chairs seemed serviceable. She could just see herself stretching out in that faded red plush wing-chair and putting her feet up on the battered pouffe after a hard day. The walls were reasonable too, so she wouldn't need to bother for a while with decorating, not until she was settled. As she was making up her mind, a train came past, causing the cups hanging from the dresser to vibrate.

"You don't notice it after a while," said Mr Dixon.

"I suppose not." Laura looked at Bert. He nodded. He thought what she thought. This was just what she was looking for. She'd need someone to give her a hand, but maybe she could get a school leaver? She made up her mind. "I'd like to take it," she said to Mr Bing, "when can I move in?"

*   *   *

Laura moved into Number Three, Trafalgar Terrace on a sunny morning in June. At the same time as the bin men, trailing cinders, humped the bins to the waiting dust cart. As the street was narrow, Laura's taxi needed to pull in behind.

The taxi driver removed their bags and bundles from the boot to a background of clanking bins and raised voices, Laura helped the excited Claire out. "Is that it, Mummy?" she said, pointing to a front door slightly further up, besides which was a wooden sign with a THREE painted on it. "Is that our new home?"

"Yes, darling. Now, will you carry this for Mummy, please?" She handed her the lightest bag. She looked up from paying the taxi-man. At the guest house window curtains twitched. She saw several avid faces, who were obviously eager to get their first glimpse of their new landlady. As she was struggling to pick up a suitcase, the front door opened, followed by piercing wolf-whistles, as smiling young men in RAF uniform, poured out of the house towards her. She blushed. Claire, clutching Primrose, her favourite doll, giggled.

"I'll carry that for you, Mrs Norris," said a good-looking lad with blue eyes and fair hair.

She straightened up. "Thanks very much."

126

"And I'll take these." A hefty airman slung two large bundles effortlessly over his shoulder. He had brown curly hair and sounded jolly. He turned to Claire and winked. "And who might you be?"

"I'm Claire. And I'm seven."

"Grown up then."

She giggled.

The rest of their luggage was gathered up too, and with the group of laughing Brylcreem boys surrounding them, Laura and Claire were escorted inside.

Mr Dixon, meeting her in the passage, straightened his shoulders. He handed her the keys, and wishing her luck, left her to it. It was straight in at the deep-end. Minutes later, with her coat off, her sleeves rolled up, and her hair wound in a turban, her hands and arms were deep in sudsy water as she battled her way through a mountain of breakfast things. Drying the last cup and dish, and setting them in their places on the shelves of the dresser, she looked down at the soaking front of her wrap-around-apron. She'd have to hang it on the line to dry it out. Making the beds came next. As she smoothed the wrinkles from the final bedspread, Claire called her. Earlier, she'd given her a new colouring book and pencils, hoping to keep her amused. This obviously hadn't worked. Or, at least not for long. Through the window she saw that the shower had stopped and the flags were steaming. If she left the back door on the latch, Claire could play out in the yard with her skipping rope. But in which bag were they packed? She hurried downstairs to their private room where the luggage was. Claire met her at the door. "I'm bored, Mummy," she whined, "can I play in the back yard?"

"Yes, you can."

Claire's face brightened. "I want to skip. I want my skipping ropes. Get them for me, please, Mummy."

"I'm just going to try and find them for you." said Laura rooting through one bag after another. "Success at last!" She

127

pulled them out and handed them to Claire. Why was it when you wanted something, it was always at the bottom of the last bag you came to?

She followed her outside and watched her skipping. "Salt, pepper, mustard, vinegar," Claire chanted.

In next-door's yard, Laura spotted a swing. If there was a girl there, perhaps they could pal up. She was certain it would make all the difference if Claire had a playmate. At the Cedars, Claire and Mollie used to amuse themselves happily for hours. Neither had been any trouble. Otherwise, she would not have been able to get through all her work.

The Cedars was nothing compared to what she now had on her hands. Then there were only four adults and two children to cater for. She needed help and fast. She decided to slip out as soon as she could and put an advertisement in the corner shop. And then she would hope and pray that someone, anyone, would turn up.

* * *

Mrs Hughes, nursing a cup of tea, looked around with satisfaction. "So you've no regrets then, Laura?"

"Never! It was the best day's work I ever did coming here. Financially and otherwise. And Claire has settled in well at Peterloo School. There's a kiddy next door, Ann. Claire and her have become as-thick-as-thieves. They're in the same class. They walk to school together. I've warned her to watch out for the army lorries when crossing the roads. I'm sure she'll be sensible. You've got to let them stand on their own feet sometime, haven't you? " Laura had no regrets apart from the fact that she now lived closer to Doris Field, which meant, once the woman knew they were back in Blackpool, that instead of a weekly Saturday visit to fetch Claire over for the day, she'd been on Laura's doorstep several evenings running. Until, losing patience, Laura had told her in no uncertain terms, that a visit once a week was enough, and then it was to be only by prior arrangement. Bert, though was a different story, he was welcome to come anytime for a chat and a cup of tea – whenever he felt he needed to escape from his wife. Grateful for his support in getting the guest house, she had bought him two packets of Players cigarettes as a 'thank you'. He'd been pleased, she knew, despite him saying it wasn't necessary. Doris Field would have been furious if she had known he'd helped her. Luckily, she was none the wiser. It was their secret!

"Yes, you can't treat them as babies forever," agreed Mrs Hughes.

Deciding on a day's shopping in Blackpool, she'd called in to see Laura at the same time. "You don't find it a bit much coping with all those young RAF lads?"

She smiled. "No, they're all perfect gentlemen as far as I'm concerned, besides the Sergeant in charge of the billet keeps them in order. I just have to conjure up the meals."

"That can't be easy, I wouldn't want to have to eke out the rations for so many. How many is it?"

"Twenty altogether. Mind you, first thing in the morning, when they're queuing on the landing, they seem more like a hundred. You should hear the racket they make banging on the lav' door and as for their comments. Well!"

"Make you blush, do they?" chuckled Mrs Hughes.

"They are a bit near the knuckle."

"But otherwise you're managing okay?"

"They're out most of the day, drilling, or doing their basic training."

"To be pilots?"

"No. Some are training to be electricians and wireless operators. The thing they've all got in common is that they're all keen to go off to take a bash at Jerry."

"Well, I wouldn't want such a motley lot to see to. My old man's enough for me! More than enough, sometimes. There must be an awful lot of work for one pair of hands, Laura?"

"It's not so bad. I send all the sheets to the laundry, and I've got a gem in Mrs Rose, who comes in of a morning to help with the beds and cleaning, and again for an hour in the evenings for the washing up. She's got a large family, so she's glad of a bit extra. The worst thing is that I'm beginning to get muscles in my upper arms from carrying so many heavy trays." She flexed her arm. "Look at that!"

Mrs Hughes laughed. "They're not big, Laura."

"They look big to me. They aren't very feminine."

"Well you are! Very feminine! So stop worrying, my girl. I'm glad you've got a woman coming in, but, even with some help, you've still got all the shopping to do. It would be bad enough without having to cope with all those ration books. I'd not fancy cutting out coupons and worrying about 'points' for so many. What a headache that must be! Then there's standing in queues for hours on end to find when you get to the front that it's all sold out. I could spit when that happens!"

"I know what you mean. I manage. I'm always up before the lark, and a good start to the day makes all the difference." Apart from breakfast, it was just dinner, 'afters', and a cup of tea to follow that she needed to find them. It wasn't easy concocting tasty dishes out of corned beef and spam, dried egg and wholemeal flour. How she wished she could get her hands on some of the ingredients that had been in the shops pre war. Still, as long as she served them up a pile of mashed potato, or steamed pudding, she couldn't go far wrong.

"But what about the business side of things?"

"It's easier since I started a book keeping course at the Technical College."

"Book keeping! How on earth do you manage to squeeze that in?"

"It's only one evening a week. Mrs Rose stays on later to listen out for Claire and to make the lads their bedtime cocoa."

"So you've got it all worked out. Well, I guess it must be nice to have young men around. I bet they're lively company?"

Laura laughed. "They are! Too lively sometimes. Especially when they gather around the piano belting out popular songs – you know, *Roll out the barrel*, that sort of thing." It was Reg, an AC2, who thumped out the tunes. Reg, who had helped her in with her case that first morning. A similar age to herself, he was rather attractive with his bright blue eyes, cheery manner and a fair quiff. Laura was more than certain that he wouldn't take much encouraging to start something with her. Not that she'd encourage him; she'd too many complications already, two men in her life was quite enough for her. But did she have two men in her life? She'd still not heard from Geoffrey. Though she had from Nigel. Before moving from Freemantle House she'd received a couple of airmail letters. Apart from the fact that he was alive and well, they didn't say much, due to the censor.

"So have they sold Freemantle House yet?"

Mrs Hughes drained her cup and placed it on the table. "They have. I can't get used to seeing strangers there when I go past. Mr Bicker feels the same. He told me when I bumped into him last week at the greengrocers."

"Mr Bicker! How is he?"

"He's fine." Mrs Hughes leaned closer. "He's courting, you know!"

"Courting! At his age? Who on earth would he be courting? Besides, I thought he was a confirmed bachelor?"

"So did I. But he's not so confirmed as we thought. He's got a young girl in tow."

"Never! A young girl?"

"Well, she's about thirty-five, but she's young compared to him. Works at the Co-op drapery. They got chatting when he was buying himself new curtains. Anyway, since then they've been tripping the *light-fantastic* at church socials. One wonders… Two hundred pound isn't to be sneezed at. She could spend his money and then skedaddle, they say there's no fool like an old fool."

Laura bit her lip. And what about young fools? Was she being a fool still daydreaming after Geoffrey? Would he ever write? Would she ever see him again? An unsettling thought resurfaced. What if he'd only been hoping to make use of her to satisfy his own physical urges? Many men would, she knew, should they get half a chance. No, she told herself. She'd not consider such a thing. He was genuine; she would stake her life on it. But if he did write, if he did return; what good would that do her? She was married to Nigel, and marriage was marriage, and not easy to get out of – not without someone getting hurt in the process. Unless, of course, Nigel didn't return from the war, but she couldn't wish such a thing on him. She would have to be a monster to wish that! No, she was well and truly stuck.

CHAPTER SEVEN

Having left Mrs Rose to see to the bed-making and the clearing up, Laura could tell that the town centre was more packed than ever. Everywhere she looked she saw Polish airmen, who were training in Blackpool and billeted around Rawcliffe Street, only a short distance from her guest house. Most of the Poles could speak some form of English. Then there were the GI soldiers in their fancy uniforms, talking like film stars, or so it seemed to her.

She reddened as a GI turned and wolf-whistled.

In 1941, Pearl Harbour brought America into the war. Now, Blackpool was buzzing with Americans stationed at Warton and the Burtonwood camp, just outside Warrington. This was to the liking of the girls of the town, if not the lads. What it is to be young with no responsibilities, to spend every night dancing at the Tower, the recipient of nylon stockings and chocolates. Not that she would wish to be without her Claire. Not even after last night.

Laura pushed open the bedroom door. "Claire! It's time you were going to bed. Good God, what a mess! I told you you weren't to paint your pictures up here, you've splashed paint everywhere, and why haven't you tidied away those comics like I told you to?"

"Don't fuss, Mum!"

"Don't fuss! They're all over the bed. I couldn't get in if I wanted to. Tidy them up immediately."

"Shan't! You can't make me."

"No? If you want a penny pocket money on Saturday you'd better had do. And when you've done that, get undressed and into bed."

Claire's brows drew together and for one moment she looked exactly like Doris Field. "It isn't fair, Ann doesn't have to go to bed until ten."

"That's up to Mr and Mrs Hill. I say nine o'clock is quite late enough. Especially when you've got school next day."

Claire half-heartedly picked up a comic. "You're always keeping on at me. You're mean, that's what you are!"

"So, I'm mean then. Now, snap-to-it."

Sighing, Laura went into the Abingdon Street market. She needed to get some vegetables. She paid the stallholder for the carrots and onions and as she was putting them into her shopping bag, she saw someone who looked familiar. They both gasped and said, "It isn't, is it?"

"It is," said Laura. "Oh, Rosemary, fancy seeing you!"

"Fancy seeing you! I've thought about you so often, and wondered how you were getting on? Are you still housekeeper to that old woman in St Annes?" Rosemary opened her arms and she and Laura hugged each other.

"No. Mrs Mullet died. I live in Blackpool. I've lived here since '41. Almost three years now. I've got a boarding house in South Shore."

"A boarding house! How on earth did you manage that?"

"It's a long story. Have you got time for a cuppa and a chat?"

"Yes, why not?"

Seated in the Copper Kettle, Rosemary stirred in a saccharin. She took a sip and pulled a face. "They say they taste the same as sugar, but I don't think so."

"No," agreed Laura. "If I can't have sugar, I'll take my tea without. You get used to it after a while." She drank and put her cup on the saucer. "So where are you nursing, now, Rosemary? I guess that you are still nursing? It's strange I haven't bumped into you before. I come up to the market at least once a week."

134

"I don't come that often, only when I need something. Today I was after some black stockings for work."

"And did you get any?"

"Two pairs and I didn't need to give up any coupons for them either."

"That was lucky!"

"I could certainly do with some."

Laura looked up sharply at the tone of Rosemary's voice. "What do you mean?"

"To make up for the bad I've had. I... I lost my fiancé in an accident on the Burtonwood base a year back. Run over by a jeep, they said; they never did say exactly how it happened."

"Oh, I'm so sorry to hear that." Laura put out her hands and took Rosemary's. "Had you known each other long?"

"No, only a few weeks. But that was enough. It was a whirlwind romance. Joe was a GI, from Texas. His father owned a ranch. I met Joe at the Tower Ballroom. He was a six footer, with a fair crew cut. He wasn't exactly handsome, but he'd something about him – he could certainly send me up to cloud nine and no mistake. And could he jitterbug! He'd spin me around and around – I'd fly out of my wits. Not to mention the fact that I showed everyone my next week's washing!" she smiled tearfully. "Oh, blow! I don't seem to have a hanky."

"Here you are, take mine."

"Thanks." Rosemary wiped her eyes. "Joe was going to take me home with him after the war. When he was killed," her voice dropped to a whisper, "I wanted to die too."

Laura nodded. She knew what that was like. She'd felt the same when she'd lost Rod.

Rosemary went on to tell her she'd been run off her feet at the hospital, and hadn't had time to dwell on what had happened; she knew she wasn't alone in suffering the loss of a loved one. Laura commiserated, saying that even with so many others in the same boat this wouldn't make her loss any easier

135

for her to bear. Rosemary agreeing, said she imagined that only time would do that.

"So you're nursing at the Victoria Hospital?" asked Laura, changing the subject.

"Yes. But it would be easier if I could live in."

"Can't you?"

"No. You see..." She flushed. "I've, well, I've got a baby, Billy – he's nine-months-old. I only found out I was pregnant after Joe was killed."

"A baby!" A love child! That must have caused some raised eyebrows in certain quarters. So Rosemary wasn't as white as she painted herself, after all.

"It caused a lot of gossip, I can tell you, but if they're talking about you, they're not talking about someone else."

"That's true. But how on earth do you manage to cope?"

Rosemary said this had been far from easy on her own. She'd been determined that she wasn't going to put Billy up for adoption, though quite a few *so-called,* well-meaning people had tried to talk her into it. The worst part for her was finding somewhere to live where the landlady would accept an unmarried mother with a child. At the digs she'd eventually found she paid the landlady to keep an eye on Billy while she worked. She didn't like it there, for a start, the food was vile. And their room was poky.

It occurred to Laura that if Rosemary could find somewhere decent, she'd move out in a flash. It'd be nice to have some female company for a change. On occasion she felt rather outnumbered with so many men under her roof. For a good old, *put the world to rights,* natter, nothing could beat another woman. If Rosemary agreed to come to lodge with her, they could relive old times. "I might be able to help you?" Laura said.

"You know of somewhere?"

"Yes, I might be able to squeeze you in with me."

"You mean at your place, Laura?"

136

"Yes. I've a room vacant. The airmen who were in it have been posted abroad. It would be nice to have another woman around. If you moved in, I could watch Billy for you while you work."

"You'd do that for me?"

"Isn't that what friends are for?"

"Oh, Laura, that'd be great. Now, come on tell me how you managed to get a guest house? Spill the beans!"

"I'm just getting to that, Rosemary. I'm no longer a widow." At least she wasn't when Nigel had last written to her. Since moving into Trafalgar Terrace she'd received two more letters from the man she'd married so hastily. In both of them he had grumbled about the heat and finding sand in everything. Could he be somewhere in North Africa? She still hadn't heard anything from Geoffrey, and in fact, now wondered if she ever would. Was he dead? A prisoner? Had he had a change of heart? She didn't know. Maybe she would never know. Laura lifted her cup and drank the cooling tea.

"So you've married again? Not Geoffrey Roberts?"

The tea went down the wrong way. "No. Not Geoffrey Roberts," she spluttered. "Nigel's the nephew of Mrs Mullet, my late employer in St Annes. I'm now Laura Norris."

"So you got over him then?" Rosemary eyed her keenly.

Laura flushed at the thought of what had almost happened between them. Good thing Rosemary couldn't read her mind. And maybe the Army's interference would prove to have been for the best in the long run. At least now, should Nigel return, she could face him with a clear conscience. In her heart-of-hearts she knew she owed it to Mrs Mullet to give her marriage a chance. She wondered if Nigel would want to run the boarding house with her? "All water under the bridge," she said flippantly.

"I gave Mr Roberts your address, you know. Did he ever come to see you?"

"Did you? Well, he must have changed his mind about contacting me," she lied.

"I see. So where's hubby?"

"Nigel?"

"Is that his name?"

"Yes. He's in the forces – abroad somewhere – he's not allowed to say where. It was partly because his aunt left me some money in her will that I was able to get my boarding house. It wasn't enough, so I tried to get a loan from the bank on the strength of it. They wouldn't! Not without a man's say-so. I'd more or less resigned myself to going back to the Fields – and you can imagine how I felt about that! Then, unbelievably, my luck turned and I came in for enough money to bridge the shortfall. This time from my side of the family."

Rosemary whistled. "Jammy beggar! I wish someone would leave me some money."

"It's certainly made all the difference to me and Claire."

"Well, good luck to you, you deserve some with having a kiddy to bring up alone. It isn't easy being mother and father. And don't I know it! How is Claire, she must be getting quite big now?"

"She is! She's almost as tall as me and she's only just ten. She's good at her lessons too. She was top of her class last term."

"You must be very proud."

Laura nodded. Anyway, if you'd like the room, it's yours."

"Great! There's no time like the present. If it's convenient, I'll come with you to see it now."

* * *

Rosemary moved in – baby Billy with her. Billy was a chubby, lively fellow, fair-haired, like his dad. Claire adored him right from the start and would play, 'One little piggy went to market', with his fingers and toes – making him chuckle. She wasn't the only one to fuss over Billy; the airmen would give up their sweet rations and feed him with thin slices of Mar's bar, so much so that both Laura and Rosemary became concerned about his teeth.

Laura never had too much trouble coping with a small child as well as the boarding house while Rosemary was at work. When it was fine, Laura would sit Billy in his pram, strapped in his safety harness, out in the back yard. He would wave his fist and shout excitedly, when, beyond the wall, trains whistled past. As Billy became older, she'd pop him with his toys into his play pen in the kitchen, where she could keep an eye on him. When Rosemary did the night shift at the hospital, Laura moved his cot into the room she shared with Claire – but he usually slept through. And it was like old times for Laura when Rosemary finished early at the hospital and they could spend a few hours together, chattering, knitting and listening to the wireless.

*　*　*

"Mrs Norris! Mrs Norris!" called Mrs Rose.

Laura dropped the garment she was pegging onto the line and hurried back inside. "What is it, Mrs Rose? What's wrong?"

She smelt it immediately. Singed material. Fire! Had her worst nightmare come true? If she'd told those lads once, she'd told them a dozen times to be careful where they put their cigarettes. Could a cigarette end have smouldered all night down the side of the cushions, or had one been dropped more recently – at breakfast time? She collided with Mrs Rose who was hovering in the lounge doorway, just in time to see the settee cushions burst into flames.

Mrs Rose, panicking, screamed and flapped a tea towel in the direction of the blaze that was rapidly spreading and from which acrid smoke was billowing.

"Don't!" coughed Laura. "Phone the Fire Brigade."

"But Mrs Norris, a bucket of water."

"No water! It'll make it worse." She recalled how as a child a neighbour had poured water onto a similar fire and the flames had leapt up ceiling-high. The woman's kitchen had been gutted. She'd been lucky to escape without being badly burnt. "We need the Fire Brigade. Ring 999. I'll try a wet tablecloth."

But Mrs Rose was entranced by the flames and made no move.

"Now! Before it gets out of hand – go!"

Mrs Rose came-to and hurried out.

Whipping off a tablecloth, Laura dashed to the scullery. Her hands shook on the taps and it seemed more than she could do to turn them. She wrung out the sodden material as she stumbled back into the lounge – it was heavy and hard to spread out – and with heart pounding – heat singeing her face and hair, and half-blinded and choking, she managed to throw the cloth over the flames.

By the time the brigade arrived, she and Mrs Rose, between them had ruined nine of Laura's best linen tablecloths, but the fire was under control.

The fire was out. The firemen gone – leaving behind them the wreck of her lounge. The two women stood there exhausted and shaking, the full impact of what had almost happened beginning to sink in. What if the whole place had burnt down? What if Claire hadn't been at school? What if Claire had been left an orphan?

Laura's hands were stinging. She looked down to see they were raw. She'd better rub in Vaseline if she didn't want nasty blisters. Putting to rights the wall behind the settee was a different matter. She tried soap and water, but she might as well have tried to wash the 'black' out of Blackpool, and as for the lino, it had to be replaced, though Bert emulsioned the bubbled walls and ceiling for free. The settee itself was a right-off, and

140

only fit to be taken away by the bin men. As she watched it being flattened in the back of the dust cart, she wished for the umpteenth time that her parents were still alive, that she had a sister, or even another aunt to turn to. But what was the good of wishing, wishing wouldn't help her. She wondered what on earth she was going to do? She had to have a settee She couldn't have her lads falling out over who should have the easy chairs. She couldn't really afford to replace it. Claire was growing so fast and needing new things all the time, and any savings she managed to scrape together went on her daughter. And as for asking Rosemary to lend her money – Rosemary, with having Billy, was as hard up as herself. She knew she could always sell Mrs Mullet's locket, but that locket, along with the shell necklace that Geoffrey had given her were far too precious ever to part with.

She'd still not solved her problem, when a few evenings later there was a rat-a-tat at the front door. To her surprise, and also unease, on the doorstep was Sid.

He raised his bowler. "Didn't expect to see me, did you, Laura?"

"Well, no."

"I've heard about your little mishap."

"My fire?"

He smoothed his moustache. "That's right. As a good Christian, I've come to offer you a helping hand. Furniture wise, that is. Aren't you going to ask me in?"

Should she? She certainly didn't want to. Especially as she was on her own. Claire and Billy in bed upstairs were no protection. What if he were to start something? And why should he want to help her? The last time they'd met, he'd promised to get even with her.

The bullet-brown eyes gleamed. "You're not frightened of me, are you, Laura?"

141

Was she? After almost being raped by him that time she supposed she was, but she wasn't going to give him the satisfaction of letting him know this. "No, of course not. Come on in. How's Prue and the children? – well, I hope? " She turned and led the way into the scullery.

He placed his bowler on the table. "They're fine. Look, Laura, I'll come straight to the point. You could do with a settee…"

As Sid spoke a train came past causing the mugs hanging from the dresser to vibrate.

"A bit trying that, isn't it?"

"You don't notice it after a while."

"Well, rather you than me. As I was saying, I can get you a three-seater settee at cost. I'll not charge you the interest I would normally. You are family, after all. Four shillings a month for thirty-six months. I can't say fairer than that. What do you think?"

It was reasonable, she had to admit. Far less than she would pay elsewhere. She would have rather not been indebted to Sid though. She felt very uncertain about the whole thing, she was sure he would have some motive of his own for helping her out, but what other choice did she have? She had to have a settee.

"Is it a decent one? Is it fire resistant?"

"It's decent, all right. But nothing's fire resistant, Laura. Get more ashtrays, that's all I can suggest. It's a bargain, do you want it, or don't you? I'm doing you a favour."

"All right then. Thank you." The words stuck in her mouth.

"I'll have it delivered first thing tomorrow morning." He made himself comfortable in the wing chair. "Now, Laura, how about a 'thank-you' for coming to your rescue?"

His leer said it all. She deliberately misunderstood him – making him tea, though she didn't join him. His hot eyes surveyed her over the rim of the cup. As if he was undressing her, she thought distastefully. The more she saw him, the more she detested him. He wiped his moustache with the back of his hand and put the cup on the table. "I've always thought you a fine figure of a woman, Laura. But now you really fill out the bodice of your dress, if you take my meaning." He licked his lips suggestively.

She froze. What now?

A tap came at the back door. "Cooee, Mrs Norris."

It was her neighbour. Mrs Hill came in with an empty sugar bowl in her hand. She looked curiously at Sid. "Sorry! I see you've company."

"It's all right, Mrs Hill." Laura took the bowl from her and filled it. Never had she been so pleased to see the woman. "My brother-in-law's just going – aren't you Sid?"

He reluctantly rose and picked up his bowler. "Yes," he said. "Can't stop. I've more calls to make – two sales to clinch."

With relief, she showed him out.

The following evening saw Laura bouncing gently on the new settee. "I've got to admit, Rosemary, that this is really comfy. You had to be careful where you sat on the old one – unless you wanted to bruise your bottom on a wonky spring." She laughed.

Rosemary laughed too. "No one's complained. Airmen have lots of 'cheek', I reckon."

"You are a caution!" Laura rose to her feet, admiring the black-and-green striped upholstery. "It's smart, isn't it? It doesn't look like Utility."

No, it's far too good a quality for that – look at those castors – reminds me of the settee in the Roberts's lounge. I think you've got yourself a bargain. I know you don't care for this Sid, but you must admit he's done you proud."

She knew Rosemary was right, but did this make her even more indebted to him?

*   *   *

Laura lifted up the pastry with her rolling pin and laid it over two large baking sheets. She took a bowl of grated sweetened carrots and spooned them into the pastry cases.

"What are you making?" asked Rosemary.

"Mock apricot tarts." Laura covered the fillings with more pastry and trimmed the edges. "It's one of Lord Woolton's. With custard it always goes down a treat."

"Sounds okay. I'm on late tomorrow. Will you save me a bit?"

"Of course, I will."

"There's a woman on my ward, Laura, with your first husband's surname."

"What, Field?"

"Yes. She's got a broken ankle and suspected internal injuries. I reckon she's been belted by her old man – she's bruised all over, though she says she got the bruises when she missed her footing and fell down the stairs."

"Fell down the stairs! That's an old chestnut. So what's this woman's Christian name?"

"Prue."

"Prue! – I suppose there could be more than one Prue Field. What's she like?"

Laura stroked her chin. "Well, she's rather sallow-skinned and in her middle thirties with mousy frizzy hair, oh, and she's got a colourless mole, just below her right eye."

"Sounds like her, I always thought Sid was a wife beater."

Rosemary went on to say she wasn't surprised, she'd thought he looked real shifty. The old battleaxe who was with him, seemed even worse, laying down the law to poor Mrs Field. Laura shook her head at Rosemary's words. The woman sounded like Sid's mother all right. And she was probably threatening poor Prue. No doubt telling her if she didn't keep her mouth shut it would be all the worse for her. Doris Field pretended her son was a saint, but Laura reckoned she knew his true nature.

"Men like that shouldn't be allowed to get away with it," said Rosemary.

"I agree, but what can anyone do? You can't interfere between man and wife."

"Who says? Men? After her visitors left, Mrs Field became hysterical. We had to give her a sedative to calm her down."

"I'm not surprised. Thank God I'm out of Doris Fields's clutches."

"But Prue Field isn't! That poor woman, Laura," said Rosemary, "she needs someone to stand up for her."

"She's got a mother, I think?"

"You're not certain?"

"I suppose she could have passed on by now. She was quite elderly."

"So what about you, Laura?"

"Me!"

"Somebody should, I reckon. That poor woman certainly needs someone in her corner."

Would Rod have wanted her to get involved? She knew the answer. She thought of the way Sid had insulted her in front of Nigel. She owed it to her self respect to see he got his comeuppance, if not for that, at least for what he was doing to Prue. She brushed aside the fact that Sid had helped her recently with the settee. He had to have some ulterior motive for coming to her rescue, she was certain. I stood up to Doris Field for myself, what's to stop me doing it again – and this time for Prue? After all, weren't we on this earth to help each other? If she'd not had financial help from Mrs Mullet and her great-aunt, where would she be now? "You're right, Rosemary. She was my sister-in-law. I think I'll go and visit Prue myself – let her know she's not on her own."

*   *   *

Clutching a bunch of tawny chrysanthemums, Laura walked across the hospital forecourt. Inside, an arrow below a sign, pointed: WARD NINETEEN – THIS WAY. She followed its direction along winding corridors, their walls an institutional green, wrinkling her nose at the smell of carbolic. People continually passed in the opposite direction, their shoes squeaking on the lino. Her throat felt tight and her chest fluttered. It was one thing to be brave when in her familiar surroundings, another now.

What would Prue's reaction be at seeing her after so long? They'd never been that pally. Prue, she guessed, had been too scared of Sid to take her up on her tentative offers of friendship. She'd be surprised to see her, that much was certain. It being afternoon, at least it wasn't likely she would run into Sid. At this hour, he'd be at his shop. But what about Doris Field? Laura wasn't particularly keen on coming face to face with her. She could just imagine what that woman would say – *'What are you doing here? You've no right to come nosing into what doesn't concern you – you're not family now. Not since you forgot my poor Rod and married again!'*

Outside Ward Nineteen was a queue. She joined it. A queue for everything, she thought, even to visit the sick!

A bell rang and the doors opened. Everyone surged into the ward. At a central desk was a posse of nurses, all uniformed caps and white starched crackle. There was a row of iron beds on either side. Her eyes slid over them. Seated by one was a sad-looking woman with a plastered-up ankle. Was this, Prue? She moved closer. One side of the woman's face was mottled yellow-and-black.

"Laura? Is that you?"

It was Prue!

146

"Yes, it's me. How are you?" What a daft thing to say! By the look of her there was only one answer.

"I fell down the stairs," said Prue, awkwardly.

"I've brought you some chrysanths." Laura gave them over. She winced at the bruises on Prue's arms.

"How kind. How lovely of you." Her voice trembled.

"Shall I ask the nurse to put them in water?"

"Yes, that would be best." Laura took them from her and went off to see if she could find Rosemary. She was sluicing bedpans. "Hallo, Laura. So you got here. How's it going?" she asked, reaching down a cut-glass vase, filling it, and arranging the flowers. "Have you managed to get Mrs Field to admit her husband is ill treating her?"

"Give me a chance, it's not so easy a thing to tackle someone about."

"No – I don't suppose it is."

"Besides she's always made excuses for Sid. Why should now be any different?"

"Well, good luck!"

"I'm going to need it," muttered Laura, carrying the flowers back to the ward.

Prue breathed in deeply. "They smell heavenly," she said. "It's very good of you to visit me. How did you know I was here?"

Laura drew up a chair and sat down. "Word gets about."

"I see."

"So you had a fall down the stairs?"

Prue looked embarrassed. "Yes."

"An accident?"

"Yes, an accident."

"Are you sure?"

"Of... of course, I am."

"Really? – you forget I've seen you with bruises before. You sure you weren't pushed?"

147

A muscle moved in Prue's throat. "No. I fell like I said. I'm... I'm accident prone – I'm clumsy, that's what Sid says."

"Does he now!"

"Yes."

"Look, Prue, why don't you admit that he's knocking you about?"

"What good would that do?"

"So he does?"

"No! He doesn't! Anyway it's none of your business. Leave me alone, please leave me alone. You'll only make things worse for me."

"But I can't leave you to suffer like this. Something must be done about it. It's wrong to let it carry on, month after month, year after year."

"It's not so bad, Sid says I deserve all I get for being so stupid. But I can't help it. The more he grumbles at me, the more mistakes I make. He's always sneering at me, just because I can't spell very well." She burst into tears.

Laura thought, the swine! Mental as well as physical cruelty! She told Prue that no one deserved to be treated like she was. Adding, that she hoped he didn't hit the children too? Prue, sniffing and wiping her eyes on the sleeve of her nightdress said that he'd never laid a finger on them. Laura relieved, said, *That's something,* thinking he'd not dare, and like all bullies he'd be crafty. He'd know the school doctors would pick up on something like that, but that his lashing out at Prue must frighten them? At this she said she thought Brenda too young to realise what was going on, but that the older three did.

"Well, let's hope they won't be affected in the future by what they've seen."

Prue's face twisted. "I worry about that, but what can I do? Then there's Tommy's and Bobby's nightmares and Betty wetting the bed. They'll grow out of it though, won't they? Most children do, don't they?"

Laura wasn't so sure. "So what happened this time? He did push you, didn't he? Go on, admit it."

"I don't suppose he meant me to fall down the stairs."

"You mean, he did actually push you! You could have been killed."

"Well, I wasn't, was I? It's when things don't go his way, he loses control, hardly realises what he is doing. And he was so furious with me."

"Furious, why?"

"Because… because his shirt still had creases in it when he went to put it on to go to his club."

"Creases!"

"He swore I'd not ironed it properly. I had; I'd spent ages on it. He yelled to me to come up to the bedroom and then he threw the shirt at me. He was in an awful temper. I was terrified. I was already aching all over from a beating he'd given me a couple of days earlier. That time he'd thrown his dinner at me, said it wasn't cooked to his liking. I tried to pacify him, I said I'd iron the shirt again immediately and I picked it up off the floor. He followed me to the top of the stairs, and then he struck me. I lost my balance, and…"

"You should leave Sid."

"Leave him!"

"Definitely!"

Prue wiped her eyes on her sleeve. "But Laura, where could I go? How could I keep myself? Anyway, he'd find me and make me go back."

"Not if you stuck up to him."

"It's impossible! I'm nothing without him. I'd lose my children. He'd have the law on his side."

"Not if you told the police what you've told me."

"I couldn't!"

"No? He'd not want the truth about himself spread over the papers – it wouldn't be good for business, would it? And he'd have to support you and the children."

"He'd certainly hate people whispering about him," agreed Prue. "He'd not want to spoil his respectable image." Suddenly all her pent-up resentment spilled out. "When the kids need new clothes, I have to plead with him for every last ha'penny. It just isn't fair, he makes a good living at the shop, but he likes to hold onto his brass."

Exactly like his mother! Laura recalled Doris Field's little black passbook and how each week she hoarded sums of money in it.

"I thought I loved him once, you know. I've never been pretty, and I suppose when he came courting, I was grateful that anyone should want me. I never realised then it was the £200 left to me by my gran, that I was to get when I was twenty-one, that he wanted. And he's got another woman. I've found lipstick on his coms. I don't care about that. At least, if he gets to do it with someone else, he leaves me alone. His mauling makes my skin crawl!"

Laura shook her head. "This is no life for you, Prue. Leave him! Be brave! And if you're worried where you and the children could go -" She made up her mind. "Well, you could come to me."

"Come to you! – have you got room for us all?"

"I've got a boarding house. Does that answer your question? I take in Air Force lads – there is always someone being transferred and leaving a room vacant. There's a family room empty at the moment. You could stop with me until you can find suitable digs. I'll take you to see my solicitor. He'll advise you. Help you get custody of the children."

"You make it sound so easy."

Laura said she thought it would be. Prue then became agitated, saying she couldn't just whip them away from their home. If she went to Laura's it would look as she was deserting them. After quite a battle, Laura finally convinced her.

"When are you due to leave the hospital?"

"If the doctor gives me the 'all clear', I can go tomorrow morning. They thought I'd hurt my insides, but the tests show I'm okay."

"That's good."

"I'm supposed to get a message to Sid at his shop and he'll send his mother to collect me."

"Don't do that."

"No?"

"No, look, I'll be here tomorrow as soon as I can. Then, if you can leave, I'll ring for a taxi."

"But, Laura, my children! What will they do without their mother? – I can't leave them at the mercy of Mrs Field."

"She wouldn't take it out on them, if that's what you're worried about. She's not all that bad." Fancy me sticking up for Doris Field! It's a wonder the ceiling doesn't come crashing down on my head!

"You really think they'd be all right with her? That my coming to you won't go against me in the long run?"

"I honestly think they'll be okay with her. And I don't see how it can go against you. And anyway it won't be for long." My God, I hope I'm right! She wasn't that certain. There were very few women, especially with children, who risked leaving their husbands, even violent husbands!

"Well, all right then, Laura, if you say so. I'll see you're not out of pocket; as soon as I can pay you something for the room, I will, I definitely will."

"Don't worry about that now. The important thing is getting you away from Sid. He's a monster!"

Prue giggled unconvincingly. "Sid and his mum will be absolutely furious when they come up here and find me gone.

They'll probably give the doctor and nurses hell – and me too…"

*   *   *

Crossing the forecourt, Laura spotted Doris Field getting off the bus. Black hat pulled low over her brow she was stepping out purposefully in her direction.

"Oh, no!"

Moving swiftly behind a group of nurses, she trembled – had she been seen?

A hand grabbed at her sleeve. "What are you doing here?"

"I've… I've been visiting one of my airmen," lied Laura.

"I've a good mind to report you."

"Report me! Whatever for?"

"For neglecting our Claire. I caught a nit in her head when she was round our house. You ought to wash her hair. All you think about is raking in money."

"I don't! I do wash her hair."

"Not enough! Use Derbac soap. And a nit comb!"

"The nurse never found anything in Claire's hair."

"You would say that. Now, think on!" She loosened her grip.

Laura turned away thankfully.

"You're sure you've not been here to see Prue?" the old woman suddenly challenged.

"Prue?" Laura froze. "I… is she here?"

Snorting, Doris Field marched off.

CHAPTER EIGHT

Laura arrived at Ward Nineteen just after eleven am.

"I've come to fetch Mrs Field," she said to the nurse-in-charge. "Can she go?"

"She can, she's waiting for you, but she must rest her ankle as much as possible."

"Thanks. I'll see she does."

Prue looked apprehensive as if she expected her husband or her mother-in-law to suddenly appear. "Oh, Laura, do you think I'm being too hasty? – my children!"

"I know. I know." She patted her shoulder. "Come on, let's be off," she said crisply, picking up Prue's bag. "Have you got everything?"

She nodded. They left the ward, Prue hobbling on crutches.

Laura called a taxi. They were both on tenterhooks until it arrived, and they were settled safely inside.

"Where to?" asked the driver.

Laura told him.

He touched his cap.

As the taxi sped past Stanley Park, Laura turned to comfort Prue – but the words froze on her lips for tears were streaming down Prue's cheeks.

*   *   *

"This is it," said Laura, opening the door. "I thought this room would suit you. It's the largest of my family rooms."

Prue looked around. "It's nice and airy," she said, taking in the double and single beds. "How welcoming those daffs look."

Laura was glad she'd brightened up the room with flowers and replaced the candlewick bedspreads with clean ones.

"I've got a folding bed that I can put up too, for you when the children come."

"And my two youngest can sleep top to tail," added Prue brightly, though Laura could tell that tears were near. Prue's problems had taken her mind off her own. At least, until now. She realised that the next few days were going to be far from easy. Had she been too hasty in offering help? She had to admit, that deep down her reasons for doing this were coloured by her dislike of Sid and his mother. Still, what was done was done. And it could all turn out for the best. Surely, it would! She opened the wardrobe door. "I've found you a few extra coat hangers. I'll leave you to settle in. Come down when you're ready. You can meet Rosemary's boy, Billy. He's such a jolly little chap. With it being warm and sunny, he's out in his playpen in the backyard. Mrs Rose watches him when I can't." She hoped meeting Billy wouldn't upset Prue?

Prue seemed to read Laura's mind. "I'll have my own kids with me soon, won't I? He'll not be able to stop me?"

"Of course you will!" She was far from certain, but there was nothing to be gained by not speaking positively.

Reassured, Prue began to unpack her bag. She paused from slipping a blouse over a coat hanger. "Rosemary?" she said thoughtfully. "Wasn't she on the ward?"

"That's right."

"Her husband? – is he off fighting?"

"No. She's not got a husband. She's never been married."

Prue's eyes widened. "I see! Like that, is it? Still, maybe she's better off without one!"

"I'm sure Rosemary doesn't feel that way. Her fiance was killed in an accident. It was terribly sad – she's still rather upset about it. They'd made such plans for their life together after the war. It was her who told me about you. Now, give me a shout when you're ready to come down. I'll come up and give you a hand."

154

"I'll be able to manage. You must be rushed off your feet with a boarding house to run?"

Laura laughed. "I must admit I don't have many idle moments. Still, if you don't mind, I'd rather come up for you. I don't want you falling with those crutches."

Prue smiled. "No, I don't suppose I want to make a habit of it."

"Too right, you don't! Then when you're down I'll make us a cuppa and a sandwich to be going on with. We eat when the lads get back, at seven."

Prue looked from wardrobe to bag and back again. "The few things I've got with me will be lost in here. I don't think I'd dare go round to my house for the rest of my clothing – not even when I'm certain Sid'll be at his shop."

"Of course you will. Look, as soon as we've cleared the breakfast things tomorrow, I'll come with you. Until then, if you need anything, ask me."

*　*　*

Despite Laura's apprehension, Prue was all right with Billy. She chucked him under the chin, making him croon with delight. She even topped-and-tailed him before he was put down for his mid-afternoon nap. Seated at the kitchen table, she helped Laura to peel a mountain of carrots, onions and potatoes, in readiness for the evening meal.

*　*　*

Having washed her face, brushed her hair and put on fresh lipstick, Prue joined the airmen in the lounge. At the sight of her on crutches, they all turned into *Sir Galahads,* rushing forward to help her into a chair and to vie good-naturedly with each other as to who should sit next to her.

Bringing in the well-filled plates, Laura smiled at the sight. To have a fuss made of her by so many well-set-up Brylcreem boys, especially after being ill-used would do Prue's confidence the power of good. Prue'd insisted that she didn't think she'd be able to eat that much, due to concern for her children and missing them. Two clean plates later, as Laura handed her a cup of tea, Prue said that what she'd just eaten couldn't have been bettered by the Norbreck Hydro's chef – not that she'd ever set foot in the swanky Promenade hotel.

Laura laughed, "Flatterer! Norbreck's chef, indeed."

"I know it was only a vegetable casserole, and a sponge pudding made with vinegar and bicarb instead of egg, served with a jam sauce, but you've got a magic touch."

"Nonsense, Prue. It always tastes better when someone else cooks it."

One of the airmen joined in. "I'd try flattery, if I'd thought it would get me seconds."

With Prue's plastered foot resting on a stool, she relaxed sufficiently to enjoy the sing-song around the old joanna.

Laura and Mrs Rose cleared the tables, carrying the crockery to the scullery. Laura had just added soda to the washing-up water, when the thud of the door knocker resounded throughout the house. She froze. They'd not wasted any time! She wasn't looking forward to this confrontation. If only Rosemary wasn't on duty at the hospital. She could have done with her support.

The thudding was repeated.

"Shall I go, Mrs Norris?" asked Mrs Rose.

She shook her head. "No. You go on washing up, I'll see to it." Straightening her shoulders she went out.

On the doorstep, stood mother and son, mouths identical steel traps.

He lifted his bowler. "I'm here for my wife," he said shortly.

"Yes, we want to talk to her. Get her for us!"

Laura supported herself on the doorjamb. "I'll do no such thing! For a start, Prue can't come to the door, she's on crutches and needs to rest her foot. Besides she doesn't want to see either of you! You're wasting your time in coming here."

"I'll be the judge of that!" put in Sid. "If she won't come out to us, then we'll come inside."

"You won't, you know!" For the millionth time she compared Sid with her wonderful Rod and wondered how two brothers could ever be so different from each other?

Doris Field sniffed. "Well, of course," she said, in an overloud voice, "if you want all your neighbours to know that you're encouraging a mother away from her children."

"I'm not! And Prue'll be able to have them with her once the truth is out." Laura eyed Sid keenly. "I'm taking her to see my solicitor tomorrow. She's had more than enough of your cruelty! I've seen her bruises. I know that her broken ankle was no accident."

"Don't you start accusing me!" he snapped. "Of course it was. She's always having accidents. Right dozy cow she is, tripping over things all the time. Of course, this latest was an accident! Nobody would believe otherwise. I'm a respected businessman. And a sidesman at St Philips Church."

"Respected businessman, St Philips Church, my eye! No one'll respect you once they know you've been abusing your wife. She's not returning to you! She's made up her mind about that."

"Has she indeed! Well, if that's what she wants, she can go where she likes. But she's not taking *my* children with her!"

"We'll see about that!"

The old woman glared. "Don't interfere! This is nothing to do with you. Since you married again, you're not even family! Now, stand aside. We've not got all night you know. I've had to

157

leave the kids with Field. He's so weak, he can't control them, they're sure to be getting into bother."

Laura flinched; *weak* indeed, better to be weak than heartless like his wife. On the opposite side of the street, net curtains were being pulled aside. She made up her mind. "All right, then. I suppose you'd best come in." She turned on her heel and led the way.

"Bout time too!" snorted Doris Field.

As they entered the room, the piano-playing and singing ceased and the airmen looked up curiously.

"I'm sorry," said Laura, "but could Mrs Field have a few minutes in private with her visitors? I don't like asking you to shift yourselves, but it isn't so easy for Mrs Field to go elsewhere with her bad ankle."

Reg nodded. He rose. The piano lid was put down. "Righty-ho, Mrs Norris! Come on, you chaps."

As one, they trooped out, saying, "I was just off for a breath of air anyway." Or, "I need to walk off my dinner."

The front door closed.

The clatter of crockery from the scullery reminded Laura of Mrs Rose's presence, and that she was a gossip. First raising a cautionary hand, she nipped along the passage. "I'll finish that. You get yourself off home, Mrs Rose."

She looked surprised, but rather reluctant. "If you're sure?" she said, drying her hands.

"I am."

"Right, see you tomorrow, then." Grabbing her hat and coat off the hook, and with a brief wave, she left.

Laura returned to the lounge. Sid and his mother, both with grim faces, he with his bowler perched on his knee, were settling themselves opposite the terrified Prue. Laura came round and placed an arm around her shaking shoulders. "All you've got to do is stick up for yourself. They can't make you do anything you don't want to."

158

She looked uncertain.

Doris Field eyed her keenly. "Well, what have you got to say for yourself, my girl? It was downright disgraceful you clearing off from the hospital like you did. Mind you, I know who we've got to blame for it," she added darkly.

Laura raised her eyebrows. "Not so much a disgrace as the way your precious son has knocked his wife about!"

"How dare you. Sid would never do such a thing. It's all lies!"

"Keep out of this, Mother!" He turned. "Prue?"

She hesitated. "I'm... I'm staying here, Sid."

"Staying here! Don't be so silly. Your place is at home with your family. Now, get your things."

"Yes, get your things. The last time Field was left with the children, they got hold of some matches, it's a mercy the house wasn't burnt down. If I'd not come back and caught them, there could have been a tragedy. He was only reading his paper in the other room."

"Nice try! But I don't believe a word of it," said Laura.

"I don't either!" Prue's fingers whitened on the arm of her chair. "No," she said firmly, "I'm not coming with you."

"Of course, you are, where else could you go? You can't stay here forever."

"Prue can stay as long as she likes. I can't understand why she's not told the police about you."

His cheeks visibly paled. "The police!"

Doris Field jerked forward. "Police! This is a family matter. We don't want them involved. We don't want everyone knowing our business."

"So will you both leave my house?"

"No! Not without my wife! You keep out of this! If she doesn't get her things together this instant and come home with me, she can kiss goodbye to her kids."

Prue gasped. "Oh, no!"

Her mother-in-law smiled smugly. "They're all missing their mother something terrible. They've been crying themselves silly. The poor mites, all this is making them poorly, little you care! How any mother can ignore something like that, I just don't know. It's downright inhuman, that's what it is."

"I can't bear to think of them being upset." Prue's lips quivered.

"Don't listen to her. She's just saying that to get to you. Don't let them win!"

Prue swallowed. "It can't be helped, can it? Me and the kids, well, we've got to be separated for a bit. It won't be for long, will it?" she looked towards Laura.

She gripped the shaking shoulders reassuringly.

Summoning all her courage, Prue said, "Laura's solicitor will get them for me. And he'll make you keep us."

"Keep you! When you're living elsewhere. What rubbish! That could never happen. *My* solicitor would see that it doesn't," he retorted.

"And how is Prue going to pay for one to act for her? That's what I'd like to know?" sneered Doris Field.

"Sid can foot the bill," said Laura.

"Over my dead body!"

"That's a thought."

Ignoring Laura, he glowered threateningly. "Now, listen to this, and take careful note. If you were to go to court to try and get the children off me, you'd have no chance. Even if you could prove that you could provide decent accommodation for them, and that'd be far from easy for you, wouldn't it?" He pointed accusingly. "You're the one who's deserted them! You'd not be allowed to take them away from their home."

She turned. "That's not true, is it, Laura?"

Laura faltered, "Of course, not, Prue. Don't worry. You're their mother. Children need a mother. Far more than a father that's hardly ever there. The courts would know that!" She turned. "Now, the both of you can get out of my house, you'll be hearing soon from my solicitor."

"And you'll be hearing from mine!"

A wail sounded overhead.

"Billy!"

Doris Field frowned. "The kiddy?"

Laura turned to Prue. "I'd best go and see, make sure he's okay. I won't be long."

"Don't go! Don't leave me with them!"

"I must!" Billy was in her charge. How would she face Rosemary if she ignored him and something was really wrong?

She dashed upstairs and went into the bedroom. Revealed by the glow of the night-light in a saucer, Billy was pulling himself up on the bars of his cot and yelling at the top of his voice. She could see what he wanted. She picked him out. "Good heavens, you're soaking wet." She patted his back, forgetting all about the drama being played out below. "I'd best get some soap and water and clean you up." Replacing him in his cot, she went into the bathroom to do just that – then found a clean terry nappy and the talc. She cuddled him close. Clean and sweet-smelling, Billy, eyes shining, and glad of the extra attention, chattered in baby talk.

She returned him to his cot and tucking his teddy in beside him, covered him up. "Now, go to sleep, there's a good boy." He yawned and his eyelids fluttered and closed.

Remembering, she groaned, and hurried back downstairs. Just in time to see Prue reach for her crutches and hoist herself up.

"Where are you going?"

"Is Billy okay?" asked Prue.

"Yes, he just wanted changing." Laura noticed Doris Field's expression. Whatever her faults, she was genuinely fond of children. "I asked you where you were going, Prue?"

Prue averted her face. "I'm sorry, Laura, I'm... I'm going home. It'd be for the best. My children need me! I can't be missing from their lives for ages. I've got to be realistic, haven't I? It could be ages, couldn't it, before the courts sorted out the custody in my favour? That's if they did. Sid's promised to treat me differently in future. He says he won't keep me short or lose his temper." She lowered her voice. "He's giving up his fancy-piece."

Laura saw Sid smirking.

"No, Prue. Don't go with him. Don't listen to him, you'll be sorry if you do. I know you will. Things won't alter, not really. They never do." Leopards didn't change their spots. Trust that slimy snake to wriggle things round to suit himself. He'd say anything to Prue to prevent a scandal. He'd not want the vicar of St Philips seeing the headlines, *Battered Wife* in the *News of the World*. She supposed he'd come out with the *old chestnut* that the woman never meant anything to him. That his adultery was just because Prue was always tired. He'd not think of giving her a hand so she wouldn't be. He was a man, after all, and for most men household chores were too belittling. It was definitely a man's world.

"I've got to!"

"You shouldn't interfere between man and wife."

"Someone's got to. Someone's got to stop her making the biggest mistake of her life. If she listens to your son's lies, next time, she might just lose it altogether. It's a miracle she wasn't killed this time."

A vein protruded on Sid's forehead, and his fingers whitened on the bowler hat on his knee. With effort, he hissed between clenched teeth. "Shut it!"

Prue turned to Laura. "I can't say I really fancy all the responsibility of the children on my own."

"You've got it already! Why can't you see it?"

There was no reply.

After all this, she was doing exactly what he'd expected of her all along. Laura felt like shaking her. Still, what good would that do? She knew she shouldn't have got involved. She shouldn't have listened to Rosemary. With someone like Prue, she ought to have known it would all be for nothing. "So, you've made up your mind?"

"I'm sorry, Laura." She turned. "I'll just get my things," she said to Sid.

"Don't be long!" He patted his bowler – making little improvement to it – and looking far from pleased.

"Yes, don't be long!" Doris Field ran a finger along the spar beneath her chair, examined it, and sniffed.

"Oh, Prue."

She turned back and took Laura's hands in her own. "I want to thank you from the bottom of my heart for all that you've tried to do for me. I can't tell you how much it's meant. You've been more than a friend."

Laura shook her head, feeling unbearably sad; she'd failed, Prue was returning to be a punch-bag once more. To maybe, even losing her life! "There's no need for thanks. I've done nothing, nothing at all!"

CHAPTER NINE

"This is London. D-Day has come. Under the Command of General Eisenhower, Allied Naval Forces, supported by strong air forces began landing Allied armies this morning on the northern coast of France." Laura turned off the wireless.

She picked up the cardigan she was knitting for Claire, remembering all the other announcements over the past five years. Was this the beginning of the end? Please, God, it was! It seemed as if this war had been going on forever. The loss of so many lives! And not only by bombing. She shuddered as she recalled that two hundred people had suffocated in an East End air raid shelter. Luckily she'd not suffered any personal loss, unlike Rosemary's friend, Ethel. It was through her that Laura had got the post with Mrs Mullet. Surviving Dunkirk, Ethel's young man had lost his life at Arhem. Then there was all the devastation of property. Buckingham Palace had taken a direct hit. Fortunately the King and Queen were unhurt. Compared to other places, Blackpool had been lucky. They'd no experience of Hitler's horrific V Ones and Twos. She could hardly imagine a peacetime Blackpool. Without servicemen, it would be so quiet. She, like all the other landladies would have empty rooms. Once demobbed, her lads would be off home to continue their lives. She would certainly miss them all. Reg, especially, who'd lodged at her guest house since she'd taken over, was more like a friend.

She laid aside her knitting and put on the kettle for a hot drink, there were a couple of lads in the lounge playing cards. Rosemary too should be back from the hospital soon – she wondered if she'd heard this latest announcement?

Spooning cocoa into a jug, she thought about the future. Once Blackpool got back on its feet as a holiday resort, it would be families she'd have to cater for. This would be very different to looking after Brylcreem boys. The kids, if her Claire was anything to go by, would be far more messy bringing back half the beach. Hopefully rationing would be a thing of the past. It would be wonderful to have no more ration books to worry about, to have the shops selling the luxury goods once more. She was sick of making do and mend. Sick of jumble sales and having to do battle to get hold of the old woollies. The unpicking and the washing of the wool was a real laborious job. She'd had to fend off a woman very much like Doris Field to get hold of the wool for Claire's half-finished royal-blue cardigan. They'd played tug-of-war with a shrunken jumper. Being younger and stronger, she'd come off best. Laura's opponent, screeching, "Leave off – it's mine!" lost not only her balance, but also her headgear, which ended up on the floor. Another struggling woman trod on the black-feathered hat, ruining it. She couldn't help but giggle as she recalled the furious woman on her backside, legs akimbo, and showing her pale-pink directoire knickers.

Her thoughts turned to the Illuminations. Blackpool wasn't Blackpool without the *Lights* each autumn. How wonderful it would be to see the prom lit up once more with the pre-war set pieces of brilliant tableaux. Cinderella's glass coach with its revolving golden wheels. The Babes in the Wood sleeping beneath emerald trees. Fluttering robins scattering red and yellow leaves which melted away as they touched the ground. Dutch girls in winged caps bowling sparkling hoops along the banks. Fairies, elves and gnomes, pirouetting among rainbow-coloured herbaceous borders.

Next time the *Lights* were turned on all those serving abroad would be home – amongst them – she had to face it, Nigel. He would no doubt expect to take up where he had left off. That might be okay by him, but would it be okay by her? He'd no doubt expect her to be subservient to him. This wouldn't come easy, she was used to being her own boss. And a wife's role was more than cooking, cleaning, washing and mending. There'd be sex. Their few hours of intimacy had been a disaster as far she was concerned. But was that all his fault? Wasn't it more likely that she couldn't respond to him because of her infatuation for Geoffrey. She had to face up to it, what she'd imagined as 'love' could very well have been infatuation. Maybe not even *that* as far as Geoffrey was concerned. If he'd cared for her at all, he'd at least have written as promised.

She poured boiling water onto the cocoa, adding condensed milk to sweeten, and stirred. The passion she'd felt for Geoffrey was a world ago. Even his features were becoming hazy. When Nigel returned, mightn't it be possible that they could become fond of each other? She owed it to him to give their marriage a try. That's if he was willing to help her run the boarding house. She'd not be keen to *up-sticks* and go elsewhere. They'd be silly to, with the chance of a flourishing business right here in Blackpool. There was Claire to consider too, Nigel might be of help there? Lately she was becoming so cheeky. It was increasingly difficult to know how to handle her. She recalled how Claire had shamed her in front of the baker.

"Can I have my plaits cut off and my hair permed, Mum?"

"Really Claire, what a thing to expect me to fork out for. You know perms aren't exactly cheap. Besides I like you with long hair." The back door opened and the bread man came in with their order. He put the loaves down on the kitchen table.

"It isn't fair! Ann's having hers done. Her parents aren't mean like you."

The baker shook his head in disbelief, saying. "I wouldn't let my kid speak to me like that. If she were mine, I'd clip her ear!"

"You wouldn't dare?" said Claire, eyeing Laura closely.

Furious at being shown up, to her own astonishment, she lifted her hand, but let it fall again – she just couldn't! – couldn't hit her, despite the older generation quoting – *'Spare the rod and spoil the child.'*

"I knew you wouldn't! I knew you wouldn't!" jeered Claire.

Shaking her head, Laura poured out the cocoa. But was Nigel the right type to be a helpmeet? When they'd married, he'd been no more than a charmer, but surely this war would have strengthened his character? And after all, hadn't he stuck up for her that time at the pub when Sid insulted her.

She wondered how Prue was getting on? And if Sid was back to his old tricks? Bert always changed the subject if she asked after her. She couldn't blame him, it was awkward for him, she guessed. After all, despite all Sid's faults, he was still Bert's son. She'd spotted Prue in the market a few weeks back. Prue, she was certain, saw her too, but turned tail, scurrying away in the opposite direction.

Rosemary entered. Flushed and giggly.

"You're tipsy!"

"Of course I'm not. Really, Laura. I've only just come off duty."

"Then you must have won the pools?"

"That'll be the day!"

"Hmm. I'll just slip this cocoa into Fred and Harry." She turned at the door. "Well, there's definitely something up with you."

"You're imagining things. Is my little Billy all right?"

"As good as gold. I put him down at six, I've not heard a peep since."

"I'll just check on him."

They both returned to the kitchen. "He's fast asleep," said Rosemary. "Looks just like an angel." Settling herself, she picked up her cocoa. "Yuk! There's a skin on mine."

"Fusspot!" Laura handed her a teaspoon.

"Thanks."

"Thanks, nothing! So what's up?"

Rosemary took a deep breath. "I've been asked out on a date." She took a letter out of her pocket.

"Oh, yes, by whom?"

"You won't tell anyone, will you?"

"Tell them what?

"That I've got a date."

"Why should I? What's it got to do with me? You're acting very mysterious."

"I've got to. You see he was a patient on my ward."

"So what?"

"Matron wouldn't like it. Nurse and patient relationships aren't allowed."

"Why on earth not?"

"Rules and Regulations, you know what the hospital is like."

"Would you really be in trouble if Matron found out?"

"Yes, I'd be dismissed, even though Tony left the hospital a week ago. Matron never gives any leeway in anything. When she does her ward inspection we all shiver in our shoes. She can spot a spec of dust on a locker at fifty paces. And woe betide the lackadaisical nurse. If you get told off by Matron, you know you've been told off!"

"Thank God, then, I didn't go into nursing! So what's he like, this Tony who's making you act so fluttery? How old is he for a start?"

"Thirty-four."

"He's not married, is he?"

"Of course not! What do you take me for? I wouldn't want another woman's husband – "

Who would? But it wasn't always that easy, as Laura knew to her own cost.

168

"If you must know, he's a widower. His wife died just before the war started – pernicious anaemia – she was only twenty-five."

"How tragic."

"Yes, we've both lost someone we loved."

"Is he like your Joe?"

Rosemary's eyes went all gooey. "His hair's not the same, Tony's is brown. But like Joe, he's full of fun and a real hunk. Tony's feet overhung his hospital bed – he's over six ft in height."

Laura laughed. "You'll have to get on a stepladder to kiss him."

"Mmm. I can't wait!"

"That good, hey?" Rosemary was really taken with this Tony. It seemed a million years since she herself felt like that about a man. These days her life was so flat. She could be ninety for all the fun she was having. "So what was he in hospital for? He hasn't got something nasty, has he? That isn't the reason why he's not in the forces?"

"Of course he's not got anything nasty, Laura!" Her mouth tightened. "And he's not a coward either, if that's what you're thinking?"

"I'm not thinking anything of the sort."

"You'd better not," she said shortly. "Tony's a plumber, that's a reserved occupation, in case you didn't know. And he was in to have a wisdom tooth out. Okay?"

"Sorry. I only wondered. So when's this big date?"

"Next Monday evening – when I finish early. We're going dancing at the Tower Ballroom. I'm borrowing a dress from one of the nurses. It's blue crêpe-de-Chine with a full skirt and a heart-shaped neckline."

Laura rinsed the cups and left them upside down on the draining board. I wish I could go dancing, too, but then there'd be no one to mind the children. "My life's dull compared to yours, Rosemary. It's all work and no play. And definitely, no romance. Well, don't forget to keep me posted on its progress."

*   *   *

Laura lay sleepless, beside her Claire breathed softly, as too did Billy from his cot. Turning her head Laura glanced at the alarm clock. It was two am. She was listening out for Rosemary. She smiled to herself. Would this Tony, as in all the romantic novels, kiss Rosemary goodnight on the doorstep?

She'd helped her get dressed in all her finery, fastening her friend's fine hair with small tortoiseshell combs into the *bangs* style that was all the rage, clapping when Rosemary twirled before the mirror. Tony came to the house to pick her up. Peeking out of the lounge window, Laura watched them go for the bus. She wanted her to have a wonderful time. She didn't want to feel jealousy at Rosemary getting whisked around the Tower Ballroom, and having a love life, but she couldn't help it. Her own life was so boring. It was all slog. It seemed like her only excitement was getting books from the library. These she read avidly in her spare moments. Having seen the autumn courses at the technical advertised in the *Gazette*, and considering the success of the bookkeeping one she'd previously taken, she was wondering whether she should enrol for a literature course? Apart from the enjoyment, she might get to make some new friends? She didn't particularly want to make men friends, her personal situation was already fraught enough. But there might be an office worker or a shop assistant she could pal up with? Even if they only saw each other at the classes, it would be pleasant to be able to chat during the tea break.

She heard a key turn, followed by movement and hushed voices downstairs. Rosemary was back. A tread creaked on the stairs as she tiptoed up them, and her door softly opened and closed.

170

As Laura was drifting off to sleep, the thought came, had Rosemary told Tony about Billy?

*   *   *

Next day, chatting over a cup of tea, Laura asked her.

Rosemary choked on her biscuit. "No, I've not told him. Not yet."

"But you've got to, you've got to tell him about Billy. If you feel things are becoming at all serious, he's got to know that you've got a child."

"I know. I know. I just keep putting it off. It's very shaming having to admit that you've had a baby out of wedlock. That you're a bad lot, a fallen woman."

Laura laughed. "Oh, don't exaggerate!"

"I'm not! You know that's how a lot of people see me. I don't want to lose Tony's respect."

"What makes you think you will? We've all done things we shouldn't have done."

"Yes, but most people hide them. You can't hide a baby! They make too much racket for a start! And when we saw a girl on the arm of a Yank in Talbot Road he said as how it was disgraceful that so many were carrying on with the GIs. Tony attends the Baptist Chapel in St Annes Road. The Baptists are sticklers when it comes to the Ten Commandments. Once he knows the truth he'll probably look down on me. And as for his old maiden aunt, well, she's very prim and proper. Hates the modern generation so Tony says. She reckons that the girls of today get into trouble because they wear short skirts and too much make-up. She'd be sure to turn him against me."

"You can't really know that. He's got a mind of his own, hasn't he? And anyway Christians are supposed to be forgiving. What does it say in the Bible? 'Don't look at the twig in your brother's eye, but at the plank in your own eye.'

171

"Maybe."

"So you'll tell him?"

"I guess so. But what if he doesn't want any more to do with me?"

"If that's the case, then you're better off without him. He'd not be worth bothering with. But I'm sure it won't be like that. So when will you tell him?"

"I don't know."

"The sooner, the better."

"I suppose so. Look, Laura, can I bring him round here to tell him?"

"You want me to be present?"

"Well, not actually in the room. But nearby. Just in case."

"All right then, and if he takes the news badly," Laura laughed, "well, I'll bash some sense into him with my rolling pin!"

*   *   *

"So you're Rosemary's best friend?" said Tony, shaking Laura's hand.

"I like to think so. She never stops talking about you."

He flushed. "Doesn't she? All good, I hope?"

"Of course. Do sit down."

He seated himself in the wing-chair. He was working-class and rather ordinary looking. It was obvious he wasn't bothered too much about his appearance, unlike Geoffrey and Nigel, the two middle-class men who'd drifted in and out of her life. He wore an open-necked shirt, a tweedy sports jacket and flannels. She couldn't really see why Rosemary was so besotted, still it took all sorts. It was hard too to tell just by appearances how he would take the news that his girlfriend was an unmarried mother. Laura hoped he wouldn't be scandalised and drop her. Rosemary would be devastated. But that wouldn't happen, would it? She had suffered enough already. *Please God*, Laura said silently, soften this Tony's heart.

"So you've got something to tell me?" he said.

"Yes." Rosemary drew up a kitchen chair opposite him.

"Right. I'll leave you to it," said Laura. She left the scullery, but not closing the door properly, put her ear to the crack.

"Things aren't as they appear," said Rosemary in a rush.

"What do you mean? There's not another bloke on the scene?"

"No. What do you take me for? I'm no two-timer."

"You've not been divorced, have you? Is that what you're trying to tell me?"

"No, of course not. I've never been married."

"Then what is it?"

"I've… I've got a child, a little boy."

"You mean you're an unmarried mother?"

"Yes. But we would have been married, but – well, he was killed in an accident before we could. And not only that he was a Yank, and I know you don't like Yanks."

"Who does? *There's only three things wrong with Yanks, they're overpaid, oversexed, and over here*! But it doesn't mean I think any less of you for going out with one, or for having a baby, for that matter."

"You don't! But I thought… that's wonderful, Tony. I just can't believe that I did all that worrying for nothing."

"So what's your little boy's name? And how old is he?"

"His name's Billy and he's eighteen months old. He's really clever for his age."

"That's what all mothers say," he laughed, giving her a dig.

"It's true in my Billy's case, he's talking already, proper sentences. And he can do those little wooden puzzles all on his own."

"Phew! So when can I see him?"

173

"You mean you really want to?"

"Of course."

Laura heard the sound of a smacking kiss.

"He's upstairs in his cot. I'll take you up to see him this very minute."

"Would you? I'd like that very much."

They were coming out! Laura shot away from the door and into the lounge, she didn't want to be caught eavesdropping. It had all turned out better than she could have hoped for. If truth be told, she'd been apprehensive about Tony's reaction to Rosemary's disclosure. Men, whether married or single could play around as much as they liked. In fact, the man's mates' mostly considered him 'no end of a fellow' for doing so. But should a woman step out of line it was a completely different story. The woman was considered a 'tart'. And often it was her own sex who were the most disapproving.

Laura heard their footsteps on the stairs, and from overhead the sound of the cot side being put down. A few moments later she heard them descending.

She went back into the scullery. Rosemary, seeing her, stuck up one thumb, signalling success. Tony was sitting in the wing-chair with a talkative Billy on his lap and his arm protectively around him.

Relieved, Laura put on the kettle. "Now that's all over. We'll have a nice cuppa, plus a plate of my hot buttered scones."

*   *   *

Laura managed to get hold of a turkey for Christmas. She and Rosemary plucked and stuffed the giant bird. A Christmas pudding covered in two layers of greaseproof paper simmered in a saucepan, needing to be topped up with hot water at regular intervals. This caused a pleasant rich fruity aroma to fill the scullery. To make the pudding, it had been necessary for her to

174

save the dried fruit ration for ages, and in place of eggs she used the equivalent in dried egg. And everyone, from all the airmen, to Laura and Rosemary, each took a turn to stir the heavy mixture – and to make a wish, too.

Rosemary was terribly excited, as Tony was coming to the boarding house to share the midday meal with them. Having popped the question and been accepted, his grandmother's diamond ring now flashed on the third finger of Rosemary's left hand. The wedding was to be the following spring. Laura was pleased for her friend, Tony seemed a good sort and it wasn't everyone who was willing to take on another man's child, even a dear little lad like Billy, but she wasn't too happy about their plans. Though it could be some time before these plans actually came off. The war would have to end first. This looked like a real possibility in the near future, as on the Home Front, not only were the blackout restrictions to be relaxed in the New Year, but also the Home Guard were to be disbanded.

Laura naturally fully expected Rosemary to move in with her husband once she was married; was resigned to losing her company and their cosy chats. But for them to be planning to go twelve thousand miles away was a different story – she'd probably never ever see her again – or Billy. Once peace was declared, Rosemary and Tony were hoping to emigrate to Australia. He had talked her into it, saying that Oz was a golden land of opportunity, where they'd have a great life in the sunshine, and that both plumbers and nurses were sure to be in demand.

They would doubtless be in great demand in this country. Plumbers especially, with all the building work that would need to be done, though sunshine couldn't be guaranteed. Not in England! Why was it people always imagined the grass would be greener on the other side of the street? In Rosemary and Tony's case, the other side of the world, Australia.

Rosemary shrieked and waved a hand covered with sage and onion stuffing. "I've lost my ring! I knew I shouldn't have worn it until I'd had it made smaller. Tony's Gran's fingers were thicker than mine and the ring was loose."

Laura, preparing the brussel sprouts, giggled. "Don't panic. It'll be inside the bird."

Rosemary plunged her hand deep within it, pulling out handfuls of stuffing onto the kitchen table, which she poked through. "There it is!" Relieved she took the ring over to the sink and washed it off under the running tap. She lifted up the ring and admired its sparkle. "That looks better!"

"For heaven's sake put that ring in a safe place. Then re-stuff that bird."

"All right, all right, I was just going to, Laura." She popped the ring into a dish on the dresser.

A few minutes later, between them, they lifted the turkey in its roasting tin and placed it in the oven.

Laura shut the cooker door with satisfaction. "Good thing you found that ring. I shouldn't have fancied swallowing it in a mouthful of stuffing."

Rosemary grimaced. "I shouldn't have fancied *you* swallowing it either!"

* * *

Christmas came and went. January turned into February, snowdrops forced themselves through the frozen earth, followed by crocuses, then daffs, as the arrangements were made for the March wedding which was to be at Holy Sepulchre Church with a party afterwards at the boarding house.

The happiness that Laura felt for her friend was tinged with a little envy as she watched her and Tony leave the church, followed by Claire in her pink taffeta bridesmaid's dress which had been run up by one of the nurses. The dress had been made

176

without coupons on account of the material being classed as coat lining. Rosemary's sunny future with a man that she really wanted, was all cut and dried, unlike hers.

As the year progressed, the shocking scenes of the concentration camps being liberated filled the newspapers and newsreels. This Nazi horror left everyone feeling disgusted and angry. At the end of April, Hitler was found dead. Surely it was only a matter of time, before peace would be declared?

Rosemary had been married two months and was living in Bispham when on the 8th of May, 1945, the Germans surrendered and war in Europe ended. The whole country went mad. Church bells rang. Schools were closed. Bonfires were lit. As it grew dark on that May evening, lads, too young to be in the forces, were kissing, and being kissed by every girl in sight, and everyone, elderly people and children, were dancing arm-in-arm around the bonfires, and singing at the top of their voices, "There'll always be an England."

Within a day or so, street parties were held everywhere. Red-white-and-blue buntings fluttered from windows and lampposts, and Union Jacks were strung across the streets. Trestle tables sagged. Where the food came from, nobody seemed to know – or care. Some of it had obviously been hoarded for years. There were meat-paste and fish-paste sandwiches – eked out with jam sandwiches – sausage rolls, blancmanges, jellies, buns and cakes, many iced with red-white-and-blue icing. There were gallons of orange juice – oceans of tinned fruit, and large enamel pots of tea – strong and black for once – for the grown-ups who waited on the happy, excited children. Healthy young appetites sated, games were played to shrieks and squeals of laughter for small prizes. Pianos having been pushed into the streets to accompany the singsongs, a few of the locals, dressed in impromptu costumes, put on tap-dancing and singing acts, and were wildly applauded for their efforts.

Claire did especially well in all these celebrations, as she attended a party in Trafalgar Terrace, and then one in her grandparents' street, winning a picture book at party number one in the three-legged race and at party number two, in the egg-and-spoon race, a rag doll, which wore a red-white-and-blue dress.

She also was taken along with Billy to Pablos Ice-Cream-Parlour by Rosemary and Tony, where she, as well as all the other children got a free ice cream.

Mrs Hill, Laura's neighbour made her laugh when she told Laura about what Peter, her twelve-year-old nephew, had been up to. Peter had gone to Pablos several times on the day this offer was on. Wearing his school blazer and cap. Without his cap and blazer. With his hair brushed back. With his hair parted in the middle. None of the staff realised that Peter had been in previously. Each time, the cheeky little varmint came out with a free ice cream.

*   *   *

On the 6th of August, 1945 an atomic bomb was dropped on Hiroshima, then three days later, on the 9th, a second one was dropped on Nagasaki. Seeing the pictures of the devastation of these cities on the front page of the *Daily Mirror*, Laura couldn't help but be shocked and sickened. Despite the harrowing tales that were filtering through of the ill treatment of Tommies in Burma by the Japanese, it all seemed so terrible that human beings could do such things to each other. But if these bombs were evil, at least the fact that they had brought about VJ Day and the end of the war with Japan, was good.

*   *   *

They were several months into 1946, when Laura received the letter that she was half-eager for – half-dreading…

Dearest Laura,

Just a few lines to tell you that I expect to be demobbed within a few days. As soon as I'm able, I'll be on the train bound for you and Blackpool.

I can't tell you how much I'm longing to see you again. I can hardly believe that the moment that I've dreamt of every night since I last held you in my arms is actually going to happen at last.

I'm looking forward to seeing Claire, too. I bet she has grown into quite a big girl since I last read her a bedtime story.

I've got lots of plans for all our futures. Great plans. Exciting plans. I'll tell you all about them when I see you.

Do hope you're both keeping well, as I am.

> Your loving husband,
> Nigel XXX

CHAPTER TEN

Clutching her platform ticket in her gloved hands, Laura paced backwards and forwards as best as she could along the crowded platform. Central Station was drab compared to pre-war. Then, there were tubs of red geraniums brightening the place, now litter was scattered across the platform and the chocolate and cigarette machines were rusty. She eyed the clock, the moment when she'd be reunited with a husband she barely knew was fast approaching. The train would come steaming into the station, and on it, Nigel. She'd not been able to make up her mind whether it would be best to meet him, or wait back at the boarding house for him to arrive? In the end, she'd decided to come to the station. She wasn't uncaring, for after all, he had been away to the war. Not only that, he was a hero. He had been awarded the MM for bravery, having rescued a comrade under severe fire.

Claire, of course wanted to go with her. When Laura said, *no*, she'd kicked up a fuss. Despite her tears, Laura was adamant, saying she should stay with Mrs Rose – she would see her stepfather soon enough. Claire couldn't really remember him that well – though she made out she could. At eleven, five years was a lifetime. Having collared the one picture that Laura had of Nigel – their wedding photograph, Claire kept it on her bedside table. This photo she would kiss nightly, after saying a prayer for his safe return, before going to sleep.

Laura's airmen having finally left, she was expecting her first influx of holidaymakers on the coming Saturday. She had put advertisements in lots of local papers – Preston, Chorley, Bolton, Bury, Oldham, Rochdale, Halifax and Todmorden. From these she'd had scores of enquiries, and replying to so many letters had given her writer's cramp. She and Mrs Rose between them had cleaned and polished everything in sight, not only in readiness for them, but also for Nigel's homecoming. Laura had moved out of the bedroom she shared with Claire and into another.

In the distance a whistle blew. The train, amidst clouds of steam, thundered in. Everyone surged forward. Carriage doors slammed. Voices called. Men with a military bearing embraced tearful women.

"Laura!"

She found herself wrapped in a bear hug as Nigel's lips found hers; in his eagerness, almost knocking off her little veiled hat, which matched her purple costume.

Stirred; after all it was five years since she'd been made love to, she felt confused. Tanned and lean, even in his ill-fitting demob suit, he was better looking than ever – now, with Geoffrey out of the picture, would the bedroom side of things be all right? Was there a chance for their marriage?

"I've got presents for both you and Claire," he said, patting his attaché case, as with an arm draping her shoulders, they left the station.

Nigel whistled up a taxi. They got in. "Where to?" said the man.

Laura told him.

The familiar streets went by in a blur.

"We're home," she said brightly in an attempt to disguise her nervousness as the taxi drew up outside.

"Is this it? – your boarding house."

"Why? – what's wrong with it?" she added, on the defensive.

"Nothing, well, this is rather a working class area."

She jerked away. "So what! I'm working class. They're the salt of the earth."

His lips twitched. "Of course they are. Anyway, it doesn't really matter."

181

"Why not?"

He patted her hand. "I've got plans."

What did Nigel mean? She decided to let his comment ride. But if he meant he expected her to give up her home to go elsewhere with him, he'd have another think coming!

The front door opened and Claire, followed by Mrs Rose, appeared.

He got out, leaving Laura to pay the driver. "If it isn't little Claire," he exclaimed, "haven't you grown! – why, you're almost as tall as your mother – and as pretty."

Claire looked pleased. "I wear the same size shoes too – size five."

"Now isn't that lucky. I just happen to have some pretty pink mules in my case which should just fit a young lady like you."

"Really! Can I see?" She clutched at his arm.

"First, give me a kiss." He offered his cheek.

She shyly kissed it. "Now, can I see them?"

Laura frowned. "Claire! Stop worrying Nigel. At least wait till we get inside."

She pulled a lip.

The case was opened to excited squeals from Claire, and Nigel brought out his presents. The fluffy slippers loosely fitted and she proudly paraded up and down in them. "I'm taller than you now, Mum."

"They're not really suitable for an eleven-year-old, Nigel. They've got high-heels."

Claire glared. If looks could have killed, well!

Laura wondered why she'd not been given a mouthful, then realised it was Nigel's presence. He was a man and good-looking and Claire wanted him to think well of her.

Laura smoothed her hand over the white silk blouse that Nigel had given her. The mules should have been for me. Beneath his shirts was a *Mamma* doll.

After Claire reluctantly agreed to go to bed, they began to talk seriously about their future. Laura's worst fears were confirmed. He wasn't a bit interested in settling down in Blackpool as the landlord of a boarding house. He'd plans of his own all right. Wild plans, in her opinion. He wanted them to move to London as he fancied getting into films. He reckoned he knew someone who could get him taken on as an extra at Ealing Studios.

Laura almost dropped the cup of cocoa she was handing him. Admittedly he was handsome enough to be a film star, but as to talent? Though she guessed luck might have a lot to do with it. And what was she supposed to do while he was chasing after rainbows? And no doubt, chasing after starlets! London was a non-starter as far as she was concerned. Southerners were to her as alien as the man-in-the-moon – the majority thought themselves superior – thought that everyone north of Birmingham were clog-wearing nitwits!

She didn't like to pour cold water over the evening by giving him an outright *no*. After all, this was the first real evening of their married life, so she just laughed. She shot an uneasy look at the clock. Its hands were on ten – bedtime.

He yawned.

She hesitated. "You must be tired? Shall we turn in?"

"Why not."

Was there a gleam in his eye? And how did she feel about that? She wasn't certain.

She took as long as she could to make sure the front door was locked, and that everything that needed to be turned off, was turned off. She even made the excuse she might have left something on the line. In the end, she could delay no longer.

As they climbed the stairs, she recalled the passionate feelings she'd felt for Geoffrey at that St Annes boarding house. If only…

With the bed between them, she and Nigel undressed. As she slipped off her bra, she felt hot all over as she sensed he was watching her. What a relief it was to pull her nightgown down over her head and scramble beneath the bedclothes and pull them up to her chin. And unlike their honeymoon night, he didn't ask her to remove her nightgown.

What she'd been dreading went better than she could have imagined. He must have learnt a thing or two since being away. Or maybe it was because her feelings for Geoffrey had faded. To her surprise, she got pleasure from his lovemaking.

She lay listening to his regular breathing. Now, as long as she could make him see sense about his way-out plans, their marriage might stand a chance.

*   *   *

Next evening, Nigel again spoke of their future. "With my gratuity and what this place fetches we can get something on the outskirts of London. Ilford, maybe? I can take the Tube for the time being. Later on, I'll get a car."

She had to try and put him off. She certainly wasn't going to London, or anywhere else for that matter. She was staying where she was, in the home and business that she had built up herself, through sheer hard work. She refused to listen to the little voice which insisted that if she felt about Nigel, as she'd felt about Geoffrey she would gladly go wherever he wanted. "Look," she said, "we can't go off just like that."

"Why not? We can rent a flat to start with until this place is sold."

She grabbed at straws. "What about Claire's schooling?" He'd a real nerve imagining he could just sell off her boarding house to suit himself. If he wanted money why didn't he ask his mother? She had plenty, she'd come into a fortune from Mrs Mullet.

"What about it? They've got schools in London, you know."

"Of course, I know. But it wouldn't do her any good changing schools at this time – not when she's about to sit her Eleven Plus."

"That's just an excuse."

"No, it's not."

He tried another tack. "I should have thought you'd have been glad to get away from your ex-mother-in-law."

That would be one thing in its favour, though she would miss Bert, also Mrs Hughes who popped over from St Annes from time to time. As far as her dear friend Rosemary went, it wouldn't make any difference. Having been accepted by Australia House, Rosemary and her family were emigrating soon. "She's not so bad." Good Grief! – this is the second time I've stuck up for Doris Field – what on earth is wrong with me! The first was when she'd been trying to get Prue to leave Sid. At her words she'd half-expected the hospital ceiling to have collapsed.

"No? That's not how she appeared from your letters. Could have been Lucretia Borgia by the way you painted her. Anyway, isn't it a woman's place to go wherever her husband wants? Head of the household and all that."

Laura sniffed. Head of the household. How Victorian could you get! "Not when it's on some wild goose chase!"

Nigel's face flushed. "Thanks a lot! So you're turning it down flat."

"I suppose I am." She'd promised to obey when they'd married. Should she? And probably end up starving. And then there was Claire. Anger welled up. No fear!

"Well, I'll be a success, with or without you, just see if I'm not. You'll have to eat your words when I'm a Hollywood idol."

"Hollywood idol! Now I've heard everything!"

The door opened. In came a sleepy-eyed Claire, in nightdress, dressing gown and furry pink mules. "Why are you squabbling?" she asked accusingly.

Laura jerked to her feet. "We're not!" She'd rather Claire didn't know that she and Nigel couldn't see eye to eye. She didn't want her daughter upset. Especially not with this all important examination looming.

"You're being horrid to Nigel. I heard you. How can you be so mean, Mum? He's a hero, you should be nice to him."

"We were just having a little talk, Claire," said Nigel. "Nothing for you to worry about. Off you go now, straight back to bed."

She gave her mother a dirty look. "I'm just going, Nigel."

"That's a good girl. Look, I'll take you to Stanley Park on Saturday."

Her face lit up. "Really?"

"I've promised, haven't I?"

She gave him a beautiful smile before pulling the door to behind her.

They listened to her footsteps on the stairs.

Laura hesitated. "I'm sorry. I'm sure you'll be a success, Nigel. You'll no doubt end up in Hollywood, if that is what you want, but, well, I want to stay here in Blackpool."

"So you don't really care if our marriage works out?"

"I do, of course I do."

"But you're not willing to do what I want?"

"I'm sorry, but I wouldn't be happy in London, Blackpool's my home now. This place will be a gold mine before long, all the boarding houses will be. Even last year, with the war barely over, Blackpool was flooded with holidaymakers." She moved over to the dresser and took from a drawer a cutting from the *Gazette* and read: 'The first Wakes Saturday of the 1945 season was an all-time record for the London Midland and Scottish Railway company who carried,

186

within twenty-four hours, a staggering 102,889 passengers to the resort'."

"So what?"

"So what? Everyone will be coming here for their holidays just like they did before the war." When she'd come to Blackpool as a child with her mother during the Wakes week in July, the place had been packed-out with mill workers from Blackburn and other northern towns. It was a mass exodus, the mill towns were left almost deserted. People had slept head to foot, four to a bed. And sometimes, even on the landing – with landladies under kitchen tables. You could have let the rooms several times over. And before going home everyone always booked for the following year. And like those earlier landladies she'd make sure that they'd come again. She would give her guests good value for their money, clean accommodation and wholesome meals that that they would really enjoy. And she'd not charge extra for the use of the cruet and sauce bottle as some landladies did in the past.

His Adam's apple moved. "They might, but I shan't be here to see it. I've always known you didn't care for me as I did for you. Why did you marry me? Was it just for the army allowance? Or because you hoped to come into something from Auntie Maude?"

"So that's what you think of me! No. Of course it wasn't. I wouldn't be that mercenary. Marrying you I lost my widow's pension. Before you say anything, I know the army allowance was far more, but that wasn't it. You were off to war, I wanted you to have some happiness before you went. I was lonely, too. I know I had Claire, but I wanted more than just a child to love me."

"But what about you loving me?"

"Of course I did. I do," she lied. She'd liked him. She'd felt at the time that perhaps *liking* was enough. She certainly not wanted to be hurt again. *Love,* like she'd felt for Geoffrey was far too painful.

"Then prove it, come with me. Sell the blasted place!"

She shook her head.

"But I want you to. I know it's in your name, but after all, Aunt Maude was my aunt, not yours. The money you used to buy this place should have been left to me."

"Your aunt must have had her reasons. Besides she only left me £100 – the rest came from my side of the family."

"Whether it did or not, as your husband, I could sell this place over your head."

Was this true? "I'd never forgive you if you did that!"

He flushed. "Think about it. Claire will be keen, I'm sure. She'll love London with all its history. It's her favourite subject. She'll be able to see Westminster Abbey, the Tower of London, Buckingham Palace."

Yes, Claire would be keen. And not just for the adventure of moving to London. She seemed to have really taken to Nigel. In fact, by the way she was behaving, it was obvious that she preferred him to her.

Nigel smiled his *bedroom* smile. "Look, we don't want to quarrel. Let's sleep on it, Laura." He took her by the hand and led her from the room.

* * *

Perhaps after all that had been said she wasn't in the mood, for this time his lovemaking left her cold. She felt his kisses and caresses were no more than an attempt to bring her round to his way of thinking. And because of this, she couldn't respond.

* * *

The next few days passed in a blur. Laura's first holidaymakers arrived. The young families were pleased with their accommodation, which made her happy. Meanwhile, Claire was becoming more and more excited about the trip to Stanley Park with Nigel. "It's a lovely day, Mum – do you think he'll take me boating on the lake?"

Laura smiled. It was a relief to have her daughter in a good mood for once.

She packed a picnic basket with hard-boiled egg sandwiches, sausage rolls and strawberry jam tarts. She added a bottle of beer for Nigel and a bottle of lemonade for Claire. She'd done all this despite being busy with providing full board for her guests. Her main course today was to be egg-and-bacon pie. How glad she was that it still wasn't *the bad old days*, when a landlady, as well as preparing a mountain of potatoes, carrots and cabbage, was expected to cook sausages for one family, fish for another, and chops for yet another. Thankfully, in most cases this system had gone out in the early '30s.

Nigel had gone out that morning to see his bank manager, promising to be back by midday. Twelve o'clock came and went, then one, then two. Still he'd not appeared. Claire began to fidget. "Where is he, Mum?" she asked.

Laura turned from washing up the dinner things. "I don't know, love." Her fingers tightened on the handle of a cup. *I'll give him a piece of my mind when he does turn up!*

He rolled in at five as she was placing the tea pots on the tables for high tea – ham salad with Blackpool tommies, white and brown bread-and-butter, and fancy cakes. "Where have you been?" she asked angrily. "Claire's really upset. I've sent her next door to see Ann. I thought it would take her mind off you letting her down."

"What do you mean?"

"What do I mean?" Laura wrinkled her nose. If not actually drunk he was far from sober. "Don't you remember what you promised for this afternoon?"

"Remember what?"

"You promised to take Claire to Stanley Park."

He slapped his hand to his head. "So I did!"

"So you remember now?"

He groaned. "Sorry, it slipped my mind."

"So you think a 'sorry' makes it okay to disappoint a child?"

"No of course not. I'm sorry if she's disappointed. I'll take her next Saturday. I really will! I bumped into an ex-comrade in town. I didn't realise it before, but Bernard's from here. He wanted us to go for a drink. I couldn't get out of it."

"Oh, yes. Don't the pubs close at two thirty? Where have you been since then?"

"The Officers' Club in Central Drive," Nigel said surlily. "He said he knew there was a good card game going. So we went."

*   *   *

Nigel was very apologetic to Claire, with a winning smile, he gave her one of her favourite boarding-school books by Enid Blyton.

The following Saturday, despite all his promises, the same thing happened again. This time, he appeared with a pretty red-bead necklace. Taking it from him, Claire, without a word, dropped the necklace into a china dish on the dresser, then turned her back.

Laura's heart went out to her. At her age, it would be a big blow to discover that even a war hero could have feet of clay. Naturally his treatment of Claire didn't help matters.

He told Laura that he had to visit his mother. As she packed his case she wondered whether there was more to this than met the eye? Had he blown his gratuity? Was he going to tap his mother? He'd stopped trying to talk Laura into parting with her cash to fund his plans – did he think his mother a better bet? The reason for Mrs Mullet not leaving any money to Nigel was now crystal clear. It was because his aunt hadn't trusted him with it. Money slipped through his fingers faster than water down a sink.

He returned a week later looking like a squashed worm. When she tackled him, he admitted that his mother would only help him out if he returned to live in Oxford.

Over the next few days, Nigel desperately attempted once more to turn Laura around to his way of thinking. When that failed, being determined to try his luck in London, he pleaded with her again to lend him some money so he could pay his way until he could set himself up.

He promised faithfully to pay her back with interest.

Laura stood her ground. She knew only too well how his promises ended. Besides what bit she managed to put by, she needed.

Two days later, returning from a flying visit to Rosemary and her family, who were about to embark for Australia, she found he was out as usual – no doubt living it up at the Officer's Club.

Some sixth sense made her go to her bedroom and examine the top drawer of her dressing table. With a shaking hand she fumbled beneath her underwear for the old black purse. The money she had put by to pay Sid his monthly instalment for the settee, buy Claire new shoes and pay her electricity and gas bills was gone.

*　*　*

191

It was two am when Laura heard Nigel creep up the stairs and enter the bedroom. A shoe thudded to the floor, followed by a rustling and springs squealing as he got into his side of the bed.

"I'm not asleep," said Laura. "Where have you been?"

"Does it matter? I'm tired."

She got out of bed and put on the light. "It matters to me. You seem to forget you've got a wife. You act exactly as if you were single. Now you're home you could give me some support – help me in the boarding house. At least earn your bed and board."

"You must be joking, if you expect me to fetch and carry. I'm not cut out to be a lackey. If you were anything of a wife, you'd put me first."

"Do what you want, I suppose? No chance!"

"You've changed, you're really hard."

"I've had to, to keep the wolf from the door. I've had no one else to turn to. If I'd gone under what would have happened to Claire? You tell me that?"

"I know things haven't been easy for you, but I'm home now. Come to London. I'll look after you and Claire. We'll be living on 'easy street' once I get started. "

"Easy street, my eye! What about my money? What have you done with it?"

He flushed. "What money? And put that light out!"

She faced him angrily. "Don't play the innocent with me. You know perfectly well. The money that was in my top drawer. The money I was saving for bills. You've gambled it, haven't you? Not satisfied with blueing all yours you've done the same with mine. How dare you!" There'd been no note left either in the scullery or the bedroom, but all the same, until she'd heard him enter their room a few moments ago, she'd half-thought he might have skedaddled off to London in pursuit of his dream. Perhaps she would have almost been relieved to have him go, if

192

it wasn't for the uneasy feeling that he might try to sell her boarding house over her head. As he hadn't left, he must have decided that her savings weren't enough to leave.

Nigel yawned. "What's yours is mine. That's what the marriage service says. Anyway, I've been on a winning streak lately, I thought I could double it. You'd have been pleased with me then."

"And did you double it?"

"Well, no."

"You lost it all?"

"I don't want to talk about it. Come back to bed. I want some sleep."

"That's just too bad! I'd promised Claire new shoes. The ones she's wearing are pinching her feet. And I've always paid my gas and electricity on time. What if they cut us off? How could I cope then with a houseful of visitors? You tell me that! I feel so ashamed. I'll have to ring up the Electricity and Gas with some excuse. I've always prided myself in paying my bills on time. Then there's the payment for the settee. What am I going to say when *he* calls round? It's all so embarrassing."

"Tell him you'll pay extra next month. You're becoming a real nag, Laura. I may as well have gone back to Rita, I'm sure she wouldn't have nagged all the time like you do."

"Who's Rita?"

He reddened. "No one."

"She's got to be someone." Suddenly Laura recalled the time, years ago now, when a photograph had fallen from his wallet at the cinema. Hadn't the name scrawled on the back of the photo been Rita? It had stuck in her mind as the film, *Only Angels have wings,* starred Rita Hayworth. There was the odd remark, too, made by Nigel's mother at Mrs Mullet's funeral. Leonora Norris had coupled her son's name with someone she'd called a gold digger. Could that have been this Rita? If so, what did it all mean?

Nigel patted the place beside him. "Let it drop! Now are you coming back to bed?"

By the expression on his face, he was lying. All the same, she was too tired to bother about it now. "Not with you. One of us is going to have to spend what's left of the night downstairs in the wing-chair." Would he just go meekly? She was beginning to realise just how stubborn he could be.

"Suit yourself!" Snatching up his clothing, he went off without another word.

*　　*　　*

After this, Nigel was out more than ever. There was an atmosphere between them. She felt he was put-out because he couldn't get his own way. She'd moved back in with Claire, and Nigel now slept on a mattress in the scullery, the reason she gave him for this was that it would release a further room for letting. In reality she knew it was because she just didn't want to share a bed with someone she couldn't trust. When Sid's collector came for the monthly payment of four shillings, muttering, he went away empty-handed. Sid would be far from pleased. She shivered. She hoped this wouldn't give him the excuse to call round? This could be just what he was hoping for all along. Why else would he have put himself out that time to help her, if not in the hope of getting something in return? She brushed aside these unsettling thoughts – with Nigel back, Sid wouldn't know whether there was any chance of finding her on her own.

A few evenings after this there was a knock at the front door. Laura, relaxing in the wing-chair thought that it was Bert, come for a cuppa and a chat. He'd need to bring his bike through the front passage; he wouldn't be able to get it past the scaffolding which was blocking the side entrance. The Hills were having some pointing done.

194

The man on the step wasn't Bert.

Sid lifted his bowler. "Yes, Laura, it's me!" He smiled thinly.

Without another word, sick-to-her-stomach, she turned and led the way into the scullery, only too aware that Nigel and all her visitors were out.

He placed his bowler on the table. His eyes raked her insolently. "You're looking good," he said.

"You've come about the payment, haven't you?" she said haltingly.

His mouth tightened. "And why shouldn't I? It is my money. I'm not a charity, you know. I've got a wife and four children to feed and clothe. And a vehicle to keep on the road. You can't expect me to let you off any payments."

She eyed him. From what Prue had once told her, she and his children were kept short. What he didn't hoard, or spend on flighty pieces, went on his own back. He looked like a dog's-dinner, in his immaculate suit, spotted bow-tie and starched shirt front. "I don't expect you to. I'll let you have it as soon as I can." She clenched her hands at her sides, finger nails cutting into her palms. "It's just this month… well, I can't. And I was very grateful to you for getting me that settee."

"Is that so? You certainly didn't show it when you tried to come between me and Prue. I've not forgotten that! Those whom God has joined together…"

Pious hypocrite! She ought to have known he would have it in for her after her trying to help Prue. "It's the first time I've not had the money for you," she put in hastily.

"And why's that? It should be easier for you to find four shillings now that that husband of yours is back. He'll have a gratuity from the army for a start. You should be rolling in it."

"I promise I'll have eight shillings for you next month." She wasn't going to admit to Sid of all people that in all probability Nigel's gratuity had disappeared, if not on other women, on drink and gambling. That he was making no attempt to get a job. That she was having to keep him.

"That's not good enough. If you can't pay me the money now, I think I should send the bailiffs in." He contemplated the room. "You've quite a decent wireless there."

"The bailiffs'!" To have them at your door was a real disgrace. All the neighbours would know. How could she face them afterwards?

His bullet-brown eyes gleamed. "Of course if you were willing to let me have it in kind." He let his meaning sink in.

"No!" Not that again.

"If you were to be kind to me, well, I could forget all about those other payments for the settee," he said smoothly.

"No! Never!"

"No?" He stroked his moustache. "If you'd acted *right* that other time, you wouldn't have regretted it. I'd have been your friend. Looked after you. You'd not have needing to go skivving for other folk."

"Set me up in a love-nest, I suppose. No thanks." She should have 'popped' Mrs Mullet's locket. She could have got it back later. She willed the front door to open, to hear her visitors' voices, or even her neighbour Mrs Hill's, "Cooee Mrs Norris," but all was quiet. The only sound was the 'plop' of the dripping tap.

Suddenly he made a grab for her. She turned and dashed towards the passage door. He chased after her and barred her path. She heard his ragged breathing, as terrified, she turned tail. Tripping over a runner, she fell, but was soon up again. "Get away! Get away!" she sobbed, and snatching a carving knife from the wall-rack, waved it in his face. He laughed mockingly and knocked it from her hand, it clattering onto the lino. She grabbed up the breadbin lid, swinging it at his head. He tore it from her grasp and flung it from him; it clanged to the floor. Cornering her, he ripped the buttons on her blouse, they flew across the room. She tried to tug the material together. He wrenched her hands away. With a deft movement, he slid down the straps of her bra, releasing her breasts. His mouth sunk greedily onto a nipple. At the same time, he pushed her down over the table, jerking up her skirt, and ramming his knee between her thighs. "My mother won't interrupt us this time," he said grimly. Laura struggled, grasping at his hair and raking her nails down his cheek. "You bitch!" He slapped her viciously across the face. She opened her mouth to scream but nothing came out. He fumbled with his clothing, she felt his hardness pressing into her. Oh, merciful heavens, no!

From the passage came Bert's voice. "Hello there, Laura. It's me. Put kettle on, lass. I'm gagging for a cuppa."

She gasped with relief. God was watching out for her, after all!

Sid froze. "Oh, hell. Dad!" He scrambled off of Laura and made a dive for the back door.

Everything seemed to happen at once. As she tried to pull her clothing together, Bert entered the room, and his foot kicked against Sid's bowler. "What on earth's been going on here?"

The back door thudded-to, Laura heard the rush of an approaching train.

Stricken, they eyed each other. A coldness swept over her. "Sid can't get out the side way – next door's pointing."

Desperately yanking open the back door, they stepped into the yard at the same moment as he disappeared over the wall and the train thundered through.

"Sid! Sid! The train!" Laura clambered onto the coal bunker and reached for the top of the wall.

Grey-faced and shaking, Bert pulled her back down. "No, lass. Don't look! Don't look!"

CHAPTER ELEVEN

Aghast, Laura read the paragraph in the *Evening Gazette*. It seemed unbelievable that such a thing had actually happened.

> BLACKPOOL MAN HIT BY TRAIN
>
> Sidney Field, aged 42, the manager of Woodhouses furniture shop, Church Street, was killed instantly last evening when he was hit by a train. He leaves a widow and four children.

With a shaking hand, she laid down the newspaper. Shock had fortunately made the events immediately after the tragedy hazy in her mind. She must have dialled 999 – though she had no memory of it – or of the police and ambulance men coming and taking Sid's body away. All she could recall was Mrs Hill holding a cup of hot sweet tea to her lips. Despite sedation, in sleep, it was then she had vivid flashbacks; Sid disappearing over the wall, the thunder of the train, sparks tangled in its smoke – even to seeing him going under the wheels. She'd good cause to detest Sid, but she wouldn't have wished something like this on him, or his mother either. Whatever her faults, Doris Field had cared deeply for Sid. Though as far as Prue was concerned, perhaps, once she'd got used to the idea of him no longer being around, what had happened would turn out for the best. She thought of Bert and it was as if a blade pierced her heart. What must he be feeling? He must be having nightmares, too, after virtually witnessing the horror and inadvertently being the cause of it. A stranger's death would be bad enough, but Sid was Bert's son – his eldest. How did you face the death of someone as close as that? Someone you had dangled on your knee as a baby? Watched proudly as they took their first tentative steps. Said their first words. When Rod was killed she had felt as if she were in the middle of a nightmare. An impossible to come through nightmare. She'd felt that the buses should have stopped, that the wireless programmes should have been cancelled. Now, thinking of Bert, and visualising his pain distressed her.

In the *Deaths* column she saw the details of the funeral. Should she send flowers? Would she be a hypocrite if she did? In the end she decided on a small spray from herself and Claire – not really for Sid, but more as a comfort for Prue and Bert.

*   *   *

Laura came out of South Shore market. As she walked along Waterloo Road, a heavy bag in each hand, she saw a woman in her thirties with a pushchair piled-high with shopping. Holding onto the handlebars was a girl of around seven with fair curly hair. As the woman drew nearer, Laura recognised her. It was Prue. At the sight of her, Laura's thoughts turned guiltily to that terrible evening – how could she face Prue? At that moment she wished herself a million miles away. Could she dart into a shop? – no, it was too late. But did Prue blame her for Sid's death? She'd always said she'd hated him, but had she really? Some women were said to have a love-hate relationship with their husbands – even to getting a sexual kick from being beaten. She herself certainly wouldn't; any violence would put her off quicker than anything. But not every woman was the same. And after all, Prue had gone back to him that time. She'd said it was just for the children's sake, perhaps it was? How could Laura know? She searched Prue's face for signs of enmity, but could find none, and instead of quickly turning off down a side street as she would have done at one time, smiling widely, she was approaching. And how different she looked. She no longer had such a hangdog expression, and not only that, she'd lost weight, and was well turned-out in the latest fashion, the *New Look*.

They came face to face. "I can't believe it. You look so well, what have you done to yourself?" Prue was not only wearing make up but her nails were painted with cherry nail polish. Laura turned to the child. "Hullo, there, Brenda; it is Brenda, isn't it? Aren't you getting a big girl?"

"I'm the tallest in my class."

"Thanks for the flowers for Sid," said Prue.

"It was nothing."

"I didn't think so. I was really touched."

Laura hoped Bert had been too. Since Sid's funeral, two months earlier, he'd not called in so often, and when he did, was rather withdrawn. This was only to be expected in the circumstances. She'd not seen Doris Field for some months, as now Claire was old enough to go on her own to her grandparents. The last time was in South Shore market. An abrupt *Good morning* was Laura's only acknowledgement.

"I can't pretend to be sorry that Sid's gone," confided Prue. "You knew how he treated me. Though I suppose I shouldn't speak ill of the dead."

I would! – if he'd knocked me about like he did you.

Prue must have read Laura's thoughts. "Why should I keep my mouth shut about what a rotten husband he was? If anyone deserves to have ill spoken of them he does. He made my life hell. I know the Church says I should forgive what he did to me, but it's not easy."

"Some things are unforgivable!"

Prue hesitated. "Like rape, you mean? I was shocked out of my wits to learn what he'd been up to. Thank God Bert interrupted him."

Laura gripped the handle of her shopping bag. Prue would be even more shocked if she knew that Sid's attempt on her

200

wasn't his first. "At least then, he wouldn't have been killed," she said faintly.

"Well, I think he only got what he deserved."

"Maybe. But as for you forgiving Sid, well, it mightn't be Christian, but by God, if I'd had a husband like Sid, well, I'd have made a wax model of him and stuck pins in it."

Prue's lips twitched. "I must admit it's great to wake up of a morning and not be aching all over. The children were terrified of his moods. They were getting worse and more frequent, despite all those promises he made to me that he would turn over a new leaf."

"He didn't change, then?"

She smiled grimly. "No, he definitely didn't! But then, I don't expect you thought he would?"

"No. I thought you were daft going back to him." I bet that swine gave you a right wallop once he got you indoors."

"I didn't see what else I could do. I couldn't risk losing my kids. My life would be meaningless without them, they're everything to me."

Laura nodded. "Like Claire is to me. No, I suppose not. Still, that's all in the past."

"Yes, thank God."

"All the same it must be hard losing the breadwinner?"

"Hard! With the way he kept me short! Financially, I'm far better off. I'm getting the widow's pension. And I've got a substantial sum from Sid's Life Insurance."

"And hasn't dear Doris told you what you can do or not do with it? Interfered, like she usually does?" said Laura.

"No. She caused a rumpus at Sid's funeral. Something she said to Bert. I don't know what it was all about. But since then, she's been different. She's gone to pieces. She just shuffles around in slippers all day, even to the shops. She's turned overnight into an old woman."

"Never!"

"I know it sounds unbelievable, but it's true."

"Well, although I know I should be, I don't think I can be too sympathetic. Not when I recall how she made my life a purgatory."

"I shouldn't have fancied living with her. She was bad enough as it was."

"So what do you plan to do with this money from Sid?" asked Laura.

"I've done quite a bit already. Sid would turn over in his grave if he knew, but I've bought myself a couple of new outfits," she smoothed a hand over her full skirt; "clothes for the kids; a new lounge suite, the other was so shabby, and despite him working in a furniture shop he'd never agree to us replacing it. I've also had the house redecorated. The remainder I've put in the bank for the children for when they're older."

"That's sensible!"

"I've even found myself a little part-time job, a couple of hours, twice a week in a newsagents."

"Well, good for you."

Prue giggled. "The newsagent's a widower of forty-five, I reckon he fancies me. He's not much to look at, but looks aren't everything, are they? He's asked me to go for a drink or the pictures with him. But there's the kids, and after what I've been through with Sid, I don't want to rush into anything. I don't want to go out of the frying pan into the fire."

"I can understand that. But thankfully all men aren't like Sid. Look, if ever you want the children minded for an hour or two, just ring me."

"I'll remember that. So how's life treating you these days, Laura? How are you settling into married life after so long?"

She flushed. "So, so." The least said about Nigel the better. He was a sore point with her. It was becoming increasingly obvious that their marriage was faltering. In fact, if it had been possible for her to scrape up sufficient money to send him off to realise his dream, she would have done so. Apart from the gambling, she suspected there were other women. Being the charmer that he was (to all but her, these days) it was likely. The desert was one thing, he'd have no choice to be faithful then, only camels there – no chance of hanky-panky unless he'd been lucky enough to meet up with a dancing girl at an oasis. She smiled wryly.

"And how's Claire?"

"Fine! She's only passed the scholarship to Grammar, she's due to go to Harold School at Bispham, in September. You should see the list of stuff she has to have. It's a mile long. It's going to cost a fortune."

"Still, you must be very proud of her?"

"I am."

"Where does she get her brains from?"

Laura laughed. "Not from me, that's for sure. Must be from Rod. If only he could have lived to know about this, still it's no good wishing for the impossible."

"Rod was a good 'un, you were lucky to have him."

"Don't I know it." She turned to Brenda and pressed a threepenny-bit into her hand. "Put that in your money-box, darling."

"Say *thank-you* to Aunty Laura."

"Thank-you, Aunty Laura."

"I just might take you up on your baby-sitting offer sometime, Laura," said Prue as they parted company.

* * *

When Bert next appeared on his bicycle with a bunch of carrots topped with leafy green, Laura made him welcome – finding out the slippers she kept for him in the cupboard – pouring him out a cup of tea and cutting him a wedge of her speciality, a jam-and-cream Victoria sandwich. These days it

203

was only mock cream, made with arrowroot, milk, a knob of margarine and a shake of sugar. Still, despite this, her cake was always praised.

He settled himself in the wing-chair, and placed his cap on the table.

How worn he looks, she thought. There are black rings beneath his eyes. He looks thinner, too. Is he ill? I hope not. She handed him the cake. "I saw Prue and little Brenda a few days ago. Prue seems to be coping well."

He crumbled the cake. "Yes, she is."

"She told me Mrs Field isn't so good. I suppose that's only to be expected." Losing a son can't be easy, especially when you've already lost one, it must bring it all back. Even someone as bad as Sid would be missed by his own mother.

"Yes. She's certainly a changed woman." Adding under his breath. "For the better, as far as I'm concerned. These days, she doesn't say *boo-to-a-goose*."

Laura could hardly imagine it.

Bert drank his tea in silence.

"You've changed too, haven't you Bert? You're different altogether to what you were – with me, anyway. There's something wrong, isn't there? It's not just the way Sid's death and the way it happened, is it?"

"I'd rather not talk about it."

"Well, of course, that's up to you, but well, I thought we were friends. Friends confide in each other."

"Do they?" He eyed her keenly. "I bet you don't tell me everything?"

Laura flushed. "I've told you that I was beginning to wonder if my marriage to Nigel was a mistake – that he's rarely in, and when he is, he's of no help at all – only eating me out of house and home, and then clearing off out again."

"Point taken."

"Look, Bert, I'm really worried about you. If you got what's bothering you off your chest, it might do you the world of good. What is it they say? – 'a trouble shared, is a trouble halved'."

"I don't know that this would be. Now, where's Claire tonight?"

"Don't change the subject, Bert."

"I only asked where she was."

"She's at guides. At Holy Sepulchre Church. She joined some weeks ago."

"And does she like it?"

"Loves it! She fancies herself no end in her guides' uniform. She's passed her Tenderfoot already. Look, you'd best tell me what's wrong."

"I don't think I can. It just doesn't bear thinking about."

"What doesn't?"

"All these years," he said, almost to himself. "I've suffered from her tongue."

"Do you mean Mrs Field's?"

"Who else? When the Great War began it became even worse. She wanted me to enlist, said if she'd been a man she would have known her duty. I wasn't a coward, though she called me one. And admittedly it would have been a relief to be free of her constant nagging. All the same, I had a wife and two young sons and I thought it only right that I should stay home and look after them. No one was compelled to join up until 1916, and then it was only single men under forty-one. Besides I didn't really want to kill anyone, not even the Hun. I was called *Conchie* for that, and not just by her. There were other names used, like *Shirker* and *Slacker*. Then in 1918, men under fifty, whether married or not, were ordered to present themselves to the tribunal. I was given a medical. And was exempt from military service for having flat feet."

"So what did Mrs Field say about that?"

205

"Too much! If I'd known forty-three years ago, what I know now – well, my life would have been so different."

"Known what, Bert?"

He hesitated. "This'll shock you. It shocked me when she came out with it."

"Well, go on."

"Sid wasn't mine!"

"Not yours! I don't understand?"

"I never *fathered* him."

"Do you mean?"

"It was some other bastard. Sorry, Laura for speaking like this in front of you. I was just the idiot that brought him up, paid for everything. Me and Doris, well, we had to get married. I thought it was me who'd got her *up-the-spout*, but it was some married man. When she knew she'd been caught, she came crying to me. She'd decided as this man couldn't wed her to put the blame on muggins. I should have been wise to her little scheme. We'd not been walking out together for some time, in fact I'd thought she'd dropped me. Well, of course, priding myself on being honourable, I thought it was my duty to make an honest woman of her – I'd had my fun – I expected to pay for it – and all the time he was having fun too, at my expense!"

"So when did all this come to light?" asked Laura gently.

"At the funeral meal. She'd been comforting herself with the port bottle. Suddenly she came out with it, saying that it didn't matter if I didn't care as much as she did that Sid was dead – and that, anyway, he was just her son and not mine!"

"Not yours!" So that was the rumpus Prue had mentioned. How embarrassing for everyone, she was glad she'd not been there.

"I didn't know where to put my face."

She patted his hand. What could she say? But perhaps he didn't need her to say anything.

"All those unhappy wasted years! My life could have been so different. Before Doris came round with her tale there'd been a pretty-little-thing in the next street whom I'd my eye on. I'd been plucking up courage to ask her out. All that went by the board! A year later, she married a milkman from Marton."

"And Rod? He was yours, wasn't he?"

"She said he was. I've no reason to disbelieve her."

Laura said brightly. "Well, if you'd not wed Mrs Field, you'd not have had Rod."

"No. That's true. It was worth marrying her just for Rod. He was a son to be proud of."

"And a husband. I always thought he took after you."

"Did you?" Bert smiled with pleasure. "No, he was taller and better looking than I ever was."

"There's a similarity though."

"Thank you for that, Laura. I used to wonder why Sid and Rod were so different. Now it's clear. It was because they were no more than half-brothers. Even as a nipper, Sid was a bit of a bully, and Rod suffered until he got big enough to hit back. Sid was always tormenting Tibbs, the cat we had then – poking it with a knitting needle. And once he got the budgie out of its cage and was pulling off its feathers."

Laura gasped. "How awful!"

"Luckily I came in and caught him before he'd done too much harm. I sent him to bed with a raw behind. It was the only time I ever hit either of the lads. But she was up in arms about it and fetched him down again. Her spoiling didn't help improve him."

"So what are you going to do?"

"Do? About what? It's too late to do anything about anything. My life's set. Besides I've got your Claire and Sid's four. They still feel like *my* grandchildren. And they're all lovely kids. No, I'll carry on the same as I always have." He rose. "I'd best get back. I don't like to leave her too long. She gets nervous on her own. Keeps forgetting things, too. She turned on the gas the other day and then forgot to light it. It could have been a disaster. Luckily I smelt the gas and turned it off. And she's got to speaking as if Sid's still alive. As if she expects him to come through the door. Dementia brought on by grief the doctor calls it."

Laura saw him out. "Let me know if you need anything, Bert. I'll always help you, you know that."

He slipped on his bicycle clips. "Thank you, Laura, my dear. I will."

*   *   *

Claire was so excited on the morning she set off for her new school, with a bulging satchel on her back... Laura felt tears pricking her eyes, as she saw her go past the lounge window, proudly wearing the grey Harold uniform and felt hat. This was kept on by elastic beneath the chin, and had a red-and-grey ribbon around it and at the front was the school badge. Beneath the grey coat, Claire was wearing a red cardigan with five buttons over a white shirt, a red-and-grey diagonal striped tie and a grey skirt. On her feet were white socks and black shoes. Despite the day's mildness, she wore the regulation red woollen winter gloves (it was white cotton during the summer months).

This wasn't all that Laura needed to purchase for Claire. Beneath her shirt she wore her first bra. Noticing Claire and Ann playing Tag in the back yard, she'd realised that Claire was running with her arms folded. Asking her why she did this, Laura was told it was because when she ran, without the support of her folded arms, her top hurt. Unbelievably, her child needed a bra. Laura had let Claire have one of her own to start with. This wasn't satisfactory, so measuring her chest with the tape measure, she got Claire fixed up at Marks & Spencers.

Mrs Rose had taken Claire up to Bispham on the bus over the previous week, so that she could learn the route. They'd changed buses outside Talbot Road Bus Station. Claire was confident that she could do this 'changing' easily on her own. After all, she was twelve next birthday, and in her own opinion, 'grown up'.

As Laura did her morning chores, she couldn't help but worry about how Claire was getting on. Was she coping? Apart from anything else, Harold was at least twice the size of Peterloo School. Taking her for an interview with the headmistress, Miss Sheldon, they'd got lost among Harold's confusing corridors – until pointed in the right direction by the school-secretary. And how would Claire get on with her new classmates? Would they be friendly? Hopefully, they would. If only Ann could have won the scholarship too. Ann was starting at Lowfield Secondary, where the majority of girls from their class at Peterloo School were also going.

Washing up from the midday meal, Laura breathed a little prayer that Claire would settle down and do well.

Laura was serving high-tea to her visitors when the phone kept ringing. Every time she answered it the line went dead. She was becoming increasingly annoyed. Who was playing *silly-beggars?* Surely it wouldn't be one of the other boarding houses nearby; jealous because she was full up, and they weren't?

Suddenly it occurred to her that it might be Claire. Though she'd been expecting her to appear for some time, she still wasn't home.

At last, when she'd picked up the phone, it was Claire on the other end of the line, a tearful Claire, she was lost!

Hiccuping, she told Laura the name of the street where she was. She had walked past the bus stop where she should have got her bus to South Shore. Spotting a phone box, but not having used one before, she had not at first pressed button A.

"I'll come and get you. Stay where you are, on no account move."

Sniffling, Claire agreed.

Leaving Mrs Rose in charge, Laura hurriedly put on her hat and coat and went outside to the taxi she had called. If only Nigel wasn't out again. If he'd been a proper husband and helpmate, he could have gone and picked up Claire.

Her thoughts turned to the men in her life. Rod, Geoffrey and Nigel. What was it with her and men? Why was she so unlucky with them?

CHAPTER TWELVE

It was just the two of them for Christmas that year – Nigel disappeared on Christmas Eve – without leaving a present for Claire – and didn't reappear until Boxing Day. Laura found that she wasn't bothered one way or the other – and she didn't think Claire was either. In fact, Laura thought they might have a better Christmas without him. At least, it would be quarrel free. She helped Claire to paste together paper chains and between them they decorated the room. They weren't the only decorations, there were two strings of cards criss-crossing the ceiling, all from her boys in blue – she chuckled to herself, the largest being from Reg in which he confided that his present landlady's cooking wasn't a patch on hers. Beneath the window was the small artificial tree she'd got Claire from the market. Placing the tree in a flower pot; covering the base of the tree in dirt, they'd hid the dirt beneath cotton wool. The pot itself was enclosed in red crepe paper. Tinsel streamers and wads of cotton wool at strategic points completed it. On the top was a tiny golden bell which shimmered in the light. Laura had had this bell since she was eight. She'd been invited to a children's party at the vicarage, back home in Chorley. It had been a wonderful party – the lady of the manor providing the Christmas crackers – dear ones that cost a shilling each. When Laura and the girl next to her pulled her cracker, she'd found a motto, a paper hat like that of a pirate, and also the bell. The following Christmas, decorating the bit of evergreen given her by a neighbour, she'd hung the bell from the top of it. Recently, tidying her drawers, she'd come across the bell.

She and Claire went together to Midnight Mass at Holy Sepulchre Church – opening their presents afterwards. As they ate their chicken and pudding, Laura sadly remembered the fun of the previous Christmas meal – the huge turkey and the jolly company. That evening, Bert managed to slip in with two packages under his arm.

He put on his slippers and made himself comfortable in the wing-chair.

"How's Mrs Field?"

"No better, Laura. She goes round the house calling, 'Sid! Sid! Where are you, son? You'll be late for school.' She's back somewhere in the past where I can't reach her."

"How sad." Should she go and see her? thought Laura. Wouldn't it be the decent thing to do?

"I never thought I'd wish to feel the sting of her tongue, but I do. It's like she's a different person. She always used to love listening to the wireless, but if I put it on she asks to have it off, says it makes her head ache. She forgets to wash or comb her hair. The other day she put her dress on back to front. She still recognises me, but for how long?" He shook his head. "She needs watching more than ever. Prue helps when she can, but she's got the kids. I wouldn't have been able to come at all if Connie hadn't agreed to sit with her to give me a break."

For a few shillings this neighbour minded Doris Field while he worked.

Pouring Bert out a Guinness, Laura sympathised and gave him his present – a warm bottle-green muffler and mittens that she'd knitted for him to wear when pushing his barrow. "I thought it would keep out the winter chill." How glad she was that he no longer pushed a barrow-load of veg round the streets – especially with Mrs Field as she was. Bert couldn't be far short of sixty-five. Selling flowers was far more suitable for someone of his age.

"It will that! It's just what I could do with!" He wound the muffler around his neck and put on the mittens. "My hands'll be as warm as toast in these, lass."

Smiling with pleasure, Laura reflected on just how much Rod's dad had come to mean to her. She loved Bert like the father she'd never known, the father whose life had been 'snuffed-out' by war. Had Geoffrey's life been 'snuffed-out' too. Was that why she'd never heard from him? She didn't suppose she'd ever know.

Claire, too, was learning to knit. Her present for her grandad was a fluffy red hot-water bottle cover.

"Do you like it, Grandad?" she asked. "Look! I've embroidered your name in blue." She pointed to a rather lopsided *BERT*.

He grinned. "Do I? It's really clever. I reckon I'm the luckiest chap alive to have two young ladies giving me such wonderful handmade gifts."

Claire smiled at his praise. She handed him a second parcel. "I've made a hot water bottle cover for Grandma, too. I'm sorry she's not well. Hers has got a *DORIS* embroidered in pink. Will you give it to her?"

"Of course I will. She'll love it."

Bert had to say that to Claire, but would Doris Field even realise what it was he was giving to her? Laura could no longer hate the woman. All she could feel for her was pity. How long would Bert be able to manage her at home? Would he end up having to put her in an institution? Life was so cruel.

"And now it's your turn to open my presents," he said.

Laura's was a box of pink lace-edged handkerchiefs. "They're lovely," she said, giving him a kiss on the cheek.

Eagerly Claire tore off the wrappings. "A book," she enthused. *"Pride and Prejudice.* I'll enjoy that! Miss Darling, our English teacher, says we must *stretch ourselves* by reading *literature."*

Bert looked pleased. Especially when he got a second kiss.

His brow isn't as furrowed as when he arrived. It's doing him good to get away from her, even if it's only for a short time.

"Now how about a game of Monopoly?" suggested Laura brightly, getting out the board, and placing it on the table between them.

"Great! Bags me the battleship. It always brings me luck." Claire placed it on the board.

"I think I'll have the top hat," said Bert. "Be a gentleman for a change and sit on my backside and do nowt all day. Sorry, Laura for the language."

She laughed. "Don't be daft! Now what shall I choose? Well, I don't want the iron. I don't want to be reminded of my least favourite chore – especially the ironing of Claire's fiddly hair ribbons."

"I help you sometimes with the ironing, Mum,"

Laura raised her eye brows. "Sometimes!"

They all laughed.

"I know, I'll have the rocking horse," said Laura.

"Let's start then," said Claire, and popping the dice into the cup, she rattled it vigorously, rolling out a six. "There, I told you I'd be lucky!"

Laura and Bert exchanged a smile. Claire's high-spirits were catching.

As the game progressed, merriment filled the room, mellowed by firelight.

*　　*　　*

Claire was in bed. Laura looked at the Christmas card from Rosemary, Tony and Bobby on the mantelpiece. The card had a picture of a kangaroo and in a fancy red script: SEASONS' GREETINGS FROM OZ. Inside, Rosemary had scrawled a few lines. Laura had got a letter from her some months back, in which she'd said that what with the seasickness they'd suffered during a bout of rough weather, she'd been relieved to see the end of the six-week voyage in the bowels of a ship, in which she and her husband had been in separate dormitories. Now she'd written, they were all well, and living in a makeshift camp in Queensland, but longing for their own accommodation. She'd added that she couldn't get used to the idea of Christmas Day being hot and sunny and spent at a barbecue on the beach.

The card next to it was from Prue and her children. On it was a Christmas pudding with a sprig of holly. Prue's news wasn't so surprising – *her* newsagent was still keen, and had invited both Prue and the kids to a slap-up Christmas dinner at a hotel on the prom.

Good for you! Laura's eyes drifted to the card from Mrs Hughes. The picture was of a robin perched on a twig. The card contained sad, if not unexpected news. Mr Hughes was dead, but her sister, also a widow, was to come to make her home with her. There was some other news. Astounding news about Mr Bicker. Against all advice, he'd married his young lady friend the previous year. And now at the age of sixty-seven, he was the father of a ten-pound baby boy. Laura recalled the sleepless nights when Claire was born. How on earth at his age, was Mr Bicker coping with the lack of sleep?

Shivering, Laura put another knob of coal on the fire, refusing to consider how small the amount was left in her bunker. She'd hoped that when the war ended, so would rationing. Fat chance! She returned to the wing-chair and pulled a blanket over her knees. It seemed ages since last summer's sweltering days. In her case since she'd been able to take advantage of the fine weather and stroll on the beach. All her summers were spent indoors, it being her busiest period.

With an empty boarding house, she should have some free time for a change, although there was the Spring cleaning to be done and bedding and curtains to be washed or dry cleaned ready for the Easter visitors. Also some decorating to be attempted. The lounge, especially, was looking shabby and would benefit from a coat of emulsion to freshen it. She didn't

215

think there was much chance of roping in Nigel. She wondered if Bert might do it for her? – after all, he had before when she had her fire. Or if not – how she could go about doing it herself.

Claire had settled in better than Laura could have hoped for at her new school and made friends – there was one she kept on about called Mollie. This girl was always phoning. In the end, Laura felt it necessary to remind Claire that they were a business, and it was important to leave the line free for bookings. Her lips twisted in amusement, as she recalled Claire's outrage at the way the teachers were so strict about the wearing of the correct school uniform. "They only pull our skirts up to check we're wearing our grey knickers, Mum."

Gloves too were to be worn at all times. Woe betide any girl without them at glove inspection. Though, one girl fooled the teachers. When everyone stuck out their gloved hands, she hid the one without a glove behind her back – and got away with it!

The chimes of Holy Sepulchre Church ringing in 1947, followed by singing and laughter from the street, broke through her thoughts. Laura yawned. She'd best go to bed – or she'd be hopeless tomorrow.

Clutching the towel-wrapped stone hot water bottle to her, she eased her feet down the ice-cold sheets, wondering what this New Year would bring? And if there was any chance of Nigel coming to his senses as regards their marriage?

*   *   *

February brought with it the coldest weather in living memory. Snow lay about for weeks, granite-hard, it formed icy potholes. In Stanley Park, skaters glided over the frozen lake. The main roads were spread with grit and sand, and ashes from fires were strewn across the frosted paths. Snowstorms stopped trains from running, and biting blizzards kept ships in port. In the first week of February, Laura, turning on the six o'clock news, learnt that Emmanuel Shinwell, the Labour Minister for Fuel and Power had informed a shocked House of Commons that the power stations were so low on coal stocks that electricity would be turned off for five hours a day to save fuel. It was so cold she filled both kettles before going to bed in case every tap in the place was frozen solid when she got up. And one morning there was even a fringe of icicles *inside* the lounge window when she went downstairs.

Wearing three layers of clothing, even in bed, she longed for the weather to become milder.

*   *   *

Having spent all morning moving wardrobes to dust behind them, she decided to take a break and go for a walk – she wasn't expecting Claire home for hours, and the exercise would do her good. As she put on her hat and coat she wondered which direction she should take. The last time she'd gone along the prom. She recalled that in March the wide stretch of promenade had been desolate, the stalls and shops shuttered, buffered against the gales. The freezing air chilling the memory of the sizzling chips and the candy-floss days of summer.

She smiled to herself as she set off in the direction of Stanley Park, considering the amount of money she'd found that morning when bottoming; pennies, threepenny bits, sixpences and even a shilling. No doubts they'd fallen out of her visitors' pockets and rolled beneath the wardrobes, when, after a few bevvies, they took off their trousers. She knew this loose change wouldn't be from the women, as they'd more sense and kept their money in a purse. She wondered what she should do with it? – after all, it wasn't hers. She'd not counted it as yet, but guessed it could be as much as five shillings. She'd seen a Barnado's charity box in the butchers. Poor kids, it must be terrible being an orphan and the charity did a good job in caring for them. Yes, she decided, she'd put the money in the box as soon as she got the chance.

To her surprise, Laura realised that her steps had taken her into Westcliffe Drive. She halted. Had her subconscious brought her here? Was she not as successful as she imagined in burying the bittersweet memories of Geoffrey? She knew she should turn around and retrace her steps. What was the good of trying to relive the past? Her happy time at the Cedars were gone forever, and best forgotten.

All the same, her feet seemed to have a will of their own.

She paused outside THE CEDARS with its neatly kept flower beds and huge cedar tree. Everything seemed unchanged. Even to the white and pink begonias. Over the front door, a hanging basket still contained trailing red freesias. It was as if time had rolled backwards to 1937. Inside the house, Gloria Roberts, with a sweet smile on her gaunt face, lay on her air bed with Rosemary in attendance. Geoffrey, an unruly lock of brown hair falling over his brow, worked at his desk. And in the rear garden, little Mollie and Claire enjoyed a dolls' tea-party with a tiny china tea service, their dolls seated in a ring about them. If Laura were to open the gates, walk down the drive and around to the back and push open the kitchen door, she would see her youthful self in a blue cotton overall rolling out pastry for a steak-and-kidney pie.

She shook herself. You can't go back! If Geoffrey had survived the war, no doubt he lived elsewhere. An overwhelming urge came over her to knock at the front door. Dare she? Excitement mixed with apprehension rose within her. What if he still lived here? If he opened the door to her, what could she say to him? She'd be struck dumb!

As if in a dream, she found herself on the doorstep. With a shaking finger, she pressed the bell. A faint musical chime came from within. Footsteps sounded. Her heart leapt, to fall again.

They were too light for a man's. The door opened. An elderly woman asked, "Yes? Can I help you?".

Laura swallowed her disappointment. "I... I wondered if Mr Roberts still lived here?"

The woman shook her head. "Mr Roberts? No, he doesn't. My husband and I bought the Cedars off a couple called Prendergast. We moved in just after Christmas. I'm sorry, but I've never heard of a Mr Roberts. You could ask the neighbours. They've been here for years, they'd probably know."

Laura thanked the woman and left. She felt deflated. Had she really expected it to be that easy? That all she had to do was knock on his door and he'd open it. And sweep her into a passionate embrace. How daft! She was old enough now to know life wasn't like that.

As she made her way home, she wondered if it had been Geoffrey who'd sold the Cedars to the Prendergasts. If he was still alive, why hadn't he ever written?

*   *   *

Laura dressed herself carefully in her best blue velvet dress, tweed winter coat and matching hat. She straightened the seams of her stockings – no way did she want to show herself up in front of the other parents.

Laura was going to her first ever Parents' Evening at Harold School. She wasn't too worried about leaving Claire on her own, after all, she was old enough now not to need minding. And Ann was coming in to keep her company. And should the phone ring with an enquiry, Laura knew Claire could handle the booking book to check what vacancies they still had and ask the caller to write in with a deposit. But all the same as she rode on the Bispham bus she began to wonder if they would behave themselves? She didn't want to get back and find her boarding house a shambles. She only hoped her trust wasn't misplaced, that they would really listen to the wireless, or else experiment with the make-up she had given Claire. She'd skin Claire alive if she touched hers! Her box of Rose Rachel face powder and her Tangee lipstick hadn't been cheap.

She entered the school. Like that other time with Claire she became lost and confused as she tried to find her way to the main hall. She eventually tagged onto a woman heading along a corridor. They came out facing the hall, with a notice outside, PARENTS' EVENING YEAR ONE.

The hall, with tall windows, was dominated by a black-curtained stage. Around the room, at intervals, were tables behind which were seated the teachers. In front of each teacher were two chairs for the parents. On the tables were piles of exercise books. Also a name-card. The teachers were mostly older than Laura, their hair in untidy buns with the grips sliding out, and they wore tweedy costumes complemented by a string of pearls, thick stockings and flat shoes. Laura shook her head in bewilderment. Which of these teachers was Miss Darling?

She was seated at the table with the longest queue. Laura joined on the end, and slowly, they moved up towards the tables. The noise was deafening as the people chattered to each other. She noticed that some of the teachers were more organised than the others – transferring the exercise books of those pupils dealt with into a separate pile, while other teachers just had the one pile which they rifled through. She rubbed the back of each of her calves with the toe of her shoe. Her legs were aching. She only hoped that all this discomfort and the headache she was getting would be worth it; that Miss Darling would tell her that her Claire was the brightest in the class and would go far. Claire had certainly been full of confidence earlier – unlike Laura in those far off days when a schoolgirl in Chorley. Smiling widely, her face reflected beside Laura's in the dressing table mirror, Claire had said chirpily, "I'm near the top of the class, Mum.

220

There's nothing for you to worry about. Miss Darling will just tell you what I've already told you."

The couple in front of her rose and shook hands with the teacher.

"I'm Laura Norris," she said, slipping into one of the vacant chairs and smiling tentatively. "My daughter's, Claire Field." Her eyes alighted on the exercise books, thinking this teacher's well organised.

Miss Darling's eyes brightened and with a friendly smile, she put out her hand, saying, "I'm very pleased to meet you, Mrs Norris. I guessed you were Claire's mother. You're very like your daughter. Or maybe, she's like you?"

"Is she?" Laura laughed. "I'm not sure that would please Claire."

Miss Darling laughed, too. "Maybe not."

"No, I don't think many young girls would think it a compliment to be likened to their mother. So how's she doing?"

"Extremely well." Miss Darling picked up an exercise book. "Yes, her English composition is outstanding." She opened it and passed it to Laura. "This one about life in a boarding house. I must admit I found it riveting. Claire can really draw thumbnail sketches of all she observes. It bodes well for her future."

"Thank you for that, Miss Darling." The pleasure Laura felt at the teacher's remark was in her voice.

The teacher placed the exercise book on top of a high pile. "I also take her for maths." She picked up another single book. "Ah, here it is." Opening it, she handed it over. "Not to be alarmed, but as you can see, Mrs Norris, Claire does need to work at this subject."

Laura noted the many crosses by the sums as she flicked through. "I see what you mean, Miss Darling." She handed back the book with a grimace and Miss Darling placed the exercise book on top of another pile.

"Yes, I'll see she applies herself. And her other subjects?"

"There's none that she's weak in Mrs Norris, apart from the maths, you've really nothing to worry about."

Laura said goodbye to Miss Darling. As a reward she'd get some chips for Claire and Ann on the way home. Knowing those two girls, they'd sure to be starving. Red-haired and freckled Ann Hill, especially. By the way you could never satisfy that girl's appetite, she was going to be the size of her mother. Betty Hill was not only taller than Laura, but round with it. And as soon as Claire came up to scratch with her maths she'd get her that bicycle she'd seen her admiring when they went past the cycle shop.

Behind her Laura heard a strangely familiar voice say, "I'm very sorry. I hope I'm not too late? My car wouldn't start."

She turned. Her chest thudded, and her knees felt all wobbly. "It can't be?" she gasped, grabbing hold of the nearest table, and hearing, as if from a distance, Miss Darling, replying, "Of course not, Mr Roberts. I quite understand."

The tall, smartly-dressed, still attractive man, with a lock of salt-and-pepper hair falling over his brow, and holding a trilby in his hand, was heavier than when she'd last seen him. But she recognised him immediately.

It was Geoffrey.

"Laura!" he said, looking astonished. "Is that you?"

With a struggle, she recovered herself. "It certainly is." They moved out of earshot. "Well, isn't this a turn up for the book," she said flippantly. "I thought perhaps you were dead. You seemed to have vanished off the face of the earth. I certainly never expected to bump into you here."

"Well, I didn't expect to see you. Look, don't run off. Did you come by bus?"

"What's that to you?"

He flinched. "You sound bitter?"

"Well, what do you expect, when you never wrote to me when you promised that you would."

Geoffrey's eyes widened in astonishment. "Is that what you think? That I just dumped you?"

"What else is there to think?"

"But I wouldn't have done that. You must have known how I felt about you?" He reached for her hand. "Still do, in fact. And I did write. Several letters. It was you who never replied."

She pulled away, her hand tingling. "I... I would have if I'd received any letters."

"Well I sent them. I'll swear that I did."

"Words are cheap! If there were any letters, then what happened to them?"

He shook his head. "I really don't know. They must have gone astray somehow."

"I suppose... where did you address them to?"

"To that place you were working at in St Annes."

"But I moved in '41. I live in South Shore now."

"I know."

She eyed him keenly. "You do, do you? Oh, well, perhaps they didn't redirect the letters. "

He nodded. "That must be it. Look, let me give you a lift home? We need to talk."

"I suppose a ride in a car might be better than hanging around a draughty bus stop," said Laura, softening. "But I can't really see what we've got to say to each other. And what about your wife, won't she mind?"

He looked astonished. "Wife! There is no wife. Why should you think there was?"

"Well that would explain why you never tried to find me when you got back to Blackpool."

"You've got it all completely wrong. I need to explain. Look, just let me have a few words first about Mollie with Miss Darling."

Laura realised that the teacher was watching them with interest. She flushed guiltily. "Mollie," she said. "I never thought when Claire mentioned a Mollie, it would be your Mollie."

"Why should you?"

"I don't think that Claire realises."

"I don't suppose she does. They were so young, hardly more than babies, weren't they? Now just let me find out how Mollie's doing. You will wait, won't you? I'll be no longer than I can help."

* * *

Laura subsided into a chair at the far end of the hall. Her head whirled and she felt slightly sick. What was going to happen now? She eyed Geoffrey talking earnestly to Miss Darling and at the sight of his clear-cut profile, excitement raced through her. Did she still feel something for him? Even after all these years. How daft! She was acting like a silly school girl. Besides she'd still not learnt why he'd not contacted her when he'd got back to Blackpool.

He came over to her with a smile on his face. "All finished," he said. "Mollie's coming on well in maths. My chivvying her to do her homework is paying off, but her English composition needs strengthening."

"That's the opposite to Claire, with her it's the maths."

He laughed. "They'll have to help each other."

Laura made no comment.

"There's my car, that Daimler. He opened the door and helped her in. A thrill ran through her at his touch, which she tried to ignore.

"So what's your excuse for not trying to find me?" she said shakily.

224

He turned on the ignition, and the engine purred into life. "I knew where you were all right. I made enquiries. I learnt you'd taken on a boarding house in Trafalgar Terrace and that your husband had returned without a scratch and with a medal. I wanted to see you. But I thought it best to keep out of the picture. I thought that if I did, it would give your marriage a chance. Remember not having heard from you, I imagined that was what you wanted."

As they sped towards South Shore she wondered if she really could believe what he was saying? At one time she would have without a second thought. Now, she wasn't so sure. Looking back to that unforgettable tête-à-tête at Lewis's, she knew that at twenty-three she'd been rather gullible. Was he really as genuine as he sounded? After all, there could have been some other reason why he'd not got in touch? If not a wife, maybe some other woman? Or even, several women! She eyed him surreptitiously. By the way his hands were grasping the wheel, this meeting was obviously affecting him as much as it was her. He hadn't lied, he did care! The car took a corner sharply, and losing her balance her shoulder brushed his. She righted herself, a tremor running through her. "Well, Nigel doesn't see our marriage in the same light as you do," she said.

"What do you mean?"

She couldn't keep the bitterness from her voice. "He's holding it against me because I won't sell up and go off to London with him. I hardly see him. He certainly gives me no support with the business. He wants to get into films. He fancies himself a Clark Gable."

"Films! Has he any experience as an actor? Been to Drama School?"

"Not as far as I know. He did a bit in the army with ENSA. But that doesn't mean he'd make it in films. Though he says his war record might help."

"It very well could." He took a hand from the wheel and tapped his inside pocket. "I kept the piece about your husband getting his medal."

"Why did you do that?" she asked surprised.

"Because it mentioned your name."

A thrill ran through her. "Well, I don't want to go to London – especially now!"

"So has he found work here?"

"No. I don't reckon he's looked either. Thinks I can keep him."

The car drew up outside her boarding house. Geoffrey came round and helped her out. Should she invite him in for a cup of tea and to meet Claire? She now knew he was genuine as regards herself. A net curtain twitched. Best not. It was late. The neighbours knew her husband. They'd see that the man getting out of a car with her, wasn't. She had to consider her respectability. It was very important to her. In her line of business she couldn't afford to lose her good name. Besides where could it all lead?

She turned to say goodnight. Would he ask for her phone number? – despite her being married. Ask if they could meet up sometime? If he did, why shouldn't she agree? The marriage she had with Nigel, wasn't really a marriage. It was very tempting. Something so hole-and-corner wasn't really her, but what other choice did she have? Now that they had found each other again, could she lose him? No, her heart told her. She'd have to be discreet though. And not just because of the business, or the people she knew at Holy Sepulchre Church. She didn't want to give Nigel *grounds*. Divorce was a disgrace whichever way you said it.

All the same, when Geoffrey asked if he could ring her, without a moments hesitation, she said, *yes.*

CHAPTER THIRTEEN

She awaited the phone call with as much eagerness as she had the one all those years ago when arranging with Geoffrey for their night of passion, which never came off. In her heart of hearts, she knew this was ridiculous. She was acting like a love struck girl instead of the mother of a twelve-year-old. Besides, despite all these feelings which were still unbelievably lurking beneath the surface, she hardly knew him, not really. She didn't even know what his favourite book or film was. Or what they might actually have in common. All this made no difference.

When the call finally came, and Geoffrey got round to suggesting a meeting, she knew that as a married woman she should refuse. Not that this was ever a possibility. She accepted eagerly his excuse of having some problem with Mollie that only she could help him with. The arrangement was that they meet at midday by Stanley Park Lake.

Since seeing Geoffrey at the school her emotions had been on a roller coaster ride. Like her younger self, she couldn't sleep at night, and her thoughts were full of him. Now as she got ready to go, her mood suddenly changed and she began to feel uneasy. A respectable woman would never agree to a meeting with another man in an out-of-the-way spot. This, she knew would be frowned on by everyone. Then she thought, why shouldn't she do what she wanted, did she really owe a husband like hers anything? She visualised the late Mrs Mullet's reproachful face – 'I was good to you.' Laura struggled with her conscience, but excitement at the thought of seeing him again had already overcome guilt.

It was a balmy spring-like day for early April. The trees were budding, their stickiness sparkling in the brittle sunshine, and spiders were knitting webs in the greening foliage. Finding a dry bench, they sat down and he lit up two Du Maurier cigarettes and passed her one. As they smoked and attempted to catch up on all that had happened in their lives since their last meeting, the unforgettable aroma that always brought Geoffrey to mind wafted around their heads. He'd been a contact for the Underground in France. His job was to rescue stranded British airmen and arrange to send them back home. "I had a few near squeaks with the Gestapo," he admitted, "it was a hush-hush job – still is, I'm afraid."

Laura shivered. She knew if he'd been caught by them, he would have been tortured and shot.

"Life's rather dull now I'm back with my old stock-broking firm, Osborne and Parkinson," he said. "Still I'm working towards the future. So how was your war?"

Perhaps he doesn't want to talk anymore about his? He was the opposite to Nigel in that respect. She knew as much about Montgomery and the Eighth Army's fight against Rommel's forces in the deserts of North Africa as Nigel did. "I was once caught up in an air raid in Manchester – that was frightening! Then there was the time one of my lads dropped a cigarette end and set my settee alight – it was a right-off." Fate was indeed strange. But for those few seconds of carelessness, she wouldn't have needed to get into debt – Sid would still be abusing Prue – and Doris Field, most likely, her dominant self. "Apart from those occasions, my war was mostly make-do-and-mend, and stretching the rations for ten to feed twenty."

"And what about all those young airmen under your roof? I bet one or two of them set your heart beating faster?" he teased.

"Not really. I'm far too old for that sort of thing!"

He threw back his head and laughed. "I don't believe it. Besides you don't look a day different than when you came to work for me."

"Get away with you," she said, but secretly was flattered. "A little while ago," she admitted with a blush, "I took a walk past your old house in Westcliffe Drive."

"Did you? How did it look?"

"The same, I suppose. Seeing the Cedars again gave me a odd feeling. I felt I could just walk in and find things exactly the way they were in 1937. Then I rung the bell and was confronted with a stranger." She wasn't going to tell him that at that moment her bubble had burst, that she'd been terribly disappointed to find he no longer lived there. Stubbing out her cigarette, she tore up some stale bread and threw it to the ducks who squawked around them. "Perhaps it's none of my business, but why did you sell the Cedars?"

He frowned. "It's simple really. When I got home, I just knew I couldn't live there anymore. Everywhere I looked, I kept seeing Gloria – and not only Gloria – I must admit, you too. Thinking that there was no hope for us, that you were happy with your husband, I found this painful. Besides the house was too big for just myself and Mollie. It seemed best to make a fresh start. A semi not far from Mollie's new school in Bispham."

"Whereabouts in Bispham?"

"Sandlea Road, not far from Bispham Village. Do you know it?"

"No, I can't really say I know that area at all."

He seemed to make up his mind. "You must come over for a visit. Bring Claire with you."

She shook her head. "I don't think I could."

"What not for a special occasion? Mollie's birthday tea. A week Saturday."

"Claire did ask me about this. But I thought it would just be Claire going." She supposed it might be okay for her go to the house with it being the girl's birthday. And who would know anyway? – she wouldn't tell anyone – and Bispham wasn't exactly on her doorstep. The fact that she'd been to Geoffrey's was unlikely to get back to her neighbours – get her gossiped about. But all the same…

"Mollie is thrilled to bits at the chance to spend more time with Claire – show her her room and all her board games and books."

"I know Claire is over the moon, too. But I still don't know whether I should come. I'm not a free agent, you know. Don't forget I'm a married woman."

He raised his eyebrows. "You won't let me forget it."

"Well, I am. You know I am!"

From his expression she could tell he was thinking: And a married woman, from what you've told me, whose husband doesn't treat her right.

"Oh, please come," he urged. "It's just for tea. Besides we'll have two chaperones, won't we?"

For a moment she wondered if there might be an extra one, a housekeeper? At this thought jealousy stabbed her. The woman might be young and attractive with her eye on Geoffrey. If that was the case, she'd want to scratch them out! She relaxed as she recalled reading somewhere that since the war it was impossible to get live-in staff. "So how do you manage?"

"With difficulty. I'm thankful for an efficient laundry service and I've got a woman coming in twice a week to do the cleaning. I've had to learn to become a dab hand with the frying pan."

She laughed. "You'll get spots if you eat too much fried food."

He laughed. "I was joking about the frying pan. I can do a mean casserole too."

"So what's this problem you've got with Mollie?" she asked.

For a moment she thought he looked puzzled. Had he forgotten! His face cleared. "I need a birthday cake for Mollie.

As I said I'm all right with simple meals, but that's as far as it goes. I know I could get a cake from a bakers, but, well, I wanted something a bit special. I thought with all your catering experience you could design me one? I'd pay you, of course."

"You've never seen any of my cakes. How do you know how good it would be?"

"I just know, Laura. I remember your delicious pies and puddings."

Flattered, she agreed not only to bake the cake for him, but also for both her and Claire to go to the birthday tea.

And so it was arranged. She said they'd take the bus to Bispham. But Geoffrey insisted it would be silly to lug a large cake tin all that way by public transport. He would pick them up in his car at the bottom of Lytham Road, where it turned onto the promenade.

"That's very kind, but I don't want to put you to any trouble." Had she really said she'd visit his house? Was she acting like a 'fast' woman in wanting, so very, very much to spend time with him? Well, if she was, she didn't care, his close proximity was causing her stomach to bounce up and down.

He smiled into her eyes. "No trouble at all – the least I can do when you're doing me a good turn."

Geoffrey walked her back from the park to the bus stop. "I'd offer you a lift to South Shore," he said, "but I need to get back. I've got a client waiting."

She eyed his clear-cut profile, and her heart missed a beat. "Don't worry about it."

He patted her hand. "Till a week Saturday, then."

"Till a week Saturday," she replied breathlessly, as the bus approached and stopped. It was one of the latest Utility buses, with sparred wooden seats. She climbed shakily up onto the footplate and found a seat inside. "Where to?" for a moment, she didn't hear the conductor. She was too busy waving goodbye to Geoffrey. Tight-lipped, he repeated his question.

"Waterloo Road," she said, flustered, handing him her fare.

He briskly wound the handle on his machine, and tearing off the ticket, thrust it at her.

* * *

It was the Saturday of the party. She clipped on the small pearl ear-bobs, then studying herself before the mirror, smiled and gave a little twirl. The wide-skirted ankle-length pink-and-white taffeta dress swirled about her. Did this latest fashion, the *Dior* New Look, suit her? She had gone specially to Hills to get it. She knew a new dress was a bit of an extravagance, but she needed to look her best for Geoffrey. Her outfit was completed with the accessories of a white veiled hat, white net gloves and high heeled white court shoes. As she slipped her feet into them, she paused. Ought she to go to Geoffrey's house? She knew only too well that this visit could lead to more than she could handle. But it wouldn't be fair to Claire to disappoint her, she convinced herself – and it was only a tea party anyway, who knows what Nigel gets up to at his officer's club. She'd suggested once he take her there for a drink. Looking awkward, he'd mumbled. "It's men only" – but was that true?

She took from her wardrobe her pre-war three-quarter length white woollen swing coat which she'd livened up with new buttons, and slipped her arms into it. On the lapel was the present Claire had given her – a small gilt brooch, its letters spelling, LAURA. A warm feeling filled her. Claire could drive her crazy, and then she could be so sweet. She had saved her Saturday pennies for several weeks and then, for no reason at all, bought Laura the brooch from the market.

Laura came downstairs. A wolf-whistle startled her. "Is that my mother?" said Claire, admiringly.

"I meet with your approval then?"

"You'll knock his eyes out!"

232

"Really, Claire. We're just friends. You mustn't speak like that about Mr Roberts," Laura said, though secretly she was pleased.

"Why not? When it's the truth." Claire looked ruefully at the floral cotton frock beneath her cardigan, her white ankle socks and Clarks sandals. "I look so childish."

"Well, you are a child."

"Oh, no, I'm not!"

"Don't start arguing." Claire's skirt hardly reached her knees. She must have shot up at least an inch since last summer. It was lucky there was a big hem to let down. It wasn't decent for a girl to show her knees. She didn't want men to get ideas about her child. "Now come on, or we'll be late."

Laura got the cake in its tin from the scullery and they set off, each holding a handle of the bag and stepping out smartly along Trafagar Terrace. They turned into Waterloo Road, and finally Lytham Road. She began to hobble on her high heels. "I never realised before how long this road was."

A car horn hooted.

"Is that Mr Roberts? – oh, there's Mollie!" She waved. "Now, Claire, you will behave yourself this afternoon? You won't show me up?"

"Of course not, Mum, what do you take me for?"

Geoffrey got out and taking the bag, placed it in the boot. He opened the car door. "Hop in," he said, with a smile.

Laura got in beside him, while Claire got in the back beside Mollie. The two girls began to chatter non-stop about the Hollywood stars that they'd read of in that week's *Picturegoer*. Geoffrey grinned and taking one hand off the wheel, put it over his ear.

Laura took in the passing scene. It being a mild day, there were plenty of people strolling along the prom. The greyish-blue sea was dazzled by sunlight that struck a path across the water. On the sands children were busily engaged with buckets and spades. Soon, the shuttered kiosks and arcades, along with the Tower and the piers, were all left far behind.

Sandlea Road was wide and the grass verges tree-lined. They turned into the drive of a semi-detached house. Compared to the Cedars it was modest. There were flower beds of daffodils and budding tulips. "I planted the bulbs myself," he said proudly. "Another skill I've learnt since being here. There's a lawn at the back. I've lost some weight in mowing it, I can tell you…"

"You're lucky," she said wistfully. "There's only a bit of yard at the back of the boarding house."

He parked the car and they went inside. The girls immediately disappeared up to Mollie's bedroom.

So much for him saying we'd have two chaperones! Through the French windows Laura could see the lawn. A mossy sundial was at its centre. Further down was a low-branched apple tree. Shrubbery and a wooden bird table completed the picture. She recognised the lounge furniture. It was from the Cedars, though here, with this room being smaller, the armchairs and settee seemed bulkier. There wasn't a newspaper or a magazine in sight, and every cushion was plumped up and in place. Mollie must be a lot tidier than her scruffy little monkey, or was it that Geoffrey had had a mammoth tidy up before setting off to meet them?

"I won't be a tick," he said. He appeared with a loaded tea trolley covered with a lace-edged pink linen cloth. On it was a teapot and part of the tea service that she recognised. On the lower shelf was a sliced chocolate Swiss roll and dainty triangular sandwiches of tinned red salmon-and-cucumber – decorated with thin slices of tomato. Her mouth watered. Surely he'd not made these? If so, if he got fed up of being a stockbroker, he could always be a chef. She imagined Geoffrey in a tall white hat and a polka-dotted neckerchief and suppressed a giggle.

He called the girls down. They looked so alike, Laura thought, with their identical fair plaits. "You should see Mollie's room, Mum," enthused Claire. She's got a bookcase full of Enid Blyton, and a gramophone, and all the latest records. We're going to play them after tea – aren't we, Mollie?"

In one corner was his gramophone. It was just as Laura remembered it. She recalled how she'd first heard him playing his classical records as she had taken him in his Ovaltine all those years ago – and those wonderful feelings that the music, added to his close proximity had stirred up in her.

The girls demolished more than their fair share of the tea. Geoffrey had indeed made the sandwiches, with Mollie buttering the bread. He brought in ice cream and wobbly red jelly from the fridge. As they tucked in, Laura thought, how wonderful to have a fridge. The birthday cake was a great success. It was four layers of Victoria sandwich mixture, filled with jam-and-mock-cream, and covered in pink icing. As a contrast, she had piped in red, on the top, Mollie's name and *A Happy Birthday*. Giggling, Mollie blew out the twelve pink candles. Laura then cut and handed out the cake. She smiled. When she'd made the cake, both Claire and Ann Hill from next door had vied with each other to clean out the mixing bowls, especially the bowl that had contained the royal icing, proving to her that neither girl were as grown up as they thought they were.

"Mmm," mumbled Mollie eating her slice with her cake fork. She licked her lips. "Can I have another piece, Dad? – after all it is my birthday."

"I suppose so, Miss Greedy-guts," he said indulgently, "and another slice for Claire too, if she wants one?"

Laura cut Mollie and Claire another piece each. Both girls tucked in.

To Laura's disbelief, when Mollie offered to do the washing up, Claire agreed to help her.

Hearing the clatter of crockery from the kitchen, Laura laughed. "How do you manage it?" she asked. "It would take a miracle to get Claire to offer to wash up for me."

He laughed too, and tapped his nose. "I made it a condition of her – and of course, you, too, coming over again."

Laura's heart leapt at the thought of a further visit, for both of them. "Now, that's an idea. I can do the same."

"Why not? It won't do them any harm once in a while to help with the chores."

Mollie put her head round the door. "All done, Dad. We're off upstairs to play records."

*   *   *

The evening passed with a little help from the popular crooner on the wireless, Donald Peers. They sat in opposite armchairs. Laura noticed Geoffrey's eyes straying towards the settee and knew by his expression he was imagining what she was imagining – the two of them rather 'wickedly' seated close together – his arms around her – their lips meeting in a kiss – if only...

They saw each other again and again after that first time.

Laura was washing up. Both girls were upstairs singing along to records.

A glass slipped out of Laura's soapy hands and broke on a plate in the washing-up bowl. "Ouch!" Grimacing, she lifted up her hand, dripping blood.

He threw down his tea-towel. "I've got some plasters in the cupboard. Good thing I did First Aid at school. Here they are. Now, let me see." He gently examined her finger. "It doesn't seem too bad. The bleeding's almost stopped. I'll just dab it with iodine and pop on a plaster. Now this will hurt me more than it does you." He carefully dabbed the finger dry with cotton wool, applied the iodine, wincing as Laura winced. He tenderly

236

covered the cut with a plaster. "There, brave girl!" He didn't immediately release her hand, but with a moan, turned it over, pressing a passionate kiss into the palm. "It's no good, Laura." He drew her towards him. She stiffened, not yielding her body. "No, Geoffrey, no, the girls; if we start this, it'll spoil everything," but already she was weakening. "Yes, yes," he pleaded, "just one kiss, Laura." With a sigh, she yielded, and he drew her trembling body into his embrace. Their lips came together. She thrilled, at the pressure of his on hers. Maybe it was wrong, but it didn't feel it. Geoffrey's kiss melted her completely. Why had she never felt as light as thistledown when Nigel kissed her? She opened her mouth welcoming Geoffrey's exploring tongue. Then she heard the girls descending the stairs.

Laura eased her conscience with the excuse that as Claire and Mollie were keen for them all to spend time together, they'd no choice. How could they refuse them? They went no further than kissing and cuddling. Perhaps, despite everything, she still felt some loyalty to Nigel? Not only that, the girls were always nearby. It was just never the right time, or place.

At Number Three, Trafalgar Terrace the decorating was still outstanding. Laura looked with panic at her calendar – it was less than three weeks before the arrival of the Easter visitors. As the Illuminations which had been suspended throughout the war years weren't due to start up again until the autumn of '48, she needed to have a bumper Easter and Summer season if she wanted to keep her head above water. The reason she was so behind was only due in part to her involvement with Geoffrey. Before Bert could start on her lounge, Doris Field's mental state had worsened. She'd wandered along Lytham Road in only her nightdress. In the end, Bert felt he'd no choice but to let her go into an asylum near to Wesham where she could be cared for properly. Laura wondered what her former mother-in-law would have thought if she'd realised that her hoarded-up money would go to keep her in such a place. She'd not considered it necessary for her or Bert to be in the Sick Club. Laura went with him to visit her. It was a disturbing experience. Shrivelled and shaking, Doris Field hadn't even recognised her own husband. Laura shrank, when clutching at her hand and calling her Dolly, the confused woman asked pathetically why Laura hadn't come to see her before? Dolly, her younger sister, had died of the consumption during the Great War. Laura's sympathy for Bert grew.

Her thoughts returned to her decorating. Bert would have more time now. She could give him a few good square meals and a cut-and-come-again cake to take home in return. When he called in she'd mention her lounge again.

Having sorted the decorating out in her mind, an idea that she'd been mulling over returned. Would the Sandbach Cafe in St Annes be far enough away for her and Geoffrey to take the girls to for afternoon tea? She suggested it on the phone. He was keen. And promised to pick them up the following Saturday on the prom by Station Road.

Laura asked Claire to be careful not to blurt anything out to Nigel about their trips to Bispham. Claire's eyes widened, "Why, Mum? Why wouldn't Nigel want you to be friends with Geoffrey?" Laura struggled to come up with an answer that her innocent child could understand. "It's because men don't like their wives having anything to do with other men – they think them their property" – adding to herself, although they, themselves, can get up to exactly what they please.

The place didn't seemed to have changed. In the discreetly-lit interior, a hum of conversation and clattering cups met them. The waitresses, moving between the tables, in their lace-edged caps and aprons over black satin dresses still had notepads and pencils attached to their waistbands by cords. Was it the same lady scraping away on the violin? They were shown to a table for four and cakes and tea were brought. Memories re-surfaced, warm looks passed between Laura and Geoffrey. They realised

238

their éclairs were untouched. They picked up their tea forks and tried to eat. The girls, however, were a different story. In no time at all, the cake stand was empty.

A waitress asked Geoffrey, "Do you need anything else, sir?"

Before he could reply, Claire put in, "I'd like an ice cream, please."

Laura pursed her lips at her daughter's cheek.

"Why don't you ask your dad if you can have one then?" said the waitress.

"He's not my dad," said Claire. "But I really wish he was."

So that was the lie of the land. She knew Claire had gone off Nigel, but Laura hadn't realised quite how much. Claire knew nothing about divorce, but from what she had said, she might very well welcome the idea of Geoffrey as her stepfather. Especially if it meant then that Mollie would become her sister. But even so, how could she get divorced? A scandal like that would ruin her business. And not only her business – would she ever be able to show her face in church? – even in an Anglican church, divorce was considered a disgrace. She had her suspicions as regards Nigel and women, but even if she could pay for a private detective to get her grounds against him, she didn't think that would be enough. She might still need to prove cruelty as well. Nigel being out more than he was in, and leaving her to cope with the boarding house alone, wouldn't class as 'grounds'. Besides there'd never been a divorce in her family. Her mother would turn in her grave at the thought.

All this was milling around in her head when Geoffrey dropped her and Claire off and they walked the short distance home.

Soon these outings would be a thing of the past. It would be the start of the season. She would be too busy, at least she hoped she would. She visualised in her front window the *No Vacancies* sign. They entered the boarding house. Just as she went to put her hand to the scullery door to push it open, she heard a clink. Could that be Nigel? It wasn't very likely, but he did put in an appearance when he thought he would. Or could it be someone else? There'd been a burglary the previous night, only a street away. She carefully opened the door of the cupboard under the stairs and took out Claire's hockey stick. Telling the wide-eyed and trembling Claire to stay where she was, she moved slowly along the passage, holding the stick up threateningly in front of her. How dare anyone break into her home!

Easing open the scullery door, she sighed with relief when she saw who was sprawled in the wing-chair, a halo of cigarette smoke around him, and a cup of tea and a slice of her cake at his elbow.

Then she saw the expression on Nigel's face.

CHAPTER FOURTEEN

The hockey stick clattered on the lino. "You didn't half give me a fright! I thought you might be a burglar."

Nigel didn't reply.

She picked up the hockey stick. "I'll just put this away."

He stubbed out his cigarette. "Not so fast." He grabbed her roughly and pulled her around to face him. "You've been seen."

"Seen?" she stammered. To think she'd been apprehensive in case Claire should let something slip. And all the time, well, it just proved she'd not been so clever, after all.

"Yes, in a car with a man."

She flinched and struggled in his grasp. "You're hurting me. Anyway, do you care?"

"You're my wife," snarled Nigel.

Tears came to her eyes. "Your property, I suppose? Who saw me?"

"That doesn't matter. Who is he?"

She sensed Claire behind her. "Leave my mum alone! You're making her cry."

"Go to your room. This is nothing to do with you."

Claire's lips tightened. "Shan't!" she retorted rudely. "You can't make me – you're not really my dad. I know how you took Mum's money that time. I couldn't have the new shoes she'd promised me. I had to wear my old ones to school and they squashed my toes, and everyone knows that too small a shoe is bad for growing feet. I could have ended up crippled."

"I don't need to explain myself to a child."

"I'm not a child! I'm big enough to know you're no good. You're just trying to spoil everything. We were better off when you weren't here." Lifting her chin, she added, "Mum's got an admirer. And he's a million times better than you. He cares about us! I'd rather he was my dad than you. Why don't you go away again?"

"Claire! Look, love, you'd best go upstairs. You can read till I come. You've your Enid Blyton book."

Claire hesitated. "If you're sure you'll be all right, Mum."

"Of course I will. Now, off you go, love."

Claire reluctantly went.

Nigel eyed Laura keenly. "And that would suit you? So what have I spoilt? You'd better tell me. How far have things gone between you and this man?"

She blinked away her tears. Should she tell him? Would it make things worse if he knew she'd known Geoffrey in the past? Far longer, in fact than she'd known him. "It isn't like that. He's just the father of Claire's school-friend. It's all quite innocent. The girls are with us all the time." If they hadn't been, things mightn't be so innocent, not when she felt the way she did about Geoffrey, but that wasn't something she was prepared to admit.

"And I'm supposed to believe a cock-and-bull story like that?"

"That's up to you."

"I'm your husband. You've got no right to go gallivanting around with other men."

"And I'm your wife. You seem to have no trouble in forgetting you've a wife when it suits you – I hardly see you for days – how do I know you're not playing around yourself? And where are you when I need some help with the boarding house?"

"You're just trying to put me in the wrong."

"It's true. You know it is. If our marriage has got off on the wrong foot, it's you who's to blame."

He flushed. "Trust a woman to say that! You always put Claire and the boarding house first – I don't reckon in your eyes. Well, I'm not one to blow my own trumpet, but I was decorated.

Let me tell you there's plenty of people, especially women, who think I'm something in this world."

"*Women*, yes!"

"I'm fed up of playing second fiddle to a kid and Northern oiks."

"Northern oiks! How dare you speak about our guests like that. They're our bread and butter. You'd go hungry if it weren't for them! Look, there's security here for me and Claire – a home! I'd be daft to jeopardise that, now wouldn't I?"

"Stop trying to change the subject. We were talking about you and 'him'. The man you insist is just an acquaintance."

"He is!"

"So you say." He seemed to make up his mind. "Look, I'll forget all about you and this chap, if you will."

"What?"

"You heard me. I still feel something for you, Laura. I'd like us to try again to make a go of it. Are you willing?"

She hesitated. Did he really care? It didn't feel like it to her. She recalled their honeymoon night. She had rather let him down – not that she could help it. She'd wanted, then, to make it up to him. Didn't she owe him. At least he'd never raised his hand to her like Prue's Sid.

"Of course I could always sell the boarding house over your head."

She gasped, shocked by his threat. "No, no, not that."

"You agree to try again then?"

"I suppose so."

"Good." He reached out to her, but she pulled back. "First though you must ring this man and tell him that I know, and that everything is at an end between you."

She swallowed. Could she do what Nigel wanted? – forget all about Geoffrey. She didn't want to, but what other choice did she have, marriage was marriage after all. And Nigel had the upper hand. She was the one in the wrong. It wouldn't be easy to tell Geoffrey though. It would be easier to cut her heart out.

"Well?"

"All right then – I'll do it." Perhaps after this, Nigel would give her more support – be a proper husband. Even at this late date, was it possible to save their marriage?

He nodded. "Now, how about something to eat – I'm starving."

She couldn't believe her ears, but she found out the frying pan – bacon and eggs – she'd been so happy when she'd come in – now it felt like her whole world had crumbled. How on earth would she manage to say the words which would break both their hearts? Geoffrey would hate her and rightly so.

*   *   *

Nigel ate the fry-up as if he'd not eaten for weeks – wiping his plate with his bread. Evidently confrontation gave him an appetite. After she'd cleared away, they had a long talk. He promised to turn over a new leaf – spend more time with her and give her a hand with the boarding house. She promised to let him share her bed again after Easter. They'd have to lose a letting room but that couldn't be helped. The hardest part would be Nigel claiming his 'rights' – but she'd face that when she came to it. She dropped a strong hint about the decorating. Would he offer?

To her surprise, he said he'd make a start first thing in the morning.

*   *   *

That night, Laura sobbed herself to sleep. At the thought of never seeing Geoffrey again she felt as upset as she had all those years ago. Claire held Laura in her arms. "Don't worry, Mum, you've still got me."

*　*　*

After Claire had left for school, and Nigel slipped out for the *Telegraph*, Laura phoned up Geoffrey.

With a trembling hand she lifted the receiver – her stomach was churning and she felt cold all over. After what seemed an age, the operator connected them.

"Geoffrey Roberts."

Oh, Geoffrey."

"Laura? – what is it, what's wrong?"

She struggled to control her voice. "It's Nigel – he knows."

The line seemed to go dead.

"Geoffrey?"

"What?"

"We were seen in the car. A neighbour, I guess. We had a terrible row. Nigel made me promise never to see you again. I don't want to, but what else can I do. He is my husband after all."

"I see."

"Is that all you can say, then?"

"What else can I say?"

"Please don't be like this, you must know how I feel about you. These last few weeks have been absolutely wonderful, I've so enjoyed spending time with you."

"And me, you. He's not in the room with you, is he?"

"No, he's not."

"Good. Look, it's all my fault. I should have been strong-willed and not asked for your phone number like I did. It just wasn't fair to you. But when I saw you again, I just couldn't help myself. I realised I still loved you, you see. I'm afraid my need to see you overcame all other considerations."

"Oh, Geoffrey."

"You won't forget me, will you?"

"No, never."

"If ever you need anything, Laura…" he couldn't continue.

He was as devastated as she was. It was obvious that he, too, had been living in a *fools paradise* – imagining that despite her having a husband, they could still be friends.

She heard Nigel whistling, and saying a hasty 'goodbye', replaced the receiver just as the front door opened.

"You've done it, have you? Finished with lover-boy."

She flinched. "Y… yes."

He nodded. "See it stays that way, then."

Shortly afterwards, wearing a shirt and trousers forgotten by a weekend 'knocker' (someone who asks for a room at the door), he enthusiastically began on the lounge. Moving and covering the furniture with dust sheets, he said he expected to be finished in next to no time. Before slipping out to the market, she poked her head around the door to see how he was doing. He was slapping away for all he was worth, but more emulsion seemed to be spraying the newspaper-covered lino, than was being applied to the walls.

An hour later she returned. It seemed very quiet in the lounge. She opened the door and was taken aback. There was no sign of him, and the room was in a real mess. The brushes lay where he'd left them beside the un-lidded tin. Even she knew that they should be washed out after use. She took them to the scullery, soaking them in soapy water. But it was too late, they were ruined.

She told him exactly what she thought of his *turning-over-a-new-leaf* later that evening. She guessed he'd been off gambling again. She was certain he hadn't been looking for work – despite him saying he would. And what good did her telling him off do? He just kept saying he was sorry, and that it wouldn't happen again. It definitely wouldn't happen again as far as any decorating went! She resigned herself to getting more new brushes and asking Bert to help her to finish the job.

Bert was only too pleased to help. With her dressed in the 'knocker's' clothing and with a turban round her head, they completed the task between them.

As Easter approached, despite all Nigel's half-hearted attempts, she wondered how much use he would be in the boarding house? That's when he wasn't missing. Even when it came to the washing up, he was slap-dash; she'd never before needed to replace so much crockery. And as for the potatoes, he peeled them to nothing.

She asked him to clean the bath. He used a whole tin of Vim, saying he thought that the more he used, the cleaner the bath would be. It took her ages to swill it away.

All this clearing up after him exasperated her. After all, she had enough to do already. This marriage didn't seem to be improving, the opposite in fact. If only her parents had been still alive, or she'd a sister, or even an aunt in which to confide her troubles. If Rosemary hadn't gone to the other side of the world, she could have chewed things over with her. But the fact was, that she had no one close enough.

Missing Geoffrey wasn't getting any easier to cope with either. Her thoughts were full of him. She couldn't eat, and despite working herself to a standstill, she couldn't sleep either.

She needed to change some recently bought gym clothes of Claire's. On leaving the school outfitters in town afterwards, she was certain that a man disappearing down a side street was Geoffrey. She dashed after him, her heart in her mouth, she just had to see him. But catching him up, she found him to be a complete stranger. As she stood there endeavouring to get her breath back, a young woman linked arms with the man. Swallowing a sob, Laura went for her bus.

*   *   *

247

Easter came and went in a blur of chores. Soon it was the Whitsun visitors who were expected. She and Nigel now shared a room and a bed, but she found it impossible to respond to him – sex with the wrong man was revolting.

Mrs Hill was down with flu. Laura slipped in to see if she needed anything. Returning, Laura was surprised to discover Nigel speaking heatedly on the telephone. Having his back to her, he didn't realise she was there.

"How did you find out this number?"

Laura listened. Who was he talking to? Could it be one of his gambling cronies?

"What! This sounds like blackmail to me," he said.

Blackmail! What was that all about?

"No, I don't want you coming here! I'll meet you…Yes, I really will… Talbot Square, outside the Town Hall… in about an hour."

He put down the phone.

"Who were you talking to, Nigel?"

He turned, his face flushing. "No one."

"That's a silly thing to say. How could you talk to no one? Was that about a gambling debt? Do you owe someone money?"

He didn't answer.

"It's no good you expecting me to help you find it if you do."

"What!" His face cleared. "Yes, that's it. It was a man I owe ten shillings to. I told him I'd meet him to return it." He put on his trilby. "See you later."

Puzzled, she returned to her chores. Nigel had looked really guilty when he realised she'd overheard him. Who was he was talking to? Was it really some man to whom he owed money? Come to think of it, by his tone of voice, it sounded more as if he was speaking to a woman. Was there more in this than met the eye?

*   *   *

She put her head around the scullery door. "I'm just off to Waterloo Road to see a girl I used to work with. Tom, her brother, was in a Japanese concentration camp. I'm taking him round a bowl of junket." When Claire had been off her food, junket made with rennet and fresh milk was the only thing Laura could tempt her with. If junket did a sickly child good, it should do Tom good too.

Sprawled in the wing-chair, listening to the six o'clock news, Nigel grunted.

The sight of Tom, the once fresh-faced lad, who was now yellow and emaciated, and Peggy, drawn from lack of sleep, distressed Laura. Tom suffered from nightmares, and Peggy would make him hot milk and sit with him. This certainly put Laura's own problems into perspective.

On the way home as she crossed the road at the bottom of her street, she saw Nigel. She frowned. He'd not said he planned on going out. Claire was at her guides' meeting and he'd implied, should she be late back, he would be there when Claire returned. He wasn't alone either. He was with a woman she knew by sight, with bleached shoulder-length hair, a leopard-skin jacket, and a thigh-high slit pencil skirt. During the war, this woman was known as 'Yankee-meat'. They went into a house. Neither noticed Laura. Minutes later, the bedroom curtains were pulled to – and against them, she saw two entwined shadows...

She was frozen to the spot. She'd had her suspicions, but to actually come face to face with them was another thing altogether. Although she knew she wasn't in love with him – never had been, her throat felt tight and her eyes prickled. She had really hoped when he'd returned from the war that their marriage might work. Not only because she needed stability in her life, but also because of the affection she would always feel for Nigel's aunt, Mrs Mullet. Her hopes had turned out to be futile, his ambitions proving to be more important to him than herself, after which, meeting up again with Geoffrey, she'd realised that what she'd talked herself into believing was 'infatuation', had all the time, really been 'love'.

What should she do? She knew she should have it out with Nigel. She couldn't just let him get away with this. Maybe she should tell him to go? But would he do as she asked? He could turn nasty.

She knew what Prue would say. Since Sid's death, Prue had blossomed and become almost a different person due to the interest of Frank, the newsagent. She often called in to see Laura for a cuppa while her children were at school – the last time had been the day before.

Prue placed her cup on the kitchen table. "So he's out again is he, this husband of yours? Leaving you to get everything ready for your visitors. "

Laura had to admit that she was right. "But I have coped before on my own."

"That was different, he was away fighting then. He's here now. He should be on the spot to help you. Bert told me about Nigel's 'latest'. Look, Laura, you told me straight when I needed a talking-to. Well, I'm doing the same for you. Tit-for-tat. I reckon you'd be better off without him. You told me to leave Sid, well I'm telling you to throw Nigel out. He's just going to be a drain on you. You could, couldn't you? The place is in your name?"

Laura didn't know what to say to this. The boarding house was in her name. But Nigel was her husband. Maybe he really could sell it over her head. The law was sure to be on a man's side. After all, it was definitely, a man's world. Always had been, and probably always would be. And even if she wanted to throw him out, it wasn't an easy thing to do. Changing the subject, Laura asked Prue if things were becoming serious between her and Frank?

Prue laughed. "He'd like it to, but I'm not keen. It's better to woo than to wed. Once they put the ring on your finger, the fussing stops."

"You don't really know that. Not all men are like Sid."

"I'd rather not take a chance."

"But what if he wants more than friendship? – loses patience; finds someone else. You could lose him, and your job as well."

"I would miss the money – no matter how much you've got coming in, extra never comes amiss. But I must admit, I would miss Frank more."

Laura went home, Nigel and the woman still very much on her mind. Through the open door of the lounge she caught sight of the white-clothed tables, over which were placed, triangularly, red paper ones, and laid up with crockery and cutlery in readiness for her visitors, each place setting having a paper serviette, folded into a Bishop's mitre.

She looked around admiring the freshly emulsioned white ceiling and sunshine-yellow walls. Everything gleamed, from the well-polished windows to the cutlery on the tables. She should have been so excited, so looking forward to a bumper new season. Why did everything always have to go wrong for her? It was like she was jinxed.

The gate squeaked. Claire already?

The knocker was rapped briskly.

Laura went to the door. It wouldn't be a visitor, she wasn't expecting anyone to arrive until the following day. Before her was a heavily made-up woman of around her own age. She wore high heels, and a black costume with a short skirt, and around her neck was thrown a fox-fur. In her ears were glittery Woolworths' clip-ons, and perched on her hennaed head was a saucy black straw hat with a spotted veil over one eye.

"Yes," said Laura, "can I help you?"

"Are you Mrs Norris?" asked the woman.

"Yes, I am."

"I've got something to say to you that I don't think should be said on the doorstep. It's rather private. Can I come in?"

"What on earth are you on about?"

"I'll explain inside."

"Tell me who you are for a start?"

"My name's Rita Morris."

"Rita Morris? I don't know any Rita Morris."

"Well, you wouldn't. I just thought you ought to be put in the picture."

"What picture? I don't understand?"

"Let's just get out of earshot of your neighbours. You don't want to give them a field day, let them know all your business, I'm sure."

"What business?"

"Nigel."

Without another word Laura led the way along the passage.

"You've got a nice place here," remarked the woman, taking-in the set-up tables as they passed the lounge.

"Thanks."

They entered the scullery.

Rita Morris looked around. "Nigel's not at home, is he?"

Laura grimaced, knowing where he was. "No, he's not. Why do you want to know?"

"Perhaps you ought to sit down, dearie. What I'm going to say will come as a big shock to you. And not a pleasant one either."

Not another one! She'd already had the shock of seeing Nigel arm-in-arm with his bit-on-the-side. "Surely nothing you say can be that bad, can it?"

"It's about the worst thing that can happen to any woman."

"What is?"

"Bigamy."

Laura stiffened. "Bigamy!!" Time stopped for a moment as she tried to get to grips with the word. "You surely don't mean...? You're not telling me that I'm not really..."

"I'm afraid I am. I'm sorry if you're devastated by this, but the man you think is your husband is really my husband. I married him at the Register Office in Abingdon in 1938. So as I married him first, I'm the legal wife."

"What!! You're married to Nigel? He's a bigamist? I can't believe it!" The woman was eyeing her rather strangely, no doubt expecting a flood of tears. Most wives would breakdown at hearing something like this. Whereas she just felt empty inside. "But you said your name was Morris?"

"It is Morris, dearie. That's the name Nigel married me under. When we met he made out his name was Nigel Morris. I'd no reason to disbelieve him. We used to go out in a foursome, my mate Ivy, and his mate, Pete. Pete let slip that Nigel was well-lined. He certainly seemed to have plenty of money. They would drive out to my village and pick us up in Nigel's car. Well, I was sick of slogging my guts out for next to nothing in a biscuit factory. I thought I'd be set up for life if I could hook Nigel. I knew he just wanted his fun without any strings. But I was after a wedding ring and I wouldn't play ball without one. Eventually he gave in. The marriage didn't last long. All I got was a weekend at a boarding house. When I woke up on that final morning, he was gone. Well, I wasn't alone for long – nine months later, I gave birth to his child."

"You mean you've got a kiddy!" This couldn't be happening to her. She couldn't be bigamously married. This happened to strangers that you read about in the *News of the World*. It suddenly came to her. This must be the Rita of the photo – Leonora Norris' gold digger.

"I certainly have, dearie. My Jimmy is eight-years-old. Thank God he's more like me – I couldn't have borne coming

253

face to face with a little Nigel each and every day. Not after what he did! It's not been easy bringing Jimmy up on my own."

"No, I know how hard that is. I've been a widow with a child to bring up."

"Well, at least you would have had a widow's pension."

"That's true. So how did you manage?"

Her mouth twisted. "The way that women have from the beginning of time, dearie. I'd no choice. And you get used to it after a while."

Get used to it! Did Rita Morris mean on her back? She'd never get used to *that*. The thought of sex with every Tom, Dick and Harry just to keep herself and Claire alive made her feel sick. "But surely you tried to find Nigel?"

Rita laughed mirthlessly. "Oh, yes, I tried, but it was hopeless. As well as giving me a false name, he lied that he lived in Didcot."

"Didcot! Oxford! What a worm!"

"There's a lot of them about, dearie. You meet a fair few in my line of business."

Laura shook her head. "So how did you find Nigel? If you couldn't trace him earlier, how did you manage to find him now."

"A lucky fluke I guess. Or maybe, unlucky as far as *our* husband is concerned. One of my gentlemen left a newspaper behind. I used it to light the fire. A photo caught my eye. I'd have known him anywhere. It was him – Nigel Morris with the MM pinned to his cheating chest and a 'wife' tucked away in Blackpool. I've been on that sod's track ever since."

"And now that you've found him, do you want him back? " Laura's voice shook. "I mean, if he is your legal husband, well…"

"Want him back! Not blooming likely! No, us women have got to stick together that's why I came. I just thought you should know the truth. Whether you decide the police should know too, is up to you."

*   *   *

Rita Morris went. Slumped in the wing-chair, Laura felt numb as she waited for Nigel's return.

Claire had been in bed for some hours. She hadn't noticed anything amiss when home from her guides' meeting. Dancing up and down in excitement, she'd told Laura that 'Captain' planned to take them to a Jamboree at the Lakes in July, that there'd be other Blackpool guides companies there, including the 5th Bispham, to which Mollie belonged, and could she go with Ann and all the others? It'd be such a wheeze. They'd be sleeping in a tent, playing games, going on rambles and singing round the camp fire, 'Ging-gang-goolie-goolie-goolie-goolie, watcha'. She gave her mother a rousing chorus of the guides' song.

Laura hardly knew what her reply had been. She must have promised to think about it.

She started, as a key turned in the front door.

Her chest palpitated. He was here!

"I didn't think you'd still be up," he said.

She got to her feet and turned to face him. She flinched. On his neck was a love bite.

"I've had a visitor!"

He yawned. "I didn't think they weren't coming 'till tomorrow."

"Not that sort of a visitor! She didn't want a room. Besides, I've got no vacancies."

He yawned again. "What did she want then?"

She eyed him keenly. "She had something to tell me."

"Tell you? Don't beat about the bush, Laura. I'm whacked."

255

Her lips twisted. "I bet you are! I saw you in the street tonight with your *Scarlet Woman*. But that pales into nothing compared to this. My 'visitor' told me you were her husband. *Her husband*! How dare you marry me when you were already married?"

He looked blank. "What are you on about?"

"I'm on about your wife, Rita Morris."

He visibly paled. "What wife?"

"Don't give me that – she's been here – can't you smell the reek of her scent?"

He sniffed. "I can't smell anything. Anyway, she can't have been – not after she said she wouldn't."

"You admit it then?"

He looked defeated. "I suppose so."

"And that phone call. That was her, wasn't it?"

"Told me if I gave her twenty pounds she'd keep clear. Bloody liar!"

"Twenty pounds! That's a fortune. How come you managed to find such a sum for her? When I've asked you for money you always said you were broke. You've never given me as much as a penny piece towards your keep."

"I had a win."

"Oh, yes. And I know where you got the money to gamble with. You've been up to your tricks again, haven't you? You thought I'd not notice that you'd taken my gold locket."

"My aunt's locket, you mean."

"She left it to me – it's mine! Have you sold it?"

"No." He fumbled in his inside pocket and pulled out a crumpled ticket. "I pawned it. You can get the locket back." He threw the ticket at her – it lay between them on the rag-rug.

"As long as I find the money to pay the pawnbroker for it," Laura said sarcastically.

"What I want to know is how on earth she managed to find me after all these years?"

"That's unimportant. All that matters is that she did. I've known for a long time that you weren't reliable, but I never thought you'd stoop so low as to do something like this. And to marry that poor women under a false name and then desert her. And she with your child! How could you?"

He shrugged. "These things happen. I certainly never thought she'd let herself get 'caught'. I wanted her, that's the top and bottom of it. The sex was so strong that I had to have her. Being a woman I don't suppose you can understand that. Besides Rita was no sweet innocent that I was leading up the garden path, she only wanted me because she thought I'd be a good meal ticket. She didn't love me, any more than I did her."

"That's no excuse. You're despicable!"

"Maybe so, but once I'd had her, I panicked. She just wasn't suitable wife material, not for me. She was so common. Do you know she would scratch herself in public. I couldn't have taken someone like her home. She wouldn't have fitted in."

"Why didn't you get a divorce? It wasn't like you couldn't have afforded it. After all, you were born with a silver spoon. It wasn't as if you were working class – with a pay packet to match."

"I meant to, but somehow or other, I never got round to it."

"But to go through a form of marriage with me. Why did you? That was really despicable!"

"It seemed the only way. I know it's not much of an excuse, but there was a war on and people were being killed in their thousands. I thought, live for the day. Didn't you?"

"Did you just *want* me as you wanted Rita?"

"No, of course not. I did want you, but I was in love with you too."

"You sure it wasn't partly because your aunt encouraged you to marry me? And that you thought if you kept her sweet, you'd come in for the lot?"

"No, of course not – though I do think she tricked me."

"You shouldn't speak like that about Mrs Mullet."

"Why not? She was my aunt, not yours."

"She had the right to do what she wanted with her money."

"You would say that."

"All I know that getting together with you was a terrible mistake. You couldn't even be faithful to me."

"I might have done if you'd really cared for me."

"So it's all my fault, is it?"

"If you'd agreed to go to London."

"If I'd gone with you to London, you'd still have been married to someone else, wouldn't you? You'd still have been a bigamist!"

"But you wouldn't have known then. So what happens now? I'm to go, am I?"

"You could stay until the morning, I suppose – down here!"

"But you'll want me out before your visitors arrive. You'd not want any embarrassment in front of them, would you? No thanks! You needn't do me any favours. I'm going right now. Just give me a few minutes to collect my things." He returned with his attaché case. "All this has worked out brilliantly for you, hasn't it?" he said harshly. "With me off the scene, you'll be able to get back with lover-boy with a clear conscience, *him* that Claire wants to be her dad."

"He's not my lover, not that it's now any of your business!"

Nigel turned at the door. "Will you go to the police?"

She flinched. How long did someone get for bigamy? She'd no idea. She didn't really want to see him in prison, maybe for years, even if he did deserve it. "I should do, but, no, though I'll have to tell my solicitor. I guess he'll inform them. I suggest you put as much distance between yourself and Blackpool as you can."

"I shall. And I shan't be sorry to wipe the dust of this place off my feet either!"

Seconds later, hearing the front door slam, Laura, collapsed into the wing-chair and wept.

CHAPTER FIFTEEN

Laura hardly slept that night as one thought after another churned through her head. What should she do? Should she ring Geoffrey? She wanted to tell him about this unbelievable chain of events, but dare she? Despite him saying he understood – that the blame of what had happened between them was his – he might feel differently after having time to think about it. Maybe he wouldn't want to know her now? After all, it did appear as if she'd chosen Nigel over him. Mightn't he say *serves you right!* and put down the phone? No, despite the hurt she must have caused him, she didn't really think he'd be quite so harsh. He was a gentleman, after all.

When she saw herself in the mirror she was shocked at the black rings beneath her eyes. What on earth would Mrs Rose think? More importantly what would her visitors think? It was Saturday morning and they were due to arrive in an hour or so. She wanted them to think of her boarding house as happy place. She didn't want them to feel there was any sort of atmosphere. They'd come to Blackpool to have a good time, to leave all their everyday cares behind them. They didn't want to see a landlady who looked as if she was about to have a nervous breakdown. Dabbing face powder thickly beneath her eyes, she outlined her lips with a bright lipstick and hoped for the best.

Claire was pleased, if surprised to know that Nigel was gone for good. Laura, reluctantly explaining the reason for him leaving, asked her not to breathe a word of what had happened, to Ann, or anyone else.

Tucking into corn flakes, Claire looked puzzled. "But surely it's best everyone knows as soon as possible, Mum. Especially a certain person. After all, it wasn't your fault, was it? You didn't lie to get married. It was Nigel."

Claire was right. Her daughter was growing up into a sensible young woman. If this had happened to anyone else, Laura would have pitied them. Still all the same...

"Everyone will be on your side, Mum."

"Will they?" Muck sticks? Doris Field wouldn't have been on her side. Far from it! When she was well she would have delighted in putting all the blame on her. It suddenly struck her that with there having been no second marriage, the woman was still very much her mother-in-law.

"Course they will. It was real mean of him to trick you like he did. Mean to his proper wife too – and his little boy. Mollie's dad wouldn't never do something so underhand. He's honest and reliable too, and if he promises something he does it. Not like Nigel. I'm glad he's gone. And Mollie will be when I tell her. Perhaps now, you and her dad can get together? That's what Mollie and I would both like."

"So you can be sisters, I suppose?"

"What's wrong with that. You know I've always wanted a sister. You'd like that too, for you and Mollie's dad to get together, wouldn't you? I'm right, aren't I? Go on, admit it!"

Laura reddened.

Claire's spoon rattled into her cereal dish. "Well, don't then!"

Dumping the dishes in the sink, Laura turned on the tap. She might like it, but would Geoffrey? Had she any chance as far as he was concerned now? Or had her old fashioned ideas about marriage being marriage, lost her, her only chance of happiness?

"See you later, Mum." Claire turned at the door. "And don't worry, it will all turn out for the best."

"Where are you off to?"

"I told you yesterday, Mum. Don't you remember? Ann and I are going to the Pleasure Beach – to the Fun House."

261

"Well, behave yourself then," she answered, her mind already centred on the lunch she was to prepare for her visitors. If she knew her daughter, Claire would be back when she was hungry, no doubt getting in the way and raiding the pantry for titbits, despite being told, time and time again, not to spoil her appetite.

The rest of the day was hectic. When Laura wasn't stirring the pans on the stove, she was answering the door and taking her guests upstairs to show them to their rooms. It wasn't until after the clearing away of the evening meal and the departure of Mrs Rose that she had a spare moment to even consider ringing Geoffrey.

Laura went into the hall and eyed the squat black telephone. Dare she pick up the receiver and ask the operator for his number? How would he react to what she had to tell him? How could she bear it, if after hearing her out, instead of showing sympathy and saying that everything could return to how it was before between them, he didn't respond.

Trying to convince herself that this wouldn't be so, she reached out and with a trembling hand, lifted it and put it to her ear.

"Number please."

Shakily she complied. She heard ringing at his end. It sounded echoey. Was the house empty? Had he and Mollie gone away for Whitsun? Claire hadn't mentioned anything about it. Still, it could have been a spur-of-the-moment thing. Disappointed, she replaced the receiver and returning to the scullery, sank into the wing-chair.

There was no point in trying to ring Geoffrey again until after Whitsun. By then though, Laura found she just couldn't be the one to make the first move, despite all Claire's urging, and insisting she was being silly. Geoffrey knew that Nigel was gone. Mollie, Claire told her, had soon put her dad in the picture. So why couldn't he ring her? Why couldn't he be more sympathetic?

The phone stayed silent. There appeared to be a stalemate between them.

As soon as she could, Laura made an appointment to see her solicitor about Nigel. Mr Clegg didn't show all that much surprise at her disclosure. She guessed that few things surprised solicitors. Her marriage had never really been a marriage. She would be a free woman officially in the near future. Mr Clegg told her that he'd have to inform the police as what Nigel had done was against the law. But still they had to find him to enforce it. Laura didn't really want to see him in prison. She didn't hate him, she just didn't want to be married to him!

She overheard Claire and Mollie on the telephone, the two girls were trying to cook up plans to get her and Geoffrey together. Laura wanted to get back with Geoffrey but she didn't see how it could be done. And the more time that went by, the harder it became to do anything about it.

As the season got into full swing, she hardly had time to breathe, let alone worry about her personal life. Some of her guests were a real trial. One middle aged honeymoon couple stayed locked in their room for the whole week. She'd made the mistake of letting the husband take up meals to his bride who was supposed to be poorly. When they went, and she cleared the room, she found cigarette ends everywhere – some of them had even been stubbed-out on the wallpaper. Empty whisky and beer bottles were under the bed. And in the wardrobe, was a whip of the type which kids whipped tops with.

Another visitor left shoes outside his door to be polished, and was indignant next morning that they'd not been attended to.

Thankfully, most of them weren't so demanding. In fact, many of her visitors were just like one of the family.

This season, Claire helped with the waiting-on for extra pocket money and proved quite a feature in a little frilly white cap and apron. It was obvious she was going to be a good mixer, which would help her in future with her chosen career.

It was July when full of excitement, she went off to her guides' Jamboree – camping near Lake Windermere, Mrs Rose's eldest girl, Meg, coming in to replace Claire.

Laura's last words to her had been, "You won't forget to send me a postcard, will you, love?"

"Course not, Mum." She hastily dropped a kiss on Laura's cheek and slinging her haversack over her shoulder, dashed off to join Ann, waiting outside.

Towards the end of the week, just as they were serving the midday meal, the phone shrilled.

Shaking her head in exasperation, Laura thought, *Some people have no consideration. What a time to ring up to make a booking!*

But it wasn't someone wanting to book a room, it was Claire's 'Captain'; and rather hysterical.

"What is it? What's wrong?"

"Oh, Mrs Norris,' came shakily from the other end of the line, "It's Claire, Ann, and Mollie, well, they've…I don't know how to tell you this, but they've disappeared."

"Disappeared!"

"Yes, I'm sorry."

An icy sensation ran up Laura's back. "How? When?"

"We were on a ramble, and they, well, somehow they wandered off. About six hours ago, now. One minute they were there, the next there was no sign of them. We've informed the police, of course, and there's a search party out looking for them."

"Police! Search party! I'm coming. I'll get the train immediately." Laura ripped off her apron.

"Don't panic. I'm sure there's no need. What about your boarding house? Your visitors? It's your busiest time, isn't it?"

"It's Claire that matters. And the other girls too, of course. I need to come."

"I understand. Look, don't go rushing off to get a train." Laura heard a voice in the background, and then another woman spoke. "Mrs Norris," she said. "I'm Freda Foster, Captain of the 5th Bispham. I've already rung Mr Roberts about Mollie. He's feels exactly as you do. He said he knows you, and that he'll ring you to say he'll pick you up in his car. The other mother, too, of course. I believe she lives next door to you. We're just going to ring her."

Dazed, Laura put down the phone. But hardly had she done so than it rang again.

"She picked up the receiver. "Yes?"

"It's me, Laura," said Geoffrey. "You've heard, have you?"

"Yes. I'm off to get the train…"

"Don't! You don't need to. I'll pick you and your neighbour up. I'll be with you as soon as I can. And don't worry, they'll probably have found them safe and sound, and making light of all the trouble that they've caused by the time we get there."

"Oh, God, I hope so. They could have fallen in Lake Windermere and been drowned. Or been taken off by some dirty old man in a raincoat."

"That's not very likely is it, Laura. Three strapping twelve-year-olds wouldn't be easy to cope with. And Claire and Mollie can swim, can't they?"

"Yes, and I think Ann can too. But…"

"There you go then, they'll be fine, I'm certain of it."

Partly consoled, she hurried off to explain the situation to Mrs Rose. It was good of Geoffrey to offer her and Mrs Hill a lift to the Lakes. But why did it have to take an emergency before he could ring?

Mrs Rose turned from the sink. "Don't you worry about a thing, Mrs N, me and my Meg will hold the fort till you get back."

As Laura hastily tidied herself, a white-faced and flustered Mrs Hill appeared. "I've left Hill in charge, something I'd not normally do, but needs must."

A car horn hooted. Geoffrey? Calling goodbye to Mrs Rose and Meg, she and Mrs Hill hurried outside. It was Geoffrey. Laura got in beside him, Mrs Hill settling herself on the back seat. They set off. With Mrs Hill present nothing personal could be said during the journey. Besides they were too tense at what they might learn when they got there for any chit-chat. As the car drew up to a field containing a score or more of tents, Claire's 'Captain', a plumpish woman in her fifties, who wore a guiders' navy beret, and a light blue blouse, covered with badges, over a navy skirt, turned with an apologetic look on her face, from stirring a pan on a primus stove. From a tent stepped another middle-aged woman, whom Laura guessed was Mollie's 'Captain'. When they got out of the car, both 'Captains' and several guides crowded around them.

Claire's 'Captain' stretched out her hands helplessly. "I'm really sorry, but there's no news of the girls as yet."

"No news." Laura choked on her disappointment. She'd talked herself into believing that they would find them, looking rather embarrassed at all the fuss they'd caused, when they got to the camp.

"But we're doing all we can. Come and sit down, have a cup of tea."

"Tea! I couldn't!" She turned to Geoffrey. "I want to go and look for Claire myself. You want to look for Mollie, don't you?"

"No, no, Mrs Norris. It's best to leave it to the experts. You and Mr Roberts don't really know your way around. We might end up having to send a search party out for you!" She laughed awkwardly.

"I don't care. I must go!"

"And I'll go with Mrs Norris," said Geoffrey.

"I can't," said an agonised Mrs Hill, easing her weight rather precariously onto a camp stool, before being carefully handed a brimming beaker by one of the guides. "My legs would never take trekking for miles over rough ground. I'd better wait here for you."

Minutes later, Laura and Geoffrey set off on foot with a map. Neither of them had any real idea about where to look, but they just had to go. Laura kept thinking terrifying thoughts. What if the girls were lying injured somewhere? Or worst still, dead? Without Claire, her life wouldn't be worth living. Even getting Geoffrey would be ashes to her. If only her parents were still alive. At least then, she'd have them. For years, she'd had no other family but Claire. She just couldn't lose her! She couldn't! She sniffed, and wiped her eyes with the back of her hand. She glanced at him. His face was white and set. He was feeling as bad about his Mollie.

Crossing a field, they climbed over a stile. As he helped her over, his close proximity, and the emotion that sparked between them, was a comfort. At least, they were in this together. He was going through what she was going through. The stile was surrounded by bramble bushes. Laura's skirt got caught up on them and when she tried to release herself, she ripped the material. They wandered around for what seemed like hours, seeing no sign of anyone, apart from a man, who with his rough-haired Collie, was driving a flock of sheep along a grassy track. "Excuse me," Laura called out hopefully, she and Geoffrey pressing themselves into the hedgerow to avoid the sheep. "Have you seen three girls in guides' uniforms?"

The man, his trouser-legs tied up with string, shook his head. "Nay, lass."

It was hopeless. Her legs were not only stinging after stepping in nettles, but aching, too. She was glad that at least she'd had the forethought to put on flat-heeled shoes.

"Look!" said Geoffrey. "They must have come this way."

It was a scrap of navy-blue material on a bush. Her heart leapt. Eagerly they searched ahead, but there was no sign of anyone.

Despondently, with him helping her along, they reluctantly retraced their steps. The sun had gone behind a cloud and it was threatening rain. She wiped her cheek. They had failed. Nothing mattered any more, not the boarding house – nothing!

By sheer good luck, they reached the tents – to be met by a beaming 'Captain', at her heels, a sheepish Claire, Mollie and Ann.

The sun came out – the dark clouds banished!

"They're all right! They turned up themselves, just after you went to look for them. They said they got lost and wandered around for ages. They were tired and ravenously hungry, but unhurt, except that Mollie has sprained her wrist. I put a cold compress on it and bandaged it up. It should be as right as rain in a couple of days."

Laura, with tears in her eyes, hugged Claire to her. "Don't ever put me through something like this again."

"Sorry, Mum. I didn't think."

"I can't tell you how relieved I was when I saw them," said Mrs Hill, struggling up from her camp stool.

All three girls hung their heads.

"It was my fault," admitted Claire. "I suggested to Mollie and Ann that we play hide-and-seek. I thought we'd easily catch the others up afterwards."

"But we couldn't, they'd gone," said Ann.

"We were chased by a bull, Dad," said Mollie, a big black brute, with blazing red eyes.

"Yes," laughed Claire, "you should have seen her run, Mum."

"Well, you ran too."

"We all did," said Ann.

"So how did you hurt your wrist, Mollie?" asked Geoffrey.

"When we clambered over a fence to escape. I fell onto my wrist. It hardly hurts now though."

Claire wrinkled her nose. "What's that stink, Mum? You've stepped in something!"

Laura looked down. There was muck from a cow pat on her shoes.

After what had happened, they decided to take the girls back to Blackpool with them. The others were returning anyway the following day. But though the tensions of the outward journey had lifted, with Claire, Mollie and Ann squashed beside Mrs Hill in the back of the car, chattering and giggling about their adventure, it was still impossible for Laura and Geoffrey to talk freely.

She hoped that this dash up to the Lakes might have broken the ice between them, and that at last, he would ring.

To her disappointment, the only phone calls were bookings. Evidently, he still expected her to make the first move.

The season continued. It was a great relief to Laura when she waved off the last of her guests. It was nice to see them come, but it was also good to see them off and to be able to finally shut her door and take the 'vacancies' sign out of the window. She was looking forward to some time to herself. She'd done well financially. Better than she could have expected. She'd also firm bookings from many of the guests, for the following year.

But with an empty house, the thoughts of Geoffrey that she had been too busy to dwell on, returned with a vengeance. If only… but she supposed it was too late now. He would surely have found consolation. Mollie mightn't know everything.

Laura refused to acknowledge the considerable length of time he'd not bothered to find a lady friend before they'd met again at the school.

It was a happy release, Laura decided, when Doris Field died in her sleep, not only for the confused woman, but for Bert. Though Laura couldn't help but be concerned about him being on his own.

The funeral was a quiet affair – with not many mourners – the deceased not being popular. Bert had brought his wife home to lie in state in their front room – so that friends and relatives, such as there were, could pay their respects.

Laura and Claire attended the funeral, Laura helping Prue prepare the food for the meal, and setting it out in readiness for after the internment. Seeing the coffin, with a wreath on top, being carried out by the undertakers to the waiting hearse, it seemed unbelievable that she'd never again hear that sharp voice laying down the law. With the vicar leading, they walked, two by two, towards the waiting grave. Bert, with Prue. Laura, following on behind with Claire. Bert seemed to be holding up well, even when throwing the customary handful of dirt onto the coffin, but what was he feeling? After all, he and Doris Field had not only had a lifetime together, but also a child. Could he be really upset deep down? She hoped not.

One evening, some weeks after this, Bert appeared on his bicycle, in his basket, a bunch of yellow chrysanths for Laura. To her surprise, he was not only wearing a collar and tie and a brand new cap, but also had a twinkle in his eyes that had certainly never been there before. As she served him with tea and cake, he explained, rather bashfully, what had put the spring back in his step. "You remember, don't you, Laura," he said, "as how I once told you that before I was married to Mrs Field, I was keen on a pretty little thing in the next street to where I was living."

She nodded. She recalled only too well the occasion when Bert had confided how he'd missed out on the girl he'd really wanted because of the scheming of Doris Field.

"Well," he continued, beaming, "I still can't believe it!"

"Believe what?"

"I've met up with Florrie again."

"Florrie?"

"Yes, the girl I was sweet on. She's as pretty as ever. Her hair's gone grey, mind you, but she's still the same Florrie."

Laura choked on her mouthful of cake and Bert had to pat her back. She recovered herself. "Go on," she urged, "tell me all about it." Surely Cupid's arrow couldn't have struck someone of Bert's age?"

"Well," he continued, "I was hawking my flowers as usual. I knocked at this house in St Annes Road, where the Missus mostly has a bunch off me, when to my astonishment the door was opened by Florrie of all people. You could have knocked me down with a feather. Her, too, I reckon. We recognised each other immediately. And to cut a long story short, she asks me in for a cuppa. It turns out she's now a widow. They'd moved to Manchester, her and her hubby. He died six months back. Florrie'd only returned to Blackpool a week earlier to make her home with her son and his wife."

"So when did all this happen?"

"Some ten days ago. Me and Florrie have started 'walking out'. Well, you can't waste time at our age, can you? We mightn't have a great deal left." He frowned. "You don't think people will talk, think it's a bit quick like, me courting?"

"Of course not. You're very well liked. Everyone will be only too pleased for you – will say, *jolly good luck to the both of you.*" Some small-minded people would talk behind his back, human nature being like it was. Still, as long as he didn't hear them. And as it was said: *when they were talking about you, at least they weren't talking about someone else!*

271

Bert looked relieved. "I was wondering if it would be okay if I brought Florrie along to meet you and Claire?"

"Of course you can. You surely know you don't need to ask. Come round tomorrow evening. I can't tell you how happy I am to hear about all this." If anyone deserved a bit of love and companionship, Bert did, especially after the life Doris Field had led him.

He rose and put on his cap. "Till tomorrow then."

The following evening, it was Claire who answered the door. It was a bashful Bert and Florrie. Coats were taken, and hands shaken. Laura took to Florrie immediately. With a nervous smile, she gave Laura a bunch of pink and white carnations and Claire, a bar of chocolate (no doubt, her week's sweet ration). Laura tried to put Florrie at her ease. Bert had been right when he said she was still pretty. She was. Despite being in her sixties. She'd gone to some trouble with her appearance. The red rosebuds trimming the brim of her cream straw hat matched her red floral frock. It was heart-warming to Laura to hear the loving way that Florrie spoke to Bert, the way she deferred to him. But what pleased Laura more than anything was learning that Florrie's son, Tom was a keen football supporter. He and Bert had hit if off straightaway – Bert having played in his youth. Tom had got tickets for the two of them for next Saturday's local Derby, Blackpool and Preston. Bert was full of it. Laura reflected that Bert going to a football match would have been out of the question when married to Doris Field. Such things, to that grasping woman, were a waste of money.

That night, as she undressed, thoughts of Geoffrey returned. What he would have thought of Bert's romance? she wondered.

* * *

The newspapers were full of the forthcoming marriage of Princess Elizabeth to her cousin, Prince Philip of Greece, which was to take place on the 20th of November 1947 in Westminster Abbey.

Laura put down the *Gazette* and shook her head. "A Royal Wedding'll cost this country a pretty penny – money we can't really afford. Her dress alone will cost hundreds of pounds. Still, I suppose we could all do with a happy and glittery occasion after all the grimness and shortages."

Claire looked up from her homework. "Miss Sheldon's said that we're to celebrate the princess's wedding with a special school concert. Each class is going sing a traditional English song in turn. Auditions are going to be held to choose which of us will sing a solo. You'll come to the concert, won't you, Mum? – especially if I'm chosen to sing on my own."

"Of course, I'll come – whether you do a solo, or not. You surely don't need to ask. But won't you be nervous if you've to sing all by yourself?"

"I don't think so. Anyway, I might not be chosen. There's thirty-five of us in the class."

"You've got such a lovely clear voice, dear. I've heard you singing in the bathroom."

"The bathroom! Everyone's voice sounds good in there. Even yours, Mother."

"Cheeky!"

"You'll not be the only parent at the concert," said Claire slyly.

"I suppose you mean Mr Roberts? Well, obviously, I'd expect that. Look, it's no good you and Mollie trying to match make, that's all over." Did she really believe that? In a little corner of her heart didn't she still hope for the opposite?

Claire laughed, bending once more to her homework. "We'll see, we'll see."

A week later, she told Laura, as she skipped around her, that she had indeed been chosen to sing a solo, *Barbara Allen.*

As September drew to a close, Claire could be heard rehearsing non stop, and not just in the bathroom, in readiness for the big occasion.

*   *   *

It was Guy Fawkes night that took the pressure off Laura. She was able to forget for a while the approach of the concert and how she would cope with coming face to face with Geoffrey. For the first time since 1939, a bonfire and fireworks display was to be held in Trafalgar Terrace. All the neighbourhood children, including Claire and Ann, were bubbling up with excitement. The bonfire, built by the older boys on nearby waste ground was to be the biggest ever, with lopped-off tree branches, rotten wood from old chicken runs and rabbit hutches and any rubbish that could be found. The heaviest contribution were abandoned railway sleepers. A real boon for the flames! All this was carried by the boys' on their soapbox trolleys to the now towering bonfire. Laura made a guy by stuffing rags into a shirt and trousers provided by Ann's father, Mr Hill; sewing them together and adding a head made out of newspaper stuffed into a brown paper bag. On it, Claire painted a face with a black moustache and a big red nose. The fire was to be lit at six-thirty when all the dads were back from work.

Claire bolted her tea, eager to get outside. Laura made her wrap up warmly in extra jumpers, scarves and gloves. Mr Hill lit the bonfire by igniting a paraffin-sodden rag that he'd shoved between the timber. Everyone cheered as it caught alight. The children's faces glowed with the heat as they leapt around, their eyes wide as the sky now lit up with multicoloured fireworks, Catherine wheels spun crazily on fence posts, and the poor old guy blazed merrily away to meet his fiery end. Hot chestnuts,

274

roasted in the embers, and tossed from glove to glove were soon scoffed. The children munched their way through Mrs Hill's parkin, and Laura's toffee apples, the gooey toffee sticking to their teeth. Parents put potatoes on long sticks into the fire. All this was washed down by Mrs Hill's home-made lemonade. Everyone had a good time, grown-ups and children alike. But Laura's toes were frozen and despite the bottle of stout provided by Mr Hill, she wasn't sorry to get back inside and toast her legs by her own hearth.

*   *   *

The papers had been full of the Royal Wedding. The Princess's beautiful ivory gown, her radiant loveliness, the rose petals which showered the bride and groom, the cheering crowds who lined the route and waited at the gates of Brooklands to welcome them on their honeymoon.

In Blackpool there'd been bunting everywhere and street parties. Neither Claire nor Ann had felt themselves too grown up to sit at the trestle tables with the younger children and gorge themselves on jelly, blancmange, cakes and ice cream. Talbot Square had been packed with flag-waving revellers as the Mayor and Mayoress in full regalia had come out on the Town Hall balcony to acknowledge their cheers before retiring to a slap-up celebratory banquet behind closed doors!

And now it was the eagerly awaited evening of the concert, and the parquet floor was solid with chairs and people, and under the strip lighting, the hall of Harold School was brilliant and festive with vases of white, yellow and copper chrysanths on the high window sills. There was a sense of animation in the air.

Despite the cushion, Laura shifted uncomfortably on her seat. Next to her were Bert and Florrie. The rafters above were criss-crossed with strings of Union Jacks, and suspended over

275

the stage was a blue cloth banner emblazoned in gold with, GOOD LUCK, ELIZABETH AND PHILIP. To the right of the stage, a grey-haired mistress was warming-up on the piano. Laura didn't think she would want to be a teacher, to have to cope with so many adolescent girls. One was enough for her, too much sometimes! From behind the curtained-stage came thuds and whispers. She turned her head to the sea of faces behind her. The ticket sales had gone well, in fact, Claire said, they could have sold twice as many. Laura's chest thudded, *he* was there, some way back, and looking straight at her. Flustered, she turned away and studied the programme. Would he come over? Was there time before the start of the show? She glanced at her watch. If he did, what could she say to him?

The pianist played a fanfare of chords. The curtains opened jerkily to reveal a shuffling, nervous semicircle of eleven-year-olds with fixed smiles. She relaxed, this wasn't Claire's class. Miss Sheldon came to the front of the stage. "Thank you all for coming," she said, "I'm sure we'll have a very enjoyable evening. The girls have been rehearsing and rehearsing, and I'm sure you'll agree with me that the end result will have justified all the work that both children and teachers have put into it. I won't say anymore except that the First Year girls will start off our little concert with *Begone! dull Care.*"

There was an enthusiastic round of applause:

In time to the piano the girls piped:

"Begone! dull Care... I prithee be-gone from me..."
Begone! dull Care... You and I shall nev-er agree..."

Laura's thoughts drifted once more to Geoffrey. In the interval, tea and biscuits were to be served in the classroom to the side of the hall. Perhaps she could manage to get in the queue behind him? He'd have to acknowledge her then. But what if he didn't? She didn't think she could bear the disappointment.

> "…my wife shall dance and I shall sing,
> So merrily pass the day,
> For I hold it one of the wisest things…
> To drive dull care a-way."

Loud applause brought Laura to herself. Year One's song was over and the curtains were swinging-to. They opened again almost immediately on Claire and Mollie's class. After they'd sung *Come, Lasses and Lads*, the teacher announced: "And now Claire Field will sing for us *Barbara Allen*.

Laura sat on the edge of her seat holding her breath. What if Claire should become tongue-tied? Her poor girl would be devastated. She willed her not to fail.

Claire, trembling slightly, stepped out to the front, and curtsied prettily, before taking a deep breath and singing:

> "In Scarlet town, where I was born,"
> There was a fair maid dwelling…"
> "Made ev-ry youth cry 'well-a-way',
> Her name was Bar-b'ra Allen."

Her daughter's voice was sweet and clear. Without stumbling, Claire sang the final verse:

> "Farewell, she said, ye virgins all,
> And shun the fault I fell in;
> Henceforth take warning by the fall
> Of cruel Barbara Allen."

The applause was deafening and women seated near to Laura, were also dabbing their eyes.

The curtain closed for the Interval. As Laura was leaving her seat, followed by Bert and Florrie, she found Claire beside her.

"You were brilliant…"

Ignoring her praise, Claire urged, "Come on, Mum," putting her hand under Laura's elbow, and hurrying Laura towards the Refreshment Room. Looking across, her eyes widened at the sight of Mollie, who was taking Geoffrey in the same direction. They came together in the doorway.

"Hello," they both said awkwardly.

Small tables covered with embroidered tea cloths had been set out invitingly. At one end of the room two trestle tables were covered with white cloths. One held plates of iced cakes, jam tarts and biscuits, and on the other, beside a pile of thick white saucers, was an array of matching cups, over which two teachers – one of them Miss Darling, were pouring from huge enamel tea pots.

"Find a table, and sit down together," ordered Claire. "We'll get your tea and biscuits, won't we, Mollie?"

"Yes, we certainly will." She eyed her father sternly. "It's time you and Claire's Mum sorted a few things out. We're both fed up with living with a parent who's forever moping. You're worse than a couple of kids."

"We'd best do as we're told," Geoffrey said in mock terror.

"I suppose we had." Laura's lips twitched.

He turned to Mollie. "Here!" He handed her a half-a-crown. "Get some lemonade and whatever you fancy for yourself and Claire."

Her face lit up. "Thanks, Dad."

Mollie placed their tea and biscuits before them, and then scuttled off to join a grinning Claire, Bert and Florrie on the other side of the room.

Laura fingered the edge of the tablecloth. One of them had to start the conversation off and it didn't look like he was going to. "I thought after we'd gone together to fetch the girls back from the Lakes, you'd ring me. Why didn't you?"

"Why didn't you ring me?" he asked gently. "And after you'd found out about Nigel."

She hesitated. "I wanted to. In fact I did try, but you weren't home. The longer I left it, the harder it became. I was frightened. You'd sounded so upset when I told you that he'd insisted I end it with you."

"Well, of course I was. But I understood your position – I couldn't really expect you, however strong your feelings were for me, to agree to leave your husband. To appear the 'guilty-party' in a divorce. As a divorcee you would have lost your good name – been looked down on by everyone. It takes an especially strong-minded person to go through with something like that. Maybe one day things will be different and no one will turn a hair. At least, let's hope so. And I never held it against your decision to try again with your marriage – give him another chance – you're that kind of woman. And I wouldn't really like it if you weren't. I love you exactly as you are."

Her chest fluttered. "You do!"

He reached out and took her hand. "Of course I do! You know I do. Have done ever since we met. What about you?"

She smiled happily. "Yes. I'll admit when I never heard from you I tried to forget you. After all, I'd thought you'd forgotten me. I tried to convince myself that I could love Nigel, but I never could, not really." She knew in her heart of hearts that it never would have worked with Nigel, even if he'd not turned out to be a bigamist. They had different goals. They were drifting further and further apart. She was sure he would have gone off in the end, anyway.

"Oh, Laura."

From the school hall, came the sound of a hand bell.

"Come on, Mum," called Claire from the doorway, "the second half will be starting again at any minute."

"But I've not drunk my tea." She took a hasty gulp and pulled a rueful face, "It's stone cold!"

Geoffrey laughed. "Neither have I. Look, why don't you sit with me to watch the rest of it?"

"I'd like that."

They left the room hand-in-hand. Florrie dug Bert in the ribs, and with a knowing grin, he changed places with Geoffrey. The rest of the evening passed in a blur. Her eyes kept straying from the stage to him, hardly able to believe that they were back together. He offered everyone a lift home – dropping Bert and Florrie off first. Laura asked him and Mollie in. As she reached for the kettle, Claire suddenly insisted that Mollie should come next door with her to see Ann.

"But it's late," objected Laura, "she might be in bed."

Claire shook her head. "No, she won't."

"I still don't think." The scullery door closed, followed by the front door.

Geoffrey smiled. "If ever I saw a put-up-job, this is it. I think our girls have decided to give us some time alone together."

Laura smiled too. "I'm inclined to agree with you."

"Well, should we take advantage of it?"

Their eyes met. She flushed. Her thoughts returned to what had almost happened between them at the St Annes boarding house. Then it would have been wrong, despite her strong feelings for Geoffrey, but now lovemaking between them would be so right. Their lips met like two amorous butterflies. Emotion swept through her. They sank to the floor. He kissed her throat in little butterfly kisses, moving lower. He unzipped the back of her dress. He kissed her again as his fingertips began to explore the silky flesh of her back. At his touch warmth surged strongly through her casting any feelings of embarrassment. She moaned as he unfastened her bra, releasing her breasts. His hand moved sideways and covered one of them and he began to tease the nipple.

Laura squirmed with desire.

She felt a hand reach beneath her skirt to caress her thigh. "Claire, Mollie," she murmured, "what if...?"

He kissed her again, zipping up her dress.

She disentangled herself and rose to her feet. "I'm sorry, I'd have liked to, but, the girls!"

"I understand."

"Disappointed?"

"I am. But it can't be helped."

She nodded.

"Will you marry me, Laura?"

She grinned. "I never thought you'd ask."

The front door opened. "Here they are," said Laura.

A tap came at the scullery door. "Have we given you long enough?" grinned Claire.

Laura and Geoffrey tried to put on straight faces, but failed. "You're a couple of little minxes, that's what you are."

"I don't know what you mean."

"I don't either," said Mollie.

"If I believed that, I'd believe anything. Now, you two, stop dithering about and come on in." He smiled at Laura. "We've got something we want to tell you."

Their faces lit up. "Is it what we think it is?" asked Claire.

"It certainly is. I've asked your mother to marry me, and she's agreed."

"Yippee!" cheered Claire, "Yippee!" cheered Mollie, and seizing each other's hands, they whirled around the scullery, "we're going to be sisters!"

Geoffrey's eyes met Laura's. *And we're going to be married lovers*, his said.

CHAPTER SIXTEEN

Laura adjusted the knot in Geoffrey's tie, and kissing him, handed him his briefcase. "Goodbye, darling, see you tonight."

"I wish we could go back to bed," he said, bringing her closer.

Wriggling away, she laughed. "Shush! The girls will hear. We're not on honeymoon now."

"So what? I'm no less keen."

"Me neither. But as you well know I've got a driving lesson at ten and there's a pile of washing up!"

Claire and Mollie appeared, still munching.

Laura shook her head. "It's a wonder you two don't get indigestion."

They reached for their coats. "Bye, Mum, bye, Dad, see you later." The door slammed behind them.

She waved Geoffrey off. Through the window as she washed up she surveyed the garden – a greenfinch fluttered down to the bird table. The apple tree which had been bare the first time she'd seen it was now laden with Granny Smiths'. This weekend, she and Geoffrey intended to pick the apples, and after keeping some to eat, they would wrap the remainder and place them in boxes in the attic. It would be good to have an apple in December, even if its skin was wrinkly.

New people were now running Number Three Trafalgar Terrace. Laura, Mrs Geoffrey Roberts since April 1948, was happy and contented with her family in Bispham. For the first time ever she was able to do all the things that she'd never had time to do before. She was due to take her driving test in a fortnight. She'd also bought herself a Singer Sewing machine and was running up dresses for herself and the girls. But what she was enjoying the most was Geoffrey taking her dancing at the Tower Ballroom. Last Saturday, feeling like a princess in her own handiwork, a pink chiffon, lace-edged dance-frock, she'd been swung around the glittering ballroom, humming the intoxicating music – held tenderly in her husband's arms.

Life indeed was good.

Geoffrey had put the money from the sale of the boarding house into shares for her. At the moment, all she wanted was to be a good wife and mother, but later on, he suggested, she might fancy trying her hand again at a business – perhaps a little cafe in the town centre, somewhere where she'd pick up the passing trade. As she put the dishes away, it occurred to her that as she was becoming so skilled at dressmaking, the business might turn out to be a high-class boutique – only time would tell.

Their wedding at Holy Sepulchre Church had been a memorable day. Laura in a cream-taffeta costume, with a red rosebud corsage pinned to the jacket, and matching hat and gloves, had been given away by a well-turned-out Bert. He wore a suit from the Fifty-Shilling-Tailors, which Florrie, smiling in the front pew, helped him to choose. Claire, Mollie and Ann, with blue ribbons in their hair, and carrying posies of sweet peas, were bridesmaids in matching ice-blue taffeta dresses. Geoffrey looked handsomer than ever in a well-cut Savile Row suit and silk cravat, fastened with a plain pin. His side of the church was packed with his colleagues from Osborne and Parkinson. His best man, his cousin Hermione's, husband. On the bride's side was a wet-eyed Mrs Hughes, with her equally wet-eyed sister. "We always cry at weddings," they told Laura afterwards at the reception at a promenade hotel. A hassled-looking Mr Bicker was with his wife and small son. It was obvious that fatherhood at such a late stage of his life was no joke! Mrs Rose, without her overall, looked a different person in a black-and-white tweedy costume and large white picture hat. Ann's parents, Mr and Mrs Hill, beamed, their eyes on Ann, as if they might burst with pride. Prue was accompanied by Frank her new fiancé – who seemed extremely fond, both of Prue and her bashful and well-scrubbed youngsters. Evidently, Prue had had a change of heart over remarrying when Frank cut his finger while opening a box of sweets. Laura was genuinely pleased for her, glad that she wasn't going to let her bad experience with Sidney ruin her life.

Now Prue was a blissful Mrs Frank Wood; she and her kids were living with him over his newsagents.

Laura and Geoffrey spent their honeymoon at a hotel, a former country house, in Scarborough. As they went up in the lift, she began to panic. What if she didn't please him in that way?

She kept telling herself she was being silly, but all the same her chest was thumping as he carried her over the threshold and laid her gently on the satin eiderdown of their four-poster bed. He stroked her hair, and their lips met in a long sweet kiss conveying promise of passionate delights. At the feel of his lips, her nervousness left her. She felt no embarrassment as she swiftly helped him to remove her clothing and his own – all that mattered was the moment – the one they'd waited for, for so very long. His mouth nuzzled her neck, his fingers tangling her hair. She moaned as he explored her full breasts with their pink-tip-tilted nipples. He caressed her neat waist and the soft curves of her bottom. "You're beautiful, even more than I imagined." He pressed his lips over every inch of her body, his tongue gently investigating the soft fair triangle between her thighs, she crying out in extreme delight and clawing at the hair of his head. Her fingers stroked his flat belly, smooth buttocks and muscular legs. She ran the tip of her tongue over his chest-hair and nipples, until he too was ready to explode.

Eagerly she spread her legs. He entered her. She gasped as he thrust and thrust again. She matched his rhythm stroke for stroke. Higher and higher their excitement mounted. On a peak of pleasure she thought – how different was this than with Nigel.

Her mind went blank, given up to delight, until finally, with long-drawn-out exquisite groans their love-act peeked in a mutual crescendo.

When she awoke she was beneath the bedclothes, with Geoffrey sleeping soundly beside her. She stretched, pulling the covers closer, smiling dreamily. She felt fulfilled. She turned and snuggled up to Geoffrey; she loved him so much. To think they could spend as long as they liked together in this bed – all evening and all night, too – and make love over and over again.

A hand slid downwards, kneading and caressing, his other moving around to her belly and slipping between her thighs. She thrilled – he was awake. Very much awake! He bent his head to nuzzle at her breast and take the hardened nipple into her mouth. Roused, she moaned, eager for him…

After dinner in the chandelier-lit dining room, they returned to their suite. The accommodation was luxurious compared to that shared with Rod on that long ago honeymoon in Southport. Then it had been a po beneath the bed, rag rugs and cotton curtaining. Now it was an en-suite bathroom, thick-pile carpet and velvet drapes. And instead of hot-pot and sausage-and-mash there was French cuisine. Such food might be expensive and highly sought after by some people, but she knew she preferred the good old English cooking. If her surroundings and food were different to when she was with Rod, the feelings of love and desire were no less.

They returned to Blackpool and the house at Bispham. Their honeymoon might be over but when they closed their bedroom door, every night was a honeymoon. In the midst of such happiness, Laura thought tenderly of Rod and of all they had shared, if briefly. It did no good to dwell on the past; it was the future that was important, but all the same… She wondered if Geoffrey ever visited Gloria's grave? – he never said, but perhaps he thought that his taking flowers to his first love might upset her? She didn't think it would, how could she be jealous of a ghost? No. Gloria Roberts had been such a generous woman and a worthy wife, why, hadn't she even hinted how suitable Laura was for Geoffrey, once she'd gone? Anyway it was herself who had Geoffrey, who slept every night in his arms.

Cradling a bunch of red roses, Laura moved slowly along Layton Cemetery's gravel paths, searching the gravestones. She halted. Here it was:

Sacred to the memory

of

RODNEY FIELD

1909 – 1934

A dearly loved husband

and son

She'd been no more than a girl on that dreadful day of Rod's funeral. Frightened and browbeaten by a battle-axe of a mother-in-law. She'd thought then that her life was over; that she could never expect to be happy again. How wrong she'd been! The grave had an air of neglect, weeds were sprouting through the chippings and the stone surround was stained with moss. Guiltily she thought she should have made more of an effort now she'd not got the boarding house; after all, Doris Field was no longer able to tidy things up. "I'm sorry, Rod," she murmured, "I'll not leave it so long next time."

She sat back on her haunches. He couldn't hear her. It was only his earthly remains in the grave, his spirit was with his Maker, waiting for the day they could be reunited, but all the same…"I'll always love you," she whispered, wiping her eyes, "I'll never forget you, but things have worked out at last for me with Geoffrey. We've married. I'm happy. Say you're pleased for me?"

A murmuring *yes* seemed to echo all around her. Had she really heard what she thought she had? Or was it just the wind in the trees? As she rode home on the bus to Bispham, she wondered about this. She had heard a voice, and one that had sounded like Rod's.

Her belief that she'd heard him speak to her that day at the cemetery, never lessened.

She draped the tea-towel patterned with a koala bear over the cooker door. One of a set which had been sent to her and Geoffrey by Rosemary and her family as a wedding present. Tony's business was booming. Rosemary was nursing part-time. They'd moved into their own house near Gladstone. The move to Australia was obviously a success, and she was as fulfilled as Laura.

She went into the lounge. Her glance fell on a photo of Bert and Florrie, taken at the tea party which she and Geoffrey had given for them to celebrate their engagement. Little had she known as she'd busied herself with the preparations, that there would be a surprise development that afternoon, brought about by Claire, which would mean so much to her.

Laura studied the table with satisfaction. In the centre of the embroidered tea cloth was a cut-glass cake stand, on it one of her special jam-and-cream Victoria sandwiches, its top iced, with *Congratulations, Florrie and Bert*, in red, pink and blue piping. Two plates of dainty brown and white triangular red salmon-and-cucumber sandwiches. There was also an arrangement of her own iced fancies. A serving dish held tinned peaches, and there was a jug of Nestles cream. At each place around the table was a cup and saucer, and a sweet dish turned upside down on top of a tea plate. There was a spoon and fork at each place, and an embroidered linen napkin, folded like a Bishop's mitre.

Geoffrey answered the doorbell. He brought in a beaming Bert and Florrie. Coats were taken and hands shaken. Florrie wore a blue crepe de Chine dress with a pleated skirt. Her hat, trimmed with bluebells. With a happy smile, she offered Laura a bunch of pink and white sweet peas. Laura smelt them appreciatively. "How lovely," she said, finding out a vase.

Claire and Mollie both got a chocolate bar (the sweet ration of not only Florrie, but Bert, too).

The sapphire ring on Florrie's work-worn hand glittered, as she held it up for inspection. It was much admired. Every one seated themselves around the table and the meal began. All afterwards agreeing that it was delicious, especially the engagement cake, which had been made with Claire's help. Florrie was visibly overwhelmed by the trouble that Laura and Geoffrey had gone to. And it was a tearful thanks that she gave them.

Geoffrey settled the couple on the settee, while Laura with the help of Claire and Mollie, cleared away. Soon Geoffrey joined them.

Returning from the kitchen Laura caught Bert kissing Florrie passionately. Bert, reddening, released Florrie. Florrie winked at Laura, who smiled widely, thinking it rather sweet. Back in the kitchen, with a smile, she whispered in Geoffrey's ear about what she'd just walked in on. Not in a million years could she imagine Bert and Doris Field kissing like that!

When the kitchen was tidied up they all returned to the lounge. While the adults chatted, Claire and Mollie seated themselves cross-legged on the rug, with the family albums. They started to put Laura and Geoffrey's wedding photos into a white-covered wedding album. Then they began going through the older albums.

Claire began to giggle. "Oh, how rude. Mum's lying naked on a hearth rug."

Laura turned from talking to Florrie. "What?"

Claire showed her the photo. "Yes, that's me, you little madam. I was only nine-months-old and that's my 'birthday suit'!"

Claire grinned. "Do you want to see?" she asked Florrie.

Florrie nodded.

Claire and Bert changed places, and with Florrie beside her, Claire slowly turned the tissue-protected pages. "That's Mum's Mum."

"You've a look of her, dear."

Suddenly Florrie started, and gasped.

"What's the matter?"

"That photo!" Florrie turned to Laura. Who is it of?"

Laura looked at a faded-and-cracked sepia photograph of a stiff-standing small boy dressed in a sailor suit. "Why, that's my dad when he was five."

Florrie clutched at her throat. "Your dad... Your dad?"

"That's right," said a puzzled Laura, 'leastways that's what my mum said."

Florrie's brow wrinkled. "It can't be! It's not possible!" She stared at the photo again. She turned to Laura. You're not going to believe this, no one is, I can hardly believe it myself, but... well, I've got the identical photograph in my album, haven't I, Bert?"

"What! Your album? How could you have? I don't understand. You say Bert's seen the photo?"

The album went across to him and he looked at it and nodded his head in assent.

Florrie touched the photograph, gently stroking it with the tip of her finger. "That's the photo of my long-lost younger brother. I'm sure of it. I've lived with it for a life time."

"Long-lost brother? You think my dad was your brother?"

"I'm sorry if this is a shock to you, but it's a shock to me, too."

Was his name Robert Brown then?" asked Laura in disbelief.

"Yes, Robert Brown. Bob and I were sent to the workhouse when our parents died in a diphtheria outbreak. I was too young to remember all that much about it. When I was eight I was adopted, and moved to Blackpool shortly afterwards with my new parents. Bob and I lost touch then. You weren't encouraged to have any contact with members of your real family. I tried to trace Bob when I was grown up. But according to the workhouse records Bob had died of fever when he was ten. But if he didn't, well, this must mean there must have been some sort of mix-up. Perhaps they had another Robert Brown there?"

"It's not an uncommon name, Brown," put in Geoffrey.

"No."

"So where was this workhouse where your brother was?" asked Laura.

"Chorley. Chorley Workhouse."

"I can't remember if my mum ever said what the workhouse was called where my dad was brought up, but it definitely was in Chorley."

"That tallies, then." Florrie turned to Laura. "So if my brother didn't die when they said he did. If he grew up to marry your mother. To have a child. Well, then we must be related."

Laura shook her head. "Related! I can't believe it. I just can't believe it. I didn't even know that my dad had a sister."

"I know that it's really wonderful for me to find you, Bob's girl. To find that I've got a niece," said Florrie, her voice thickening.

This couldn't be happening, thought Laura dizzily. It was unbelievable. Could she really have discovered a family member, whom, a few moments before, she'd not even realised existed? It appeared it was true. For years she'd thought she was completely alone in the world apart from Claire. And now, with Bert meeting Florrie again, and having his life changed by it, all of a sudden, it appeared that hers was to be changed too. She had to keep pinching herself. She's my aunt, my aunt! Laura could hardly take it in. She'd have to get used to calling this new-found relation, of whom she was already fond, Auntie Florrie. The more she thought about having an aunt, the more pleased she became at the idea. They could do the things together that Geoffrey wouldn't be interested in – go shopping for clothes – exchange recipes. It suddenly struck her that all this wasn't really so unbelievable – it was the Lord's work. 'He' had answered all those prayers and hopes of so many years.

Letters dropping onto the mat brought Laura back to the present.

That evening she and Geoffrey took the girls to Robinson's Cafe for a cream bun tea. Afterwards they went to the Roxy cinema to see, *Warriors of the Iceni,* a newly released Hollywood movie. The lights faded. The film title appeared on screen, accompanied by a musical soundtrack. This changed to a band of Iceni, who covered in wode, uttered blood-curdling cries as they leapt from the cover of trees to attack a Roman legion.

Laura, sat bolt upright, almost dropping her ice lolly. One of the half-naked warriors, who hurtled a spear at a centurion and then turned and fled was the spitting image of Nigel – despite the wode. Hardly had she come to this conclusion when Claire voiced her thoughts.

"It's Nigel, isn't it, Mum?"

"It can't be!"

"Well, it looks like him to me."

Had his dream of being a Hollywood 'actor' come true? Laura rather hoped it had. She fingered the necklace around her neck, its pink and yellow tinted shells complementing the pattern on her dress. It was the necklace that Geoffrey had got from the gift shop all those years ago. After all, she'd got what she'd wanted, the man she loved.

Later, as she lay happily beside Geoffrey, she wondered again if it really could have been Nigel? She'd watched the rest of the film carefully, but never saw anyone remotely like him again.

She snuggled up to Geoffrey's warm back. She wondered if he'd be pleased with the news she'd yet to impart? Earlier that day the doctor had told her something she'd suspected for some time. She ran a hand over the slight curve of her belly.

Geoffrey stirred.

"Are you awake?" she asked.

"Only just."

"I've got something to tell you."

"Can't it wait till morning?"

"It'll only take a minute… It's just that we'll probably need a bigger house before very long."

"A bigger house! Why?"

"Because Mollie and Claire are going to have a little half-brother or sister. I'm expecting."

"What!" He shot upright, and wide-awake, he took her into his arms. "Oh, darling that's wonderful news."

"Isn't it just," she said happily

THE END